The Con Company

DOUBLE ACTORS IN BUDAPEST

GÁBOR DOMOKOS

THE Con Company

DOUBLE ACTORS IN BUDAPEST

Translation by
Andrea Hellman

"The Con Company: Double Actors in Budapest" (English Translation)

Originally published in Hungarian as "A nagy parádé. Kétszínűek."
(Jaffa Kiadó)
Original Hungarian work © 2025 Gábor Domokos
English translation © 2026 Andrea B. Hellman
Published by Duna Books LLC

Duna Books, Springfield, Missouri, USA https://dunabooks.com/
Cover art, cover design, book design: Andrea B. Hellman
Editor: Andrea B. Hellman
Contact: Publisher@DunaBooks.com

Film, television, and streaming adaptation rights available.
A feature-length screenplay based on the novel is completed and available.

Library of Congress Cataloging-in-Publication Data
Domokos, Gábor, 1972–, author.
[A nagy parádé. English]
The Con Company: Double Actors in Budapest / Gábor Domokos ; translated
from the Hungarian by Andrea B. Hellman.

ISBN: 978-1-970934-02-1 (paperback)
ISBN: 978-1-970934-03-8 (e-book)

Printed in the United States of America.

When luck suddenly smiles on you,
beware—you may be the one it's laughing at.

Part One

The Inheritance

At times like this, he always felt as though he were an actor in a movie. Some spy thriller or whatever. Sitting on a park bench in blazing sunlight—kids racing past, couples in love, a gray-haired, fragile old woman feeding pigeons, a hot-dog cart in the background, the fountain splashing—while nobody had any idea he was on a secret mission.

He had to pass something to a stranger. Well, not exactly a stranger—they'd met three times already—but still, all he really knew was that the guy worked for the municipal government and helped make sure B&B LLC won certain contracts. Supposedly named something like Morvai. Handled the smaller construction bids.

But it all added up. That's what his father told him six months ago, when he first sent him here with a fat envelope.

That one had held two million. This one, three and a half. That's what the weasel got from that thirty-five-million-forint playground renovation they'd scored last week. With a little help. And everyone came out ahead. A real win-win situation, as the cultured Frenchman would say.

He remembered his first time—sunglasses on, palms sweating. Like some rookie scared-shitless loser. Which he was, of course. Any second he expected someone to pull a gun, yell *Police! On the ground!*, cuff him, drag him off for interrogation, and lock him up for thirty years. When he told his old man about it later over a beer, the guy laughed and said he watched too many movies. And not to worry—everything was greased.

That was the elder Bartha's favorite expression: *Everything's greased.*

So no need to worry—and now he didn't. In fact, he downright enjoyed it. He was glad his father trusted him with this. The first B in the second B. In the younger B. His future successor. He just needed to learn the ropes. Like how to pass a little grease money without drawing attention. Because that had its own precise choreography too.

His father had worked it out with this Morvai guy at their first and only face-to-face meeting. According to the plan: on the first Tuesday morning after the contract announcement, at ten-thirty sharp, at this bench, an envelope would change hands containing ten percent of the contract value—an intermediary included. And no email, no phone calls—nothing that left a trace.

Smart.

Then someone sat down next to him.

A man around forty, glasses, soft-looking, reeking of sweat—a stranger he had no intention of getting to know. The guy was practically dripping. The armpits of his synthetic shirt bloomed with spreading stains; his hair was so greasy that when he anxiously pushed it back, his palm gleamed. The motion released a small shower of white dandruff across his shoulders.

An outright disgusting impression. And why he chose this particular bench when three others nearby were completely empty, Bartha Junior couldn't imagine.

"Is that you?" The hoarse stranger's voice startled him; the man was staring straight ahead, not at him. "Are you... Bartha?"

"Yes..." he managed, brow furrowing.

"Thank God." The man wiped his sweat-sheened face with a paper tissue. "I forgot where to start counting from."

"What?"

"The benches. Balázs said go to the third one, but whether the third from here or..."

"Who's Balázs?" Bartha cut in, though he already suspected the answer.

"My brother-in-law." The sweaty one blinked at him. "Balázs Morvai. I thought you knew him."

"Let's say I do," he hissed, shifting away with barely concealed disgust.

"He called an hour ago—his daughter came down with a fever, so he had to pick her up from daycare."

"I see."

"Then he asked me to come here..." The man chewed the corner of his mouth. "But I don't like this."

"Why not?" Bartha raised an eyebrow, though he didn't like it either.

"Because... the whole thing's weird." The man stumbled over his words, glanced around, then shifted a few centimeters closer. "If he couldn't make it, why didn't he just call you?"

Their thighs nearly touched. Only one of them cared. Bartha slid toward the edge of the bench.

"He doesn't have my number," he said. This needed to be over.

"That's what I'm saying." The man nodded, narrowing his eyes. "Who meets someone without having their number?"

Hm. Point taken. Among ordinary people, sure—this kind of thing was rare. But this wasn't an ordinary situation. And he wasn't an ordinary person.

This flaky-scalped, wheezing wreck beside him, though—he was. And that wheezing was now happening five centimeters from his face.

"Maybe I don't have a phone," he muttered.

"Very funny," the brother-in-law snorted. "And that package"—he leaned in, finally getting to the point—"that I'm supposed to collect... what the hell is it?"

Instead of answering, Bartha pulled the envelope from his

pocket and tossed it into the man's lap. *Well, buddy, he thought, you wouldn't make much of a conspirator either.*

And now he wasn't the rookie scared-shitless loser. That role belonged to the fidgeting creep next to him.

The minority—if we want to be precise, one-percent—owner of B&B LLC let out a contemptuous sigh. The moment had arrived. When, as an experienced old fox, he would run a delicate transaction like this.

"There's money in it, right?" the creep said, his voice climbing half an octave.

"Don't worry about it." Bartha waved him off. "Just put it away and give it to your brother-in-law."

The man eyed the envelope, then snatched it and shoved it into his pocket.

"Fine. But... I'm not doing this again."

And he was gone.

Bartha Junior—only seconds away from experiencing one of the greatest traumas of his life so far—watched him leave with relief.

What an asshole. Total amateur hour. A miracle he didn't have a stroke.

But he had kept his cool. Handled things for the fourth time. Like a boss. By the book. A real professional. His father would be proud.

He stood, radiating predatory satisfaction. When a familiar figure appeared by the fountain, hurrying toward him past the old woman scattering crumbs for the birds.

"I'm sorry," the newcomer panted when he reached him. "I almost ran into someone just now, and I thought— But why are you so pale? Are you all right?"

"Uh... Mr. Morvai?!"

That was all the experienced old fox could manage.

*   *   *

The smell was the worst part. Oszkár could never get used to it, nor understand it. Wherever he went—the seventh floor of a housing project on the outskirts, a rundown block behind Keleti Station, or, like now, a hovel in Csepel (and that was just today; the countryside was no better)—the same thing greeted him.

Cheap food. Unwashed dishes. An inadequately ventilated bathroom. Belched-up canned beer. Chinese deodorant powerless against body odor. The reek of a mop never wrung out quite enough. And who knew what else contributed. The stench was always the same.

Poverty smell.

It reminded him of cabbage stew left to rot for two days.

But why specifically cabbage? Why didn't this particular combination of components produce something else? He could never figure it out. As he studied the stains hideously spreading across the wallpaper, he imagined boiled cabbage hung instead, replacing the peeling paper entirely—pale, limp, pointless.

But at least that would explain the smell.

Of course, he thought—and miming a cough, he pulled out his handkerchief, carefully saturated with his favorite perfume.

"Are you feeling ill?" the fat woman asked, alarmed, turning from her husband, with whom she'd been huddled in the corner like they were splitting lottery winnings.

"Just this dust..." Oszkár shook his head and cleared his throat. "It's irritating my throat."

"Would you like a glass of water?"

Before his eyes rose the image of the kitchen cabinet: glasses lined up, smudged with fingerprints and other things. He imagined raising one to his lips.

"No, thank you," he said quickly, swallowing. "It'll pass in a moment. Let's move on to the financial side, if you don't mind."

They didn't mind at all. They'd been waiting half an hour for him to finally mention the money he'd offer them—for this pile of garbage. Because all that rank furniture, putrid paper, and moldy junk the old man had crammed into the two tiny rooms of the crumbling house was, according to everyone who'd seen it, nothing but trash begging to be hauled away.

And that was true.

Almost.

His hosts believed they'd struck gold with Oszkár. And that, too, was almost true. Because yes—he was even paying for all of it. Not much, of course. Never enough to raise suspicion.

First he'd say a hundred thousand, then allow himself to be "talked up" to a hundred twenty. But he knew the phrase *takes everything* on the flyer mattered at least as much to most heirs as the final number. Meaning that once he left, nothing would remain but bare walls.

"If I remember correctly, we said a hundred twenty," the man in the athletic tank top began, licking his lower lip. He was the one who'd called Oszkár three days earlier, on a what-have-we-got-to-lose basis, to ask if he'd come look at his father-in-law's things.

"That's what I recall too." Oszkár nodded and reached into his back pocket for his wallet. He always carried it there in the field—more authentic that way. As were the pants with the appropriate pocket, the shirt that didn't match by accident or otherwise, and the wallet itself: an ugly, worn, fake-leather billfold straight out of the not-so-good old days of restaurant waiters.

He counted out six twenty-thousand-forint notes and, folding them neatly in half, held them out toward the couple. They both grabbed for it at once—then both felt embarrassed.

"You take it," the woman muttered, her hands trembling slightly.

"Fine," the man nodded. "After all, I..."

He stalled, confusion dawning as he caught his wife's contemptuous glare.

"You what?!"

"Well..." he stammered, "I called the junk dealer... I mean...

sorry..."

"No problem." Oszkár stepped in magnanimously. "Lots of people say that."

"Idiots," the woman nodded. "Who can't read."

"Now what's your problem?" the tank top asked, genuinely mystified.

"That it says right here." She waved the flyer she'd been crushing in her fist. "See? Oszkár Balogh, antique dealer."

"All right, already. I apologized."

"Besides, what difference does it make?" she went on.

Her husband stared, once again having lost the thread. "What difference does what make?"

"That you called."

A small, confused silence followed. Then the man in the tank top tried again.

"Oh, that? Well, nothing, it's just... since I talked to him, I thought... uh..."

He didn't finish, because his wife snorted.

"You thought the money was yours too, right?!"

So much accusation and hatred poured out of her voice that Oszkár suspected there was more at stake here than a few twenty-thousand-forint notes.

"So you could spend it on your whore," the woman added, practically spitting.

The Curse of the Inheritance, or *Love Triangle in the Latrine*, Oszkár mused, because he enjoyed giving tabloid headlines to events for his own amusement.

But then his attention shifted to the two movers returning from the truck.

As they hoisted the huge armchairs—linings shredding in several places—the arguing couple stepped aside without noticing, still planted on the filthy carpet sticking out from under the ramshackle couch, continuing exactly where they'd left off.

"That's over," the man groaned, hoarse. "You know that. And this—of course it's yours." He pressed her father's inheritance into her hand. "I just... wanted to help."

Feigning offense, he pulled out a cigarette. He lit it with a match, shook the matchstick irritably to extinguish it, and dropped it beside him.

Oszkár froze as the moron stepped on the still-smoking matchstick and ground it into the floor with his full weight.

Or rather—

into the carpet.

The fortune-worth, genuine Persian carpet.

The stupid prole.

"I'm sorry, but—" Oszkár blurted before he could stop himself. He bit his tongue, reconsidered, then tried a gentler approach. "—we'd move faster if we helped the guys out a bit."

They exchanged a look and nodded.

"Okay."

"Just tell us what to do!"

"Maybe... let's push the couch against the wall. And this—" He pointed at the carpet. "Let's roll it up."

The man in the tank top nodded, shifted his cigarette to the corner of his mouth, and got to work. Then he froze, as if suddenly remembering something.

Foreboding crawled up Oszkár's spine—he cursed himself for not being more careful—but when the man grinned and launched into an old rock-and-roll tune, maybe to cheer up his wife or lighten the mood, Oszkár realized there was no danger.

"Roll up the carpet tonight, roll up the carpet..."

Trapped in character, Oszkár hummed along.

* * *

Damn good legs, the older man thought, and rejuvenated by the observation, he set off after them.

Her ass is perfect too, he decided a moment later, sighing when a stray breeze lifted the young woman's skirt a few centimeters higher. Not as much, unfortunately, as another breeze once lifted a certain Marilyn Monroe's—but still. A divine gift. One brief moment to admire those dreamlike calves. Worth getting out of bed for.

The owner of the calves looked to be in her early thirties, with long, golden-brown hair rippling in the wake of her steps. She was clearly in a hurry, a large, decoratively wrapped box in her hands.

Where's she headed? wondered the newest member of her fan club. Definitely to her lover. Some young stud who couldn't wait for her to arrive, and... Or maybe not so young?

Maybe middle-aged? Or as old as him? Why not. Plenty of women liked older men. Could be the poor thing grew up in a broken home and had daddy issues—nothing was off the table.

As he wove through the pedestrians, closing the distance, he could already smell her. Clean, fresh, early-spring floral—maybe with a touch of cinnamon. The old man suddenly couldn't decide what that little extra was that made the air sweeter, so, searching his memory, he closed his eyes for a moment—

—and ran into her.

The angel had stopped right in front of him. A step away. Or half a step. Maybe a pebble had gotten into her shoe; maybe something else entirely—it didn't matter. One moment she was practically running, the next she planted herself in place, and the old man collided with her at full momentum.

Awkward.

The thirty-something staggered, just managing to catch herself. The box, however, slipped from her hands and hit the ground. Something inside shattered.

"Oh no!" The young woman clapped her hands to her mouth and knelt.

The box lay on its side. At first she didn't dare touch it. Finally she drew a deep breath and eased it upright.

A faint clink of shards.

"This can't be happening," she groaned, tearful. Then she whipped her head back toward him, her eyes flashing. "What was in it?"

The elderly gentleman murmured an apology, having already concluded that her eyes—and, in fact, her entire face—were beautiful.

And anger suited her exceptionally well.

"A vase," she said, her voice tightening. "I just bought it. For my parents' anniversary. I saved for six months. And you knock it out of my hands!"

Someone sucked in a breath through their teeth. Several people shook their heads. A small crowd had gathered by now; even a few customers from the nearby café drifted over to see what was happening. And the mood was firmly with the brunette beauty.

The old man understood that, of course—but for heaven's sake, there was no need to lynch him over one misstep. Besides, it wasn't entirely his fault.

"I'm sorry," he muttered, hesitating, "but you stopped so suddenly."

The brunette huffed.

"So now it's my fault?"

"I didn't say that, but—" the old man began, when a spectator cut in.

"Traffic code says the one in back is always at fault," a man announced. "Doesn't matter if the person ahead slams the brakes—if there's a collision, the rear driver pays."

The crowd murmured approvingly. Great, the old man thought. A volunteer firefighter too.

From the corner of his eye, across the street, he noticed a delicate-featured, frail gray-haired woman leaning on her cane. She turned from a shop window, curious, and lifted her glasses for a better look.

This can't be happening.

"Exactly." The bombshell shrugged. "People don't have eyes in the back of their heads."

Then, muttering: "Some apparently don't have them in front either."

A middle-aged housewife joined in, a large woven basket hooked over her arm—she'd been on her way to the market and had seen everything.

"Or if they do..." she said, savoring the moment, giving a tiny dramatic pause, "...they're focused on something else."

She puckered slightly and pointed at the woman's legs.

A few people laughed. The old man flushed.

"I take offense at that," he stammered. "I'm a married man, and never—"

He cut himself off. He didn't believe it either.

Resigned, he jerked his chin toward the box. "All right. How much was it?"

"A hundred thirty-eight thousand," the woman shot back.

The old man stared.

"For a vase?"

"A Biedermeier vase. Porcelain. Hand-painted. *Was.* If you don't believe me, I can show you the receipt." She began rummaging in her bag.

"I'm sorry, but I don't have that much on me."

"Bad excuse," the housewife said.

"Sure is," the volunteer firefighter chimed in. "Don't let him off, sweetheart."

"I didn't say I won't pay," the old man protested. "I just need to find an ATM."

"There's one on the corner," a teenage boy in a baseball cap said helpfully—he'd been staring at the woman's chest the whole time.

"Want me to show you?"

"Yeah," another spectator nodded. "Let's escort the gentleman. Before he takes off."

"I have no intention of taking off," the old man said—and for once he wasn't lying. "But if you want, come along."

With that he headed toward the corner. Three people went with him—plus the angel, who now carried her parents' shattered gift under her arm.

"I don't have the heart to throw the box away," she sighed, as if she needed to explain.

Then she smiled at him—softly, unexpectedly—and he felt immediately lighter.

And that was when he realized what that scent was that had just made him a hundred thirty-eight thousand forints poorer.

Not cinnamon.

Vanilla mixed with honey.

The recognition filled him with a ridiculous sort of

satisfaction, so when he spotted the gray-haired old lady in the background putting away her glasses—the show apparently over—he didn't know why, but he gave her a nod.

*   *   *

The two men shook hands.

"Still hurt?" the older one asked, nodding toward the other's ribs.

"Only when I breathe," the younger muttered wryly, then crossed to the bar cabinet. "Want something?"

"Gin and tonic. No ice. And yes—cracked ribs can be worse than breaks."

"I deserve it," said the man who, two days earlier, had stepped in front of a car driven by a municipal representative named Balázs Morvai, just to keep him from making it to a meeting on time.

"Come on," said the other—the one who *had* made it to the meeting. "You did it perfectly."

His partner shook his head.

Like hell he had.

He was supposed to step out from behind the van, fall onto the hood, and slide off with a convincing moan. They'd rehearsed it at least fifteen times.

With an almost stationary car.

But that asshole either didn't know the right-of-way rules or didn't give a damn, and he'd barely slowed down. He must have been doing thirty—maybe forty—when Viktor "appeared" in front of him.

All things considered, Viktor had gotten off cheap. And that was how he saw it.

"Three and a half million for a little bruising isn't such a bad deal," he sighed, mixing the drinks.

"That's bullshit," the older man replied. His hair wasn't dandruff-covered now like it had been in the park—of course, it hadn't been dandruff then either, but baby powder sprinkled onto a paraffin-oiled wig and the shoulders of a thrift-store shirt stuffed with padding. "We risked too much. And I'm the one to blame."

"Stop it, Dénes. How could you have known that idiot would—"

"I should have thought of it," his partner cut in sourly. "It was in the cards. And don't tell my aunt, because—"

"I already told her."

Dénes hissed.

"And what did she say?" he asked, suddenly cautious.

Viktor shrugged. "That we should have done it at a speed bump. Or a stop sign."

"On the street where the guy usually parks, there's neither."

"I know. I told her."

"And?"

"She said we should have put one up."

Dénes sighed. "True," he said wryly, and his mind drifted—as it often did—into some dusty corner of trivia he'd once read: that stop signs didn't only have that distinctive color

and shape for visibility, as most people assumed, but also because, back in the day, you could cut the most octagons with
the least waste from large sheets of wood or metal.

Economic reasons. Naturally.

And he'd continued the thought at the time—because even
when he didn't fully grasp something, he loved math, especially geometry—that regular hexagons would have been
even more efficient. With octagons you still ended up with a
bunch of useless squares. But the old-timers probably found
some use for those too.

He didn't share this with Viktor, who would only mock him,
saying that with all this useless data in his head he should
be on quiz shows. Dénes wouldn't bother explaining—pearls
before swine—that in America there are four-way stop inter-
sections, where everyone stops and only then creeps forward,
partly because liability is automatically fifty–fifty. Similar to
how in Hungary you can get up to three years in prison for
stealing any traffic sign, drunk or sober.

Okay—none of this had much to do with the Morvai business.

But one day it might come in handy.

"Come on," Viktor objected. "It would have looked suspicious if a brand-new—"

"Everything in the world," his mentor interrupted, "happens overnight."

"You know what I mean." Viktor waved him off, then added,
"But it's nice you worry about me."

He'd worried the same way when he saved him.

Even though they hadn't known each other yet.

Viktor had been sitting in a bar, nursing his eighth vodka, broke and hopeless, when someone sat down across from him and asked what was wrong.

It had been Dénes.

And Viktor had started talking. He still didn't understand why—he'd never seen the man before—but he'd been glad he did. The words poured out: frantic, bitter, incoherent. Hard to make sense of.

But this guy made sense of them anyway.

When Viktor, exhausted, finally wound down half an hour later, Dénes summarized:

"Let me see if I've got this. You were a hotshot banker—assistant branch manager at a smaller bank—with a bright future, until your supposed love screwed you over. For almost one hundred eighty million. Your entire fortune. Which then became the bank's, since you'd co-signed the loan she took out before disappearing. So now you've got no job, no apartment, no car—"

"No reason to live," Viktor finished, his voice scraping the words out. "But you summarized it well."

"I tried. So... what next?"

"I was planning to kill myself."

"That's one solution," Dénes nodded—

and then, in five minutes, sketched out another.

That had been almost three years ago.

And now here he was—satisfied, energetic, ready for action (he almost said happy, but that was a stretch)—working in an entirely different profession that had nothing to do with banking, and not much to do with freight forwarding either, despite that being the main profile of his official workplace: the front company run by his mentor's old friend.

On paper, they even made a living from it, thanks to that friend, who managed things well. It helped that he had two silent partners who invested money but never asked for a penny: the invisible personnel director and the invisible finance director—at least according to their business cards, minus the "invisible."

Not that the friend needed to meet them often. They were busy doing something completely different.

Something far more interesting than freight forwarding.

And Dénes taught him the tricks of that trade.

Well—Dénes and his aunt.

One of the world's most remarkable old ladies. Viktor hadn't met anyone like her.

Though the nephew wasn't far behind.

"...Never mind. We'll be more careful next time," the nephew in question said, snapping him back. "Is that gin and tonic ready yet?"

"Yeah," Viktor said apologetically. "I zoned out, sorry." Then—though he knew Dénes hated it when he quoted movies—he added, "Shaken. Not stirred."

Dénes rolled his eyes and took one of the glasses.

"Godfather?" he asked deadpan, though Viktor knew he wasn't serious.

"Almost."

They clinked glasses.

* * *

Mici néni tried shooing the pigeons away with her cane so the poor sparrows might get a few bites too—she liked them better—but the effort was hopeless. The big, aggressive birds shamelessly devoured every piece of bread she scattered while she sat on the bench. Not a crumb for the little ones.

The law of nature, triumphant.

She knew the law of nature. She just didn't agree with it.

So she decided on a harder method. She picked up a few larger pebbles, chose the one that fit her hand best—or, as her nephew would say, the most handy—took brief aim, and threw it at the leader of the pigeons. Then three more in quick succession. The first missed. The second came close. The third whistled past barely half a centimeter from the boss's head.

Practice makes perfect.

With indignant wing-flapping, all the birds fled. The sparrows too.

The plan seemed to have failed.

But Mici néni didn't lose heart. She simply waited, several pebbles ready in her palm. She knew the sparrows would return sooner, and they'd get a second or two of peaceful eating before their more cautious... species-mates—classmates, she corrected herself at once, because birds form a class, every schoolchild knows that—assuming they were taught properly and don't promptly forget it, the way she herself had been forgetting more and more things lately, which was worrying, the way her thoughts wandered like this—before the pigeons appeared again to chase them away.

Well, the sparrows would have to make do with that second or two. Better than nothing.

It was the same in her profession.

There too, timing was everything. Well—not everything, since a successful parade required many other things—but it was certain that if you didn't hit the right moment, the whole act fell apart.

Like that bribe-money business the other day. A simple swap trick, really—a classic shell game. The corrupt Morvai disappeared, Dénes appeared. But the illusion only worked in that ten-minute window while Viktor performed his swan song...

and that stupid boy had actually done it.

Instead of calling off the operation. Which would have been the correct decision in this case.

But he risked his life! How was that normal?

Mici néni gave him a thorough scolding and made him promise never to take unnecessary risks again. The boy tried to argue, of course—that they'd planned that ten-minute window for months, which would all have gone to waste if he'd backed out at the last second, and anyway the guy was barely going twenty—

but Mici néni didn't budge.

You do not risk your physical safety, she told him sternly. And certainly not your life. No operation was worth that much.

They could have performed the routine when the next rigged contract came up—true, that wouldn't be for almost six months, if it came at all, since anything could come up at any time—but still.

You don't manufacture life-or-death situations out of nothing.

Privately, she would have bet that the twenty kilometers per hour Viktor mentioned was more like thirty. Or forty. Knowing that reckless idiot.

Then the sparrows returned and ate a few bites. The pigeons watched from a distance, then gradually came closer and took control again—until a few well-aimed pebbles, Mici néni indulging in her favorite hobby, cleared the field once more.

And everything started over.

Because if something worked once, it would work a second time, and a third—at least here, on the bird front.

With people, the formula wasn't so simple. There you always had to... change up the show a little, often on the fly. Even if you were performing the same number that was practically coming out of your ears by now, you still had to adapt.

To the situation. To the mark. To the current audience.

And you could not make mistakes.

Otherwise...

Mici néni sighed. She hated even thinking about those eighteen months she'd spent in the penitentiary of the Hungarian People's Republic, yet the memory surfaced almost daily. The mistake she'd made too. Her last mistake—which, considering almost fifty years had passed since then, wasn't so bad.

It was just that she was getting old.

Her nephew always laughed at this—that someone almost eighty would complain about such a thing, in the present tense no less—but Mici néni knew better. A few years ago the problem hadn't existed at all. Not physically, of course—she'd needed a cane for quite some time, and her heart couldn't take strain like before ("display-window disease," she called it, because when she got too tired walking, she'd stop as if admiring a storefront, hoping it wasn't too obvious she was gasping for air)—not to mention other inconveniences.

But her head had always been crystal clear.

Lately, though, she really did forget things sometimes. A name here, a date there, what she'd had for lunch yesterday, where she'd put her keys—little things that seemed trivial, but in her profession even a trivial thing could be fatal. And not just for her. One slip-up and she could endanger Dénes and Viktor too.

So for a while now, Mici néni had participated in performances only as an observer—footage they then analyzed together afterward, like game tape in serious sports.

Together—just as they planned new operations together.

Like the one coming up, in which Mici néni would, exceptionally, have an important role.

And one that would require her to use the knowledge she'd acquired in prison.

She hoped it was like riding a bicycle.

Or whatever it was you supposedly couldn't forget.

* * *

The pharmaceutical executive—fifties, well maintained—was a regular. Six visits in the last six months. Maybe seven.

Exactly four million eight hundred seventy thousand forints.

Oszkár kept a running tally in his head. What he'd sold and when? No idea. But the price? Always. Every time. Like a cash register lodged in his skull, endlessly ringing, branding the numbers into permanence. Not that he'd ever want to erase them.

This was what fed him. Made him happy.

It gave him something close to what other people called sexual satisfaction. *Close* being the operative word, since he had no idea what the real thing felt like. Women didn't interest him. Neither did men. Not like that. As customers, sure—money was money. But sex itself left him cold.

Even as a child he'd preferred button soccer to the real thing.

Fine dining, exotic destinations, hunting, good wine, better books, sailing—who needed more? People thought he was strange. Couldn't wrap their heads around it. Oszkár counted that a blessing. No jealousy, no longing, no heartbreak, no disappointment—the shit that destroyed ninety percent of humanity. No thanks.

He had his work.

Buying something for x, selling it for ten x, twenty x, a hundred x—nothing compared.

Like now.

If this went right, the register would ring again. The executive's total would break six million forints. By a hundred twenty thousand.

The executive was studying the carpet closely. Worth studying. The price tag read one million two hundred fifty thousand, but that clearly didn't faze him. Good sign. Anyone who checked prices first didn't shop here.

"In disguise?" the regular smiled, running his fingers over the carpet's floral and vine patterns. "Like King Matthias?"

Oszkár shrugged. The origin story was often as important as the object. Some customers loved the romance.

"They trust me more when I dress like them."

"According to last year's fashion?"

"Thrift shop."

"Good God."

"Tell me about it."

"Track pants? Hawaiian shirt?"

"Plus a tracksuit top." Oszkár pulled a face. "The shiny kind."

"Don't envy you."

"Business is business. When I show up there looking like this..."

He spread his arms and stepped back, letting the executive take in the Cesare Attolini suit—one hundred percent wool, nearly a million forints. He'd hated buying it. A damn piece of clothing—and not even the most expensive option (were these people insane?)—but necessary.

Presentation mattered. Here, in this environment, with this clientele, this was the uniform.

Really, there was no difference between the Práter market and Falk Miksa Street—he couldn't even remember that Csepel address—not in essence. Everywhere, you dressed for the customer.

"Same thing in pinstripes," a voice said behind them.

"My dear fellow." Oszkár turned, forcing a smile. "What brings you here?"

Early seventies. Tall. Straight-backed. Tremendous energy packed into that elegant frame. Hooked, aristocratic nose. Silver-white hair setting off thick, coal-black eyebrows.

Dyed, Oszkár noted. Like every time.

"Passing through." Easy delivery. Impossible to tell whether he was lying. "Didn't want to interrupt. You were mid-story."

Oszkár ignored the mockery curled around *story*.

"Just wrapping up."

"I know. I've been here a while."

"Didn't see you—"

"I came in at the chameleon bit." The white-haired man smiled. "Next you'll tell me you're Leonard Zelig reincarnated." The executive frowned. "Who's—" Then snapped his fingers. "Oh. Right. Woody Allen. Christ, I'm slow."

"The only question is," the newcomer continued, ignoring him, "which one's the real you. One of them has to be."

"What do you think?" Oszkár sighed. He already knew the answer. And it contradicted everything he projected.

"You're in disguise now. Those other rags? That's you going home."

"What's he talking about?" the executive asked, bristling.

"Just that our friend Oszkár's grandfather made his pile at the Garay Square market. Such as it was. Thread, buttons... rabbit-fur hats?"

"Everything," Oszkár said. He pictured kneeing him in the balls.

"Just like here." A pursed-lip sweep of the room. "Flea market with pretensions."

"You come every month."

"Law of large numbers."

"Right."

The white-haired man drifted toward the display cases—paper antiquities.

"There's another reason."

"What's that?"

"Eternal optimism. In defiance of all evidence." He smiled.

"Same thing," Oszkár muttered.

"What?"

"Large numbers, optimism. Both mean you've never found anything interesting here—but keep hoping."

"Not as dumb as you look."

"Thanks."

"So?" Fingers tapped old postcards. A bored sigh. "Would I find anything if I wasted half an hour?"

"There's one where a Hungarian soldier wrote his wife from the Don Bend, exactly on the day—"

But the man was already setting it down, heading for the exit, shaking his head.

Oszkár swallowed.

"If you're looking for Stefan Zweig's suicide note, wrong shop." A small jab, allowed. "Can't help with Ludwig's hand-written love confessions either."

Merchant's blood surged.

"But I do have an original Imre Steindl architectural drawing."

The man paused. Tilted his head—bad hearing, that familiar angle. Turned back slowly.

"Parliament?"

"Church renovation. Beautiful, though."

"I'm sure." Interest evaporated. "I'd be happier if you surprised me with an actual rarity. What are the odds?"

Purely rhetorical. He didn't wait for an answer.

"Right."

He left.

"Who *was* that arrogant prick?" the executive asked, almost reverent.

Oszkár had forgotten he was still there.

"Antal Sólyom," he said quietly. "*The* Antal Sólyom."

"The billionaire?" The executive lowered his voice. "I read about his collection. Elvis postcard, Einstein letter, Al Capone notes, autographs from Diana, Gagarin, Menuhin..."

"Once sold him an envelope," Oszkár cut in, sour, "addressed by József Nagysándor to Kossuth. Sixty thousand." He sighed—the particular ache reserved for lost profit—then continued. "The letter was gone. Still special. Especially once I found out he'd collected similar items from the others. All twelve."

"Sorry, but—"

"Martyrs of Arad."

"Oh."

"Their handwriting. A few lines each. Together—only visible in one place on earth."

"What's something like that worth?"

"Last year a Hungarian-American oil guy supposedly offered a hundred fifty thousand dollars. Sólyom said no."

They let that sit.

"Smug bastard," the executive said finally. Then, shaking his head, he changed tack.

"But you still haven't explained how an expensive, hand-knotted silk Persian carpet ends up in some broke old man's Csepel shithole."

He stroked the pattern again.

Oszkár shrugged. "Who knows. Gift. Theft. Lucky find. Purchase. Could've won it at cards."

"Daughter didn't know?"

"Didn't ask. Would've tipped her off. Not the plan."

The executive laughed. "You're a real piece of work." Admiring. "No offense."

"Please." Oszkár grinned. "Flatter away."

"How much did you give those poor bastards? Trade secret?"

"One hundred twenty thousand. Whole estate. Had to take everything so it wouldn't look suspicious. Ended up paying another forty just to haul the rest to the dump."

"Am I crying for you yet?"

"That's a hundred sixty total," Oszkár said. "Plus fifty-five for rug cleaning."

"My heart bleeds. You know what this reminds me of? An episode of *Tales of the Unexpected*. Old TV series—"

"Seen it. Read it. Half the dealers I know trace their origin story to that show."

"Didn't end well for the protagonist."

"Sometimes you take a hit. If you're careless."

"But never you. Just the customers. Like those Csepel folks."

"They were thrilled with that hundred twenty. Like winning the lottery. Best day of their lives."

"Thanks to you."

"They pray in my name now."

"Careful," the executive laughed. "You'll get canonized."

"Wouldn't shock me."

"And if they find out you're clearing over a million?"

"They never come to this neighborhood." Oszkár waved it off—the Saint.

"And even if they did, they wouldn't know this carpet from that one."

He shifted. "So—are you buying?"

"For sure. Gorgeous. Wrap it."

"Right away." Oszkár nodded.

To be precise, he was clearing thirty-five thousand more than a million on the markup.

But who was counting?

*　*　*

The brunette who'd dazzled that daydreaming old man a few days earlier sat at the table, screwing the cap back onto the glue tube. She studied the more-or-less restored vase.

Not bad, she thought, running her finger along one faint crack. Barely visible.

Her name was Anett Kertész. For the past four and a half months she'd been using her maiden name again—when she had to give a name at all. She hated providing information to anyone. Her husband would track her down eventually anyway, take back what he considered his, what Anett had "stolen" from him—his version, naturally.

Because what she'd taken from that multimillion-forint villa in Debrecen, pool and all? She had every right to it. A court would probably agree—if the man didn't have lawyers billing a hundred thousand an hour who could prove red was green. And he had people who could convince others to swear the same. Under penalty of perjury.

Anett didn't judge them.

As her husband liked to say, money isn't everything, but a lot of money is something. And he paid well. When that wasn't enough, alternative solutions appeared. Baseball bats. Chains. Dogs. Sooner or later, everyone came around.

Except Anett.

She'd gotten out in time. Before he deployed the heavy artillery. And when she left—straight to Pest, where he had less pull than back home, where she could disappear into the crowd—she'd taken something with her. If she'd left empty-handed, one of Debrecen's underworld kingpins might not have come after her. Might not. She wasn't certain.

In his circles, the rule was simple: once you acquired something, you did what you wanted with it. *Till death do us part.* So he'd probably hunt her down regardless—just maybe not as persistently. Not as fiercely.

Once, he'd almost caught her.

Close call.

Three months earlier, heading home one evening, she'd spotted one of his men sitting in a parked car across the street. The guy lit a cigarette; the flame flared and automatically caught her eyes. She recognized the face in the glow. Security from an upscale Debrecen "hostess club." They'd eaten there once or twice with friends, back when Anett had blonde hair—straight, styled—when she dressed to provoke. The jewelry. The makeup.

That was what made her look like a whore, really.

These days she didn't even line her eyes. No lipstick. Except for the tiny earrings from her mother, nothing on her caught the light. The villa had held rings and necklaces worth a fortune—still worth a fortune. She'd left them all in the bedroom drawer.

What she'd taken was worth more.

Point being, the bodyguard hadn't recognized her. He'd looked her over, though. Anett felt his gaze as she walked past the building, heart pounding in her throat, keeping the same pace she'd had before—though every instinct screamed to run. She forced calm. Only started gasping once she'd turned the corner. Got on a bus, didn't check which one, rode until her pulse settled.

How had they found her?

She'd been careful. No official business that required documents. Working under the table at a small cleaning company that paid cash per job, like they did the Transylvanians—which is what she claimed to be. She'd only given her real name when she rented the apartment.

Probably the mistake.

Her husband had favorite sayings (he had several). One went: if you don't learn from your mistakes, there's no point making them. Anett learned fast. Hit reset immediately. Left the rental. Left the suitcase of clothes she'd brought from Debrecen—she'd buy new ones. Lucky she'd kept her documents and money in her bag. Didn't need to go back for anything.

The treasure was already somewhere safe.

She'd called a coworker from a street phone, asked if she could crash at her place for a few days. Told her the landlord had kicked her out for refusing to sleep with him. She'd always been a good liar. Never lacked imagination.

She'd been living here since. Two months now. Alone.

The coworker had gone home to Transylvania to care for her sick father—supposedly not much time left—but following Anett's advice, she'd paid six months' rent upfront on the miserable District VIII apartment. So she'd have somewhere to come back to.

The coworker paid, of course.

But this gave Anett an untraceable base.

Only the money was running out. Cleaning wages covered nothing. She needed work she could do without papers. Off the books.

So after witnessing a real accident once—no con, a genuine mishap, except it was a record player that hit the floor, not a vase—she'd developed the concept. Worked out the broken-vase trick. Refined the details through practice.

She'd performed it twelve times now.

Same gift box.

The shards wrapped in crumpled paper had originally belonged to a simple twenty-first-century—meaning, made a few years ago—unremarkable mass-produced item from the Chinese market. Eight thousand forints. After the first successful performance she'd bought five more; two still waited intact in the cabinet.

Because you could reuse a vase multiple times.

Dropped right, they shattered into eight or ten large pieces—nice and loud—making the damage seem irreparable. With glue, though, you could sometimes restore them enough to deploy again. They wouldn't hold water. But they'd break just as well, with a satisfying crack—and in that state they didn't look much different from pricier Biedermeier cousins.

So if someone wanted to inspect the box after the drop—and the swap—they could. Usually unnecessary. The sound effect alone was convincing enough.

This particular specimen—seven performances and counting—was the absolute champion. Still held together well enough for an eighth run. Probably the last, though.

As Anett's grandmother would've said, besides the glue, only the Holy Spirit was keeping the poor thing together now.

* * *

Oszkár—back in worn jeans and an oversized jacket from some Communist-era suit—stopped in the middle of one of District VIII's ugliest streets. He sighed, looked up at the sign above the entrance.

This would be it. Third address today. Probably pointless going in.

But necessary.

The gate stood open. Inside, two rows of trash bins waited for collection. Farther back, a woman around sixty, in a housecoat, scrubbed the floor tiles with a filthy rag on a long handle. The water in the bucket by her leg was coal-black.

Here we go, Oszkár muttered.

"Huh?" the woman barked, looking up suspiciously.

"Just—uh—saying hello."

"Oh. God bless you too." She went back to scrubbing.

Oszkár moved to the mailboxes and began scanning names.

"Who you looking for?" the woman called from behind him.

"A certain Mr. Horváth," Oszkár said, already tired. "You know where he lives?"

"Up there." She jerked her chin upward.

Oszkár groaned—no elevator, naturally—but she continued:

"I mean heaven. He's dead, sir."

Very funny, Oszkár thought, though he wasn't sure she'd meant it as a joke.

"And while he was down here?" he asked, adding a mild smile, playing along—if there was anything to play along with.

"Mezzanine. Three B."

Oszkár nodded and trudged up the dripping-wet stairs.

The man who answered the doorbell was in his mid-thirties, unshaven, generally unkempt, with a blue-black shiner under his left eye. He was eating something. Salt pork, from the smell. With raw onions. His right hand held a beer, probably not his first that day.

"Told you I'd clear it out by Monday!" he bellowed, mouth full, before Oszkár could speak.

"Uh... excuse me?"

"The apartment." Quieter now. Then, uncertain: "Or—you're not here about that? To remind me about the deadline again?"

"No. I'm here about the estate. We spoke yesterday on the phone. Oszkár Balogh." He extended his hand.

The man with the shiner pulled a face, shifted the beer to his left, wiped his greasy fingers on his shirt.

"Right, yeah. Gergő Horváth." He slapped Oszkár's palm. "I remember now. You're the one who takes everything."

"If we can agree on terms."

"Sure... that's what I meant. Come in."

Suppressing a belch, Gergő stepped back, let Oszkár through, closed the door behind him—and kept talking.

"And sorry about before, but they keep hassling me from the municipality to hand over the keys. Since the old man rented on social assistance, and supposedly people are already lined up for it."

Inside was dim. The tiny entryway was littered with boxes—most still empty, some already filled with books. Oszkár glanced at the spines. Mostly horses. Covers with racehorses jumping obstacles, stampeding herds mid-gallop.

"Beer?" the host asked, finally pausing.

"No thanks. I'd rather look around."

"Go ahead."

Oszkár stepped into the cramped, mildewed living room. The walls were covered with old yellowed posters, paintings, framed photographs. Most depicted horses. The empty spaces were filled with horseshoes, stirrups, bridles, other stable paraphernalia. Even the vases, sculptures, and decorative objects followed the same theme.

Surreal.

"I see your father loved horses."

"How'd you guess?"

"When you've been in this business as long as I have..."

Gergő snorted—then started neighing. Both sounds fit the environment perfectly, but that didn't make them any less unpleasant. Especially when he slapped Oszkár heartily on the back while laughing.

"You're funny."

"I have good days."

"Actually he was my grandfather. Barely knew him. I mean, visited a lot as a kid, but since Dad died, I saw him maybe twice. And Dad died, like, fifteen years ago."

"So you didn't keep in touch."

"Not really. Made it pretty weird at the funeral when his buddies—a bunch of trembling-handed bald geezers—offered me condolences."

"Happens when you're the only relative," Oszkár said, bored, moving toward a massive oil painting. "Did he paint this?"

The canvas showed an enormous black mare rearing beside a well—probably the Hortobágy—but everything was so

disproportionate the animal looked like a failed genetic experiment.

"Yeah." Gergő sounded sour. "Ugly, right?"

Oszkár just shook his head and moved on—

then froze.

In a shadowy corner of the room hung a much smaller
horse portrait.

Jesus Christ.

Lucky his back was to the other man. The shock on his face
stayed hidden—but the telltale stillness, his feet rooting to
the floor, needed covering.

He shifted, found something else in that direction, feigned
interest, stepped to the black-and-white photograph beside
the painting.

For variety, it showed two boys—maybe ten years old—grinning at the camera in front of an ornate wrought-iron gate.
Above it, a decorative coat of arms: a scrollwork *H*, flanked
by two lions. The boys were half-naked, looked like brothers.
Behind them, a manicured park and the silhouette of an old
villa.

"That's my grandfather." Gergő stepped beside him, pointing to the boy on the left. "The other one's his best friend.
Supposedly a real count's kid. From that castle."

"What happened to him?" Oszkár asked hoarsely.

It took everything he had to keep staring at the perfectly
uninteresting photograph instead of the masterpiece hanging directly beside it.

"Think he went to America." Gergő shrugged.

Then something started beeping.

He pulled out his phone, checked the caller.

"Yo." Flat delivery. "No, still at the old man's place... Hold on..."

He shot Oszkár an apologetic glance. Oszkár nodded.

Gergő hurried toward the kitchen.

"Sorry..."

From the other room: "...just there's this sucker here who might take the whole setup..."

The sucker glanced toward the kitchen—he could hear every word despite the distance—then pulled out his phone with careful clumsiness and snapped several quick shots of the horse portrait.

No flash.

He hoped the essentials showed.

His pulse still hovered around two hundred.

"...and I'll still make a profit," Gergő continued. "If I'm lucky... Some junk dealer... No, sold the fridge to the neighbor already, he's broke... Didn't want that one, says it's a tube TV and he only likes plasma... Crazy, right? A ticket inspector... Whatever. Still hitting the party tonight... I'll contribute, relax. Telling you I've got money. Might even have more by then... Gotta go now..."

By the time Gergő returned, Oszkár was examining the far side of the room, poking idly at a horseshoe-shaped ashtray.

"Hideous, right?" Gergő took a swig of beer.

"Certainly... interesting," Oszkár said carefully, setting the ashtray down. "Like the rest of it." A chin gesture took in the apartment.

"The old man wasn't playing with a full deck," Gergő said reluctantly. "Not dangerous or anything," he added quickly. "Never hurt anyone. Just... had a thing for horses."

"Right. A thing."

"Okay." Gergő shook his head. "Overdid it. But nobody died from it, right?"

Then he cleared his throat, suddenly nervous.

"So... what do you think? About this whole... situation?"

The small, defeated tilt of his head encompassed the apartment.

You'll never know, buddy, Oszkár thought, expressionless. At least I hope not.

What he said instead:

"Well... at first glance, not much you can do with this stuff." He paused, shrugged. "But at the flea market, anything can happen. Someone might even like it."

He picked up the ashtray again.

Gergő frowned. "You're kidding."

"God's zoo is big, my friend. Bigger than you think." Oszkár set the ashtray down. "So if you want, tomorrow morning I'll take the whole mess off your hands for—say—two hundred thousand."

The other stared.

"You mean," he said slowly, "you'll clear out the dump and

give me two hundred grand?"

Oszkár nodded.

Gergő let out a sharp breath, tossed the empty beer can into the trash, and grinned as he extended his hand.

"Deal."

* * *

The old man in the trench coat wasn't giving up easily. He really dug in once he heard *one hundred thirty-eight thousand forints.*

Anett understood. That was, in fact, what a Biedermeier vase cost in a downtown shop window she'd passed recently—anyone could check. She'd been shocked too, but this was Pest. A world-class city.

Only three onlookers remained at the corner of the elegant, café-lined street; the others had drifted off. Still, as always, the crowd took her side. Especially since the other party was particularly unlikeable.

The bald old man huffed and stared at the receipt clenched in his hand, suspicion hardening his face. He pushed his glasses up to his forehead and squinted at the tiny print. When he finally deciphered it, he growled.

She wasn't surprised. She knew exactly what it said. She'd written it herself, in a word-processing program. Everything checked out. Even the date.

The devil lived in the details.

"I'm not paying this." The man—in his seventies, wrapped

in a long gray belted coat—shook his head.

"But that's what it cost!" Anett protested, letting her mouth tremble on cue.

"Don't care."

"Aren't you ashamed of yourself?!" The wife from a middle-aged couple rushed to Anett's defense. "The poor thing spent all her money on this... Baader-Meinhof vase to surprise her parents..."

She fixed a hard stare on the beautifully wrapped box lying on the ground.

"Sweetheart..." her husband murmured.

"What?"

"Please don't talk nonsense."

"What do you mean, non—"

"Because," the old man in the puffy coat cut in, "those were two German terrorists. Who never dabbled in... vase design."

He delivered this with such scorn that the woman's face twitched—though the old man was only warming up.

"They preferred bombing, you know. Ever heard of the Red Army Faction?"

"Of course..." the woman said uncertainly, then frowned. "But didn't you say they were German?"

"Yes."

"And they teamed up with the Russians? Because the *Red Army*—"

"Good God!" the old man shouted. "Are you really this stupid?!"

"Hey." The husband stepped forward, indignant. "Don't insult my wife!"

"I'm just stating facts. How can anyone confuse Biedermeier with—"

"Actually..." the woman cut in, rallying, "they do sound pretty similar."

"Right. Like one egg sounds like another bread roll."

"I meant the, uh... phonetic resemblance. Anyway—don't change the subject!"

"Me?!"

"You. This isn't about bread rolls or terrorists." She paused, then added pointedly, "Though you're starting to act like one."

"Like a terrorist?"

"Yes. The way you mowed down this nice lady here, after destroying her valuable art object—"

"But she came at *me*," the old man protested—without much conviction now.

"That's not true!" Anett stomped her foot, relieved they'd at least abandoned international terror groups. Still better than if they'd started swinging bags at each other. That was always in the deck.

"You really did hit her," a uniformed worker said from the sidelines, having enjoyed the show so far. He gave the old man an apologetic look. "Saw you turn the corner and nail her straight on."

"Or her me."

"But I was standing still!" Anett said, turning to the witness with grateful eyes.

"Four to one," the woman declared, buoyed by victory.

The old man had a cutting remark brewing—something about quantity versus quality—but when he looked around at the small group, he thought better of it.

He sighed.

Reached into his pocket.

And pulled out his wallet.

*   *   *

Mici néni sat at the computer, browsing the internet.

She'd gotten addicted.

Though she'd resisted at first, the way she resisted most technological inventions—most of which she considered direct attacks on the profession. Those cursed mobile phones, for instance. They remembered everything. Who called you, when, from where—because nowadays they could triangulate (if she remembered her nephew's explanation correctly) the precise location of a device's owner, even retroactively. Three weeks ago. Tuesday. Four twenty-five.

Sodom and Gomorrah.

Like having a tracking chip implanted under your skin. At least you could leave the wretched things at home when necessary—or, like Dénes did, stock up on dozens of disposable, prepaid, untraceable SIM cards. Whatever those were.

But what she hated most were the cameras.

At first they crept in slowly—then all at once—until they

seemed to cover the entire planet. Space too, supposedly. Satellites that, people claimed, could read the tiny flickering letters on a screen thousands of kilometers away. Letters she herself could barely make out at twenty centimeters, peering through her glasses.

So even though she didn't care for sentences that began with *back in my day*, she caught herself using them more and more. Along with the instructive sayings and proverbs that drove her nephew up the wall.

Because back then, in the old, honest world, life wasn't tangled up in these science-fiction contraptions.

But now she had to watch everything, lest some modern hocus-pocus expose her.

Or her son—because for the last twenty-some years, Dénes had been there too, insisting since graduation that he participate actively in operations. Despite her efforts to steer him toward becoming a doctor, lawyer, engineer, or... firefighter, cop, astronaut—the usual things normal kids wanted to be.

Of course, he hadn't been a kid anymore by then.

And nothing about his circumstances had ever been normal.

Not since the age of four and a half, when he lost his parents and came to live with her. With the then thirty-five-year-old, unmarried Mária Hadnagy, whom he called *Titsie* until the age of six—because *Mici* made no sense to him—shouting it in public and causing countless awkward scenes, plus no small amount of hilarity, on buses, trams, practically everywhere.

And Mici néni, though she hadn't planned it, transformed overnight from aunt to honorary mother.

Suddenly there was a little boy snoring beside her at night, pressed close. And she gradually realized her life had changed forever—because from now on, she would be the one caring for him.

Not easy to accept.

But since the alternative was the orphanage, she didn't hesitate.

Besides, whenever she drifted toward self-pity, she reminded herself that someone else had it harder. A four-and-a-half-year-old orphan whose only living relative she was.

Then she'd feel ashamed and swear again that as long as the world turned, she would love the child and raise him as best she knew how.

True, her knowledge belonged mostly to a less respectable segment of life—she was, after all, one of the most successful con artists of her generation—but Mici néni, God as her witness, fulfilled her mission.

And she was damn proud of the result.

Because Dénes was perfection.

Perhaps a biased opinion—very biased—but not far from the truth. He was kind, intelligent, talented, handsome, brave, honest... in his own way, since the general public insisted on regarding swindlers as common criminals.

But what did that matter?

Everyone admired politicians, after all.

And what a sweet child he'd been. Sweet—and exhausting. Everything interested him. How lead got inside a pencil, why elevators didn't fall when cables snapped, why the sun and moon looked the same size when one was far larger, what the crane operator did when he needed to shit, and what happened to his body if—God forbid—he died up there.

She'd worried briefly about why a six-year-old contemplated such things, then reassured herself it was normal and focused instead on answering the questions—because her nephew demanded answers, not evasions.

Facts. Data. Scientifically grounded explanations.

So she often had to look things up.

She never regretted it. She learned something new every time. Whether it was useful was another matter entirely. To this day, she hadn't found any practical application for her knowledge of crane operators' toilet logistics.

But she remembered with a smile that some questions he solved himself, through logic—and those were his happiest triumphs. Like when, at ten, he suddenly figured out why traffic rules required a small arc for right turns and a large one for left.

At least in civilized countries.

Thanks to him, Mici néni learned a great deal about how the world worked—far more than most people. Almost as much as Dénes himself, who still investigated everything he didn't understand, accumulating by now a working grasp of subjects ranging from mathematics (the alpha and omega of everything, in his view) through psychology (also important) to space exploration and the history of various sports.

And he knew a thing or two about computers as well.

You had to keep up with the times, he claimed, if you couldn't stay ahead of them.

True enough—but Mici néni felt too old for such things. Fortunately, after a few failed attempts, her nephew stopped pushing. He did, however, teach her some simpler tricks.

Like how to use the internet.

So now she sat before the screen, indulging her new hobby alongside feeding birds. Reading stories—some exciting, some entertaining, some downright instructive—about colleagues.

The web was full of them.

Stories about con artists, exposed scams, and the occasional genuinely brilliant scheme. All of them proved there was nothing new under the sun. Every scam had a prototype someone had already invented—just as movies, novels, plays, musical compositions... everything in the creative world rested on archetypes.

The difference lay in how you deployed those archetypes.

Well or badly.

That alone separated inspiration from theft.

Mici néni drew inspiration from everything. Watching television, reading newspapers (even online now), listening to strangers on the bus—part of her mind constantly analyzed information for potential use.

That was how she first heard about Morvai.

Over lunch in a popular diner, half-listening, she over-heard two municipal office women in the next booth vilifying a third colleague—younger, and probably prettier, than both. And the bitch was exploiting it, going after Balázs, the best catch in the office, judging by his condo and car.

Which far exceeded a simple government employee's means.

Why, they exchanged knowing looks.

Mici néni hadn't known—but once Viktor dug into it, pub-lic records revealed plenty. The rest required deeper digging, but nothing contradicted expectations.

Over the next two and a half months, they tracked the man. Taking turns. They saw everything—gym visits, dates, movies, friends, dog-walking, trash disposal.

And they saw him, on the Tuesday morning after the next contract announcement, accept an envelope in the park from the son of a construction company owner who just kept win-ning bids.

In fact, they saw him accept two fat envelopes. On two dif-ferent Tuesdays.

So they decided they would take the next one themselves.

The old classic scams were a solid foundation. There were plenty of them—though not all were usable. The rest need-ed fine-tuning to work in Budapest in the third decade of the third millennium.

That new choreography required a special, almost artistic

sensibility.

Which she had always had.

And Dénes had it too. Even more so.

As he should.

Just a pity he sometimes didn't know where the line was.

The one thing his aunt couldn't teach him.

There was always a safe point—you could go right up to it. Cross it, and things could turn brutal in an instant. Mici néni had learned that on her own skin and didn't want her nephew learning it the same way.

So no matter how much he sighed when she raised the issue for the hundredth time, she raised it again.

The boy was simply too reckless.

As she mulled this over, her eyes drifted across the list of links on the screen. She opened a few, skimmed the articles, then clicked back to the page of results her nephew had pulled up with a handful of keywords.

One headline finally snagged her attention:

Corpse Robber.

Curious what kind of trick could fleece the dead, she clicked.

"Bastard," she muttered a few minutes later, leaning back with a sigh.

The article described a con artist who targeted the next of kin of recently deceased patients. He sent them carefully addressed packages—fake, of course—claiming, with the help of hastily forged documents, that the deceased had placed the order shortly before dying.

Cash on delivery.

Nine families out of ten paid. Out of curiosity. Piety. Who knew.

The idea itself wasn't bad, Mici néni conceded.

It was simply too base—at least by her standards.

And there was no heart in it at all.

* * *

Oszkár stood before the painting, hands clasped behind his back, nodding at the price tag with satisfaction.

He'd remembered right.

The owner of the Újlipótváros antique shop—specializing mainly in paintings—stopped beside him.

"Like it?" he asked, voice lowered with reverence.

"Now I do," Oszkár said, giving nothing more as he met the man's eyes.

"Tell me."

The man's name was Szilárd Fischer, and he had a serious reputation in the trade. Far more serious than Oszkár's. Not that Oszkár cared—he wasn't chasing reputation; he was chasing money.

Everyone knew that.

Fischer too, though he never judged him for it.

"You know painting's not really my table," Oszkár said with rare honesty.

"But you know plenty of other things," Fischer cut in.

"Furniture, books, jewelry, sculptures..."

"Don't leave out the envelopes," Oszkár muttered.

Fischer laughed. "God, let it go already!"

"I'm trying."

"You're acting like the fourteenth martyr of Arad."

"That's how I feel."

"You're an idiot."

"Exactly."

Neither meant a word of it. The ritual was too old to skip.

"Speaking of which," Fischer said, "what's up with that Nazi worm?" He hated the billionaire as much as everyone else.

"Last week he supposedly bought a Renaissance coconut cup for one and a half million."

"Who drank from it—one of the Borgias?"

"Could be."

"Still hunting for Beethoven's scalp?"

"As far as I know. But let's not talk about Sólyom. Let's talk about these."

Oszkár gestured to the three paintings hanging side by side.

Each depicted a horse in profile: one white—pardon, gray, the official term, he'd looked it up—one brown (bay), and one black, finally uncontroversial.

All three stood before the same bright green fence. All faced right.

A series, judging from the elegant labels beneath them:

Antal Ács, Horse Portrait, 1923

And, most importantly:

12,000,000 Ft.

Yes. Twelve million.

"What about them?" Fischer asked, intrigued.

"Just that yesterday..." Oszkár paused. "I ran into one just like it."

"Impossible." Fischer shook his head.

Oszkár pulled out his phone and held it toward him. The dealer leaned in, skeptical—then froze. He snatched the phone from Oszkár's hand. Oszkár let him. Even enjoyed watching his old friend zoom in on the photo, on the artist's signature in the lower right corner, his face draining of color.

"Unbelievable," Fischer whispered. "This really is him. But how the hell—"

"No idea," Oszkár shrugged. "Just saw it. Thought of you. And these. Want it?"

"Of course I want it!" Fischer nearly shouted. "An unknown Antal Ács turning up out of nowhere would be a sensation. Especially a horse portrait—that's what he was best at. He painted them with a technique that appeared with the avant-garde in the—"

"For who?" Oszkár cut in.

Fischer blinked. "What?"

"I mean," Oszkár clarified, "was he commissioned? Or did he just paint them?"

"Just painted them," Fischer said. "But they sold quickly. These three, for instance, were owned by the Helvéczy family until the sixties, when—"

"Helvéczy?" Oszkár cut in, mind flashing to a black-and-white photo, two boys, an ornate gate. "Big *H*. Two lions?"

"Yes," Fischer said slowly. "That was their coat of arms. How do you know?"

* * *

The passenger behind the tinted windows of the custom-modified Volvo could barely wait to get home and place the newest treasure of his world-famous private collection in its rightful spot.

For now it lay on the seat beside him, nestled in a double-clasped, velvet-lined pigskin briefcase.

Sólyom had been sharpening his teeth on it for years, but the banker who'd owned it for the past two had rejected every offer—right up until yesterday. Even fifteen million hadn't moved him.

No use.

So came Plan B.

And now the beauty was his.

And he'd paid pocket change for it, as his only true confidant—his secretary—liked to say. Oddly enough, the young man hadn't lied. True, that "pocket change" turned out to be an 1895 ten-korona coin in mint condition, long coveted by the banker and purchased for nearly thirty thousand euros from a former minister whose legendary love of coins had finally collided with a sudden need for cash—and a demand for absolute discretion.

Still, the fact remained: in practice it had been a simple swap.

One tiny coin for a twenty-seven-centimeter, silver-colored cylinder.

Because at first glance, that was all the object offered.

And, his secretary insisted, at second glance too.

"So you have no idea what this is?" Sólyom asked pleasantly, studying the man across from him.

Or rather, the kid—because in the billionaire's world anyone under thirty still counted. This one—one-seventy-five, blond, blue-eyed, solidly built, named Richárd—looked, not by accident (it had been a hiring criterion), like an SS officer from an American movie.

At the interview he'd technically already been thirty; Sólyom remembered noting the date on the résumé, off by two weeks.

So yes—back then he'd still been a kid.

Today, nearly eight years later, he wasn't anymore.

A shame how quickly youth evaporated.

"Of course I have ideas," Richárd said. "Plenty."

"Let's hear them." Sólyom smiled and adjusted his hearing aid—never in public; vanity forbade it. But with no one watching (staff didn't count), he allowed himself the tiny, clever device.

Richárd, genuinely intrigued by the mystery item his boss had shown him moments earlier, straightened slightly, his hand hovering near his hip.

"Uh… sword hilt?"

Sólyom shook his head.

"Some kind of kitchen tool?"

Another shake.

"I didn't get a good look at the engravings, though. That would help…"

"Nice try," the billionaire said, smiling.

"But not nice enough?"

"No. Go on."

Running out of inspiration, Richárd sighed but tried again.

"Part of a larger device?"

"What kind?"

"Actually… no idea. Just whether it belonged to something or stood on its own."

"On its own."

"Paperweight?" A sudden guess. Another head shake. "Glass… test tube… snuff box…"

"No, no, and no."

"Children's toy? Like a rattle—"

Sólyom waved this off.

"Then adult."

"Adult toy?" Sólyom mused.

"Vibrator, maybe," the secretary ventured, not quite meeting his eyes.

The billionaire laughed. "Very cold."

Richárd's shoulders slumped. "Candleholder?" he offered at last—

—and froze as Sólyom's thick, coal-black eyebrows rose.

"Warming up."

"Thank God," Richárd muttered. "But I'm sure that's as warm as it gets."

"Except," Sólyom said, opening the briefcase, "it didn't hold a candle, but a torch."

He lifted the object with reverent care.

"This, my friend, is a torch holder made of silver-plated nickel alloy. It traveled hand to hand over more than three thousand kilometers, from Olympia to Berlin."

He paused.

"You know when, don't you?"

"'36?" Richárd breathed. He knew the era—and the country—that were his boss's favorites. The one where, as Sólyom liked to say, for a few good years there had been order.

And cleanliness.

"Indeed." Sólyom nodded, pleased, running his hand over the relic. "And this one even appeared on television. You can watch it on YouTube—the exact moment when, using this—or rather, the torch housed in it—on August first, 1936, in Berlin, they lit the Olympic flame."

The billionaire stared ahead, treating the object with an almost ceremonial touch as his fingers drifted over the artifact from one of the Krupp factories—lingering on the five rings engraved on its side, clasped in the talons of the German imperial eagle.

* * *

"And the truck's here too, just looking for parking." Oszkár jerked his thumb behind him and stepped into the apartment.

"That's good..." Gergő said uncertainly, closing the door. "But the thing is, yesterday... there was this poker game, and when... uh... the old man's stuff came up..."

He trailed off—because Oszkár wasn't listening.

Oszkár was already at the living room doorway, where he froze for a beat.

"...so anyway, Lala said he's got this appraiser buddy who works at a pawn shop, and if he were me... uh..."

But Oszkár had understood enough.

The deal was blown.

Someone stood by the window.

"...Not that I don't trust you, but you know how it is..."

A grim man in his forties, in a herringbone jacket. Slicked-back hair. Rimless glasses. Behind them, a stare that promised nothing pleasant.

"...When someone comes all this way," Gergő kept apologizing, wringing his hands, "for free... to help out... I hope you don't mind."

"Why would he mind?" the newcomer asked, his voice dipped in mockery. "After all, nobody wants to cheat you. Right, colleague?"

He fixed Oszkár with a cold, deliberate stare.

Goddamn it, a voice groaned inside Oszkár's head. This is going to be worse than I thought.

He could already see the tabloid covers: *Treasure That Wasn't*, or *Junk Dealer Gets Played*.

"Of course not," he said, spreading his arms.

What else could he say?

"But in today's world," the other man went on, unhurried, "you can never be too careful."

Then—suddenly—he smiled and stepped forward with an outstretched hand.

"Péter Halmos."

Oszkár stared at him just long enough to read the intention.

The man wanted to toy with him. A cat with a mouse. Could end it with one clean bite, but preferred to watch the little creature squirm first. Supposedly the blood tasted sweeter afterward—if that idiotic article Oszkár had once read online was even true. Something about bullfights, too, where gourmets lined up to taste the enraged meat of the freshly killed animal...

Sounded nice.

He'd never quite believed it.

But you won't eat me, his thoughts snapped back. *My meat's not on the menu.*

Nothing had actually happened yet. He was a peddler buying a pile of junk. Doing Gergő a favor. And as for one of those paintings being... better executed than the others—well, he had no knowledge of that.

Let them prove otherwise.

No reason to be afraid.

"Oszkár Balogh." He slapped the man's palm, matching the smile. "Had a chance to look around yet?"

Halmos shook his head. "Just getting started, but... there are a couple of interesting pieces here. Like this one." He chin-pointed toward the horse portrait.

Go ahead, Oszkár thought, heat rising, arranging interest on his face.

But Halmos wasn't talking about the painting at all.

He drifted to the photograph beside it.

"In this one, our friend Gergő's grandfather appears with one of the Helvéczy counts. I assume you've heard of the Helvéczy family."

"Rings a bell," Oszkár said carefully, flicking a glance at their host.

The air in the room had shifted. Maybe he'd misread this. Maybe it wasn't exposure at all. Halmos's voice carried an undertone that didn't fit the disaster scenario in Oszkár's head—hinting at an entirely different story.

He didn't yet know what.

But suddenly he was, painfully, curious.

"Great patrons of the arts," Halmos went on, fingers steepled like a lecturer. "Several figures in the Hungarian avant-garde owe them their—"

He stopped mid-sentence and turned to Gergő as if struck by a thought.

"But didn't you mention coffee earlier?"

"Coming right up," the host stammered, still rattled. He

looked to Oszkár. "Would you like some?"

"Please. Black, one sugar."

Gergő nodded and vanished into the kitchen.

Finally, they were alone.

"Now where was I?" Halmos said, returning with theatrical innocence.

Oszkár felt it more clearly with each second: this was a performance.

And he'd soon learn his role.

"Oh yes." Halmos's memory returned. "I was about to get to"—a pause, relished—"Antal Ács."

Okay, pal. You've got me, Oszkár thought, still unsure of the angle.

"And his famous horse portraits from the twenties." Halmos continued, showing off, but the point still didn't land.

Until now.

"A gallery's selling the three best-known ones as we speak." He met Oszkár's eyes. "Twelve million each."

A beat.

"But you already knew that."

Everything clicked.

So that's the game.

No tabloids after all. Unless it was next month's *Antiques World*: *Deal of the Year*—full-length portrait, long interview where he held forth on professional ethics—

"How much do you want?" Oszkár asked quietly.

Halmos stepped closer. "For my silence?"

Oszkár nodded.

Halmos sighed toward the kitchen, as if calculating on the fly.

"Considering," he said slowly, "that a previously unknown Ács would fetch, at minimum, fifteen million at auction... I think thirty percent is reasonable."

He's right, Oszkár thought grimly. He'd still pocket over ten million.

But he hated paying.

Whenever he had to, he heard his grandfather: *Always negotiate. Come hell, high water, or Gypsy children falling from the sky—even on your deathbed. You can only win. And if not—at least you tried.*

"You want to make four and a half million for five minutes' work?" Oszkár shook his head like a man personally wounded by mathematics.

"You're right," Halmos said, forcing restraint. "Let's call it four even. Final offer."

Oszkár knew better than to push further. Mentally patting his grandfather's back, he nodded.

"And I want it now. In cash," Halmos added quickly, nerves leaking through. "Otherwise no deal."

Gergő returned, wobbling slightly under a tray.

"I need to go to the bank," Oszkár muttered fast, then turned to the host with a polite smile as he stopped beside them.

"Gentlemen—your coffee."

"Thank you." Oszkár took his cup. "But while it cools, I'll

check on that truck."

He shot a look at Halmos.

Halmos sipped, hissed, and immediately set the steaming cup on the windowsill.

"Go ahead," he grimaced, touching his burned lip. "We'll wait here."

* * *

When Anett spotted the two men, she dropped behind a parked car as if she'd been shot.

Did they see me?

Panic dried her mouth instantly—not just dry, but Sahara dry. Three days without water. The nearest oasis a hundred kilometers away, reachable only by crawling.

She would have given her left arm for a sip. And if they *had* spotted her, that arm was gone anyway.

Because Zsolt Bereczki was capable of anything.

She'd heard plenty during the two and a half years she'd lived with him. About the illegal poker club the authorities shut down—and about its boss, whose body later turned up in a garbage dump.

Without his head.

Never found.

The man had been at their house the night before. Anett had watched him enter Zsolt's study. Heard the shouting. About what, she never asked. Didn't want to know.

Business, obviously.

But this would be personal.

Twice-divorced Zsolt Bereczki considered wife number three to have betrayed him. And robbed him. Both unforgivable—especially the second. What Anett had taken mattered far more to him than she ever had.

Not that he hadn't loved her.

At the beginning he'd been obsessed. That was why he married her—among other reasons. Nearly five years had passed since his last divorce; it was time for another wedding. And another ironclad prenup, because without that there'd be no ceremony.

Anett hadn't minded then.

He took her to Bali, Paris, Tuscany. Showered her with gifts—clothes, jewelry. For her twenty-fifth birthday he bought her a car. She used it to drive to Budapest once a month to visit her mother in the Cheerful Sunset nursing home. Twice, really: she stayed the weekend at a nearby guesthouse and checked in again on the way home.

To see her mom and her roommate, loudmouthed Aunt Luca.

The two old women had grown so close they spent their last year and a half like sisters, giggling and whispering like ridiculous schoolgirls, to the amusement of both families. They thrived on it. Anett and Luca's only son, András, agreed immediately.

He worked as some kind of civil servant at the Interior Ministry and kept thanking them at their foursome dinners, convinced his mother owed her recovery from depression to

Anett's mother. That she'd become her old self again.

For this, he said, he'd be forever grateful.

When Anett repeated these dinners at home, Zsolt teased her that András was only so nice because he wanted into her pants. She never knew how much of that was a joke—and how much was jealousy. Sometimes she caught something in Zsolt's eyes that looked like the latter.

It hurt.

It also felt like proof of love.

András's eternal gratitude didn't last. A quick heart attack ended it. Ended the trips too. Anett had visited the cemetery maybe three times in the past two years. Always alone.

Her husband disliked the city. Disliked her mother. He sent candy and flowers at first—later just flowers for the grave—but stayed home. He paid for everything, though. The facility. The funeral.

In some respects, Anett had a good life.

Materially.

But that wasn't the scale she used.

After he got bored—four or five months after the wedding—Zsolt began cheating openly. Call girls. Hostesses. Waitresses. Prostitutes. He didn't even bother hiding it.

That was the most humiliating part.

When she confronted him, he was genuinely offended. Didn't understand the problem. In his mind, his wife had everything a woman could want. A house. Vacation homes—two of them. Comfort. Staff.

He could list for hours everything money could buy.

She should have left then.

She hadn't had the courage. She was afraid to start over. Afraid to admit to acquaintances that her marriage had collapsed. Afraid of being alone.

And afraid of Zsolt.

Whether he'd even let her go.

Maybe he would have—except the situation changed. Complicated. The moment slipped away. Love vanished. Then even basic affection.

She had no one to confide in. Everyone in Debrecen orbited Zsolt somehow—especially the men—and she didn't dare be honest with any of them.

Then she remembered Aunt Luca.

Kind. Warm. And crucially—someone who had never met Zsolt.

So after one All Souls' Day visit, she detoured to Cheerful Sunset. The old woman welcomed her with the same affection as always. So did her son.

András genuinely liked her. Was more than willing to comfort her—in an older, more traditional way.

And Anett, though she knew he was married with three children, let him.

She peeked around the car's brake light.

The two men in sunglasses and dark suits were approaching a black Mercedes that had just pulled up outside the restaurant next to her building. An elegant couple emerged.

The woman had long red hair—looked familiar—but she wore sunglasses too, and they were on the street for no more than a few seconds.

One bodyguard scanned the area, opened the rear door. They climbed in. He followed. The other gorilla took the passenger seat.

The car pulled away.

Anett closed her eyes.

Not them.

As she straightened, her gaze snagged on an advertising column. A poster for a new Hollywood action film: one of the hottest A-list actresses leaping over a burning spaceship-looking thing, laser pistol in hand.

Blonde hair in the poster.

The long red suited her better.

Anett continued toward her apartment, thinking only of a tall glass of water—and of the day it became undeniable that she couldn't stay in that house anymore.

That the house was no longer safe.

Not even as safe as before.

Zsolt's earlier enemies were small-time compared to the Serbs who had appeared months earlier to seize control of Debrecen's underworld. Now even Zsolt Bereczki's life was no longer guaranteed.

The hand grenade someone tossed through one of the villa's windows proved that.

Not just any window. The nursery window.

* * *

"You're sure?" Oszkár's voice had gone tight.

Szilárd stared back, apologetic, the painting balanced in his hands.

"That it's a fake? Absolutely."

He set the canvas down on the table with something close to contempt—nearly threw it.

The gesture alone told Oszkár he'd lost. Literally and figuratively. And he couldn't even tell which hurt more: the four million he was down (*call it four even*—may that pus-filled garbage can rot in hell), plus the two hundred thousand for the giant pile of horse shit they'd hauled off, plus another forty to dump it—

four million two hundred forty thousand—

or the fact that he'd been played.

"Plus," Szilárd went on, his mouth twisting, "pretty amateur work."

"But..." A groan slipped out of Oszkár. "Yesterday you said—"

"Based on a five-centimeter, overexposed photo?" Szilárd cut in, irritation sharpening his voice. "I couldn't even see the colors."

Because the cursed thing was in shadow, Oszkár thought—but he stayed still.

"Much less the brushwork, or the—"

Szilárd snatched the painting up again and held it out in front of Oszkár, as if presenting evidence in court.

"And this canvas," he said. "Ten years old. Max."

Oszkár didn't react. It could've been twenty, for all he cared. Or a hundred and twenty.

"So you really blew this one," his friend said at last.

Oszkár didn't argue.

* * *

This was the day's high point. French champagne, dimmed lights, soft music—Beethoven, naturally—and here he sat in a comfortable armchair in the middle of the museum. Because this hundred-square-meter room in the Sólyom villa's basement *was* a museum, housing a collection whose value was literally incalculable. The insurance company calculated it anyway—at just over two billion forints—but that covered only the legally acquired treasures. The public knew about those; a few upscale magazines periodically showcased some of them (and justifiably so), each new addition as sensational as the last. Sólyom had even allowed a British TV crew ten minutes with their cameras once, to give the plebs their due. Bread and circuses.

A few exhibition pieces, however—kept in the special chamber beneath the cellar, conveniently missing from every blueprint—never came before foreign eyes, though they were worth twice as much. Minimum. You just couldn't really sell them—except on the black market. Not that he'd part with even one. Each was a treasure. And not only the paintings, sculptures, and jewelry—most spirited away during the war by the Germans or the Russians, and these were the collection's showstoppers—but also the handwritten, paper-based documents closest to Sólyom's heart. And we're not talking about the signed 1926 *Mein Kampf*, acquired legitimately at a Los Angeles auction for sixty-two thousand dollars—no problem there—but the others. The problematic ones.

Like that gorgeous four-hundred-year-old Geneva Bible stolen from a museum and sought worldwide for ten years, fruitlessly, naturally, because it sat here with him in an airtight display case. If that ever came out, he'd find himself splashed across front pages—or in prison. That wasn't ruled out, especially if anyone examined the other exhibits. A few were even more compromising. Some had been sought for eighty years by relatives of the original owners—assuming any survived the "unpleasant summer camp years," as he casually called them, which, in his opinion, happened more often than it should have.

So apart from three initiates like himself—fellow big-game hunters who also possessed certain fortune-worth treasures of... questionable provenance—no one had ever seen the complete collection. No one ever would.

Sólyom knew most people wouldn't understand. Wouldn't understand if they knew—but they wouldn't, because he'd taken every precaution, including deliberately discrediting rumors of the special chamber with exaggerated lies. As he aged, he increasingly didn't give a damn. What did it matter what all those primitive proles thought? About this or anything? After work they ate, drank, slept, screwed, and voted—if he hadn't missed anything important. Change his life because of them? A joke. They weren't even in the same weight class. A bus driver, cook, manual laborer? God forbid a Gypsy? Please. Some days he doubted they even belonged to the same species—him and the others.

Not because he was a Nazi, as many accused him—he considered himself the most reliable judge of that—and he wasn't. Maybe just a tiny bit. He simply liked keeping things where they belonged, including people—most of whom didn't impress him. He judged by merit, and damn few had any.

He subscribed to a self-designed hypothetical caste system based on reputation, influence, and wealth, where he naturally ranked high—but not highest. Not even close. Not in the top three tiers, at least not globally, where bank directors, arms and pharmaceutical moguls, hotshot brokers, producers, minor-nation dictators and their ilk crowded the podium with private jets, hotel chains, private islands, and whatnot in their pockets. Domestically, yes—here he belonged among those at the peak, knowing maybe two dozen people richer than he was. Which meant nothing, since he never appeared on the top-hundred lists. Cost him plenty to keep it that way. He'd never wanted publicity.

He concentrated on the Ninth Symphony's final bars and angled himself toward his favorite Rembrandt—hearing aid or no, the Dolby Atmos was perfect only at that precise tilt—when a magazine cover from the previous day drifted onto the inside of his closed eyelids, blurry at first, then sharpening. Also Beethoven-related, whom Sólyom adored. Every work. Knew them all, note for note. Had read everything ever written about him. As for the Martonvásár museum—where a lock of the composer's hair was preserved—he'd made pilgrimage there almost every year to make an offer. Always refused. Not for sale, they said. Though it would be among the most precious relics in this room. A piece of the Master himself.

Few people sensed the emanation of objects, but Sólyom was among them. He believed that a handwritten letter, a glass someone drank from, shoes they walked in, even a ring they wore held something of the person. Which is why he had such a massive collection of diaries, letters, and personal effects. But nothing from Beethoven yet—nothing truly major. Something referencing the old man's Hungarian connections, for instance. Not exclusively the letters documenting his hopeless love for Josephine Brunsvik; he'd acquired one of those already.

But when he saw that magazine cover—a slightly yellowed paper sheet front and center—his heart had stalled for a moment. Then he read the article... and again. If he could obtain that, he thought, one of his last dreams would be fulfilled. He would own something that bore the imprint of a true genius's hand—thus a piece of the man himself—and spoke specifically to *us*, to Hungarians.

Besides, he already kept here a piece of Petőfi, Horthy, the

Arad martyrs, Kádár, along with countless others—including Adolf Hitler. But he could cite Kodály, Bartók, or Wagner if he wanted to list composers. In other words, good company. Both he, Sólyom—and Beethoven.

* * *

The little boy lifted his face toward her with a smile, reached for his mother's cheek as if to stroke it—and twisted her nose so sharply her eyes watered.

"Hey, what was that for?" Anett laughed, suddenly aware of how long it had been since she'd last seen him.

Almost three days.

Could he have grown in that time? He seemed bigger.

"No," her friend replied—though Anett hadn't spoken. "Same weight as the day before yesterday. To the gram."

"But I didn't even—" Anett's brow creased, but the other woman waved it off.

"You always ask. Anyway—what's the situation?"

Anett let out a breath.

"If everything goes well, we'll have the money in a month. Month and a half, tops."

As long as she kept performing that little amateur number three times a week—easy enough—she'd have the five million together and could finally buy the tiny house in Transylvania her roommate had found. No gas or sewer, true, but electricity, two rooms, a miniature kitchen, a bathroom. On the forest's edge, in a village Zsolt Bereczki had never heard of—and never would, if things went according to plan. Exactly right for her. And for almost-eighteen-month-old Dani, now asleep in her lap.

What a beautiful child. If not for that strange, almost perfectly five-pointed star birthmark—deep crimson-purple, about a centimeter wide—right in the middle of his left shoulder, he would've been flawless.

He still was. Not because clothes usually hid the mark, but because the star itself was beautiful—whatever his father had said.

Zsolt had wanted it removed when the baby was three months old. Joking, supposedly, that they might lock the poor kid up one day for "using prohibited totalitarian symbols." He'd even scheduled the surgery. Anett had dug in her heels, thrown such a fit he backed down—which wasn't like him. So the birthmark stayed.

She gazed at the peacefully breathing boy. He'd worn himself out on the giraffes—that Africa-themed playground with four different-sized, surprisingly lifelike plastic giraffes you could actually sit on. Dani always got excited there, though not as much as he had at the zoo back home, where the giraffes were a regular pilgrimage. In Debrecen they had to go at least once a month, ignoring tigers and monkeys, which left him cold. Only giraffes mattered.

"Guh-waf!" he'd shout, unable to manage the *j* or the *r*, to his father's delight. Whenever Zsolt came along, he'd slap his forehead in mock disbelief—*That's a gray wolf to you?*

Jeeeesus!—and everyone laughed.

Anett smiled at the memory. She resolved that next time they'd visit the Budapest giraffes—then wondered whether Dani, once grown, would forgive her for "pawning him off." Or whether he wouldn't remember at all that for four and a half months—so far—her friend had raised him. Or, more delicately, looked after him.

Anett had met Eszter on a Balaton vacation at twelve. Both liked the same boy—a flash-toothed, half-Italian kid from the campground—who promptly hooked up with some "old" girl already past fourteen. Their shared disappointment bonded them instantly, and they'd been inseparable ever since. Mostly summers, but they kept in touch by phone and online until Eszter left for Dubai. From there she checked in less often; for two years they barely communicated—fortunate, really, because those years coincided exactly with Anett's marriage. Zsolt never learned Eszter existed.

Which was precisely why he'd never look for the child there.

That was why Anett entrusted her with what mattered most—beyond loving Eszter and trusting her fully. It was sheer luck that Eszter came home from Dubai just when Anett needed a place to land. A few days after the escape, they ran into each other downtown, clung to one another, and told everything. Eszter spoke about the Arab oil magnate she'd "secretaried" for, alongside eight other Eastern European girls, earning enough to rent a nice apartment in a gated community. Anett talked about Zsolt. And about Dani—whom she wanted hidden from the world. Especially from his father.

They devised the plan. Temporarily. Until things settled. Eszter would take the little boy, whom she'd come to love as her own.

But that had been over four months ago. Since then, Anett only visited—in a wig and sunglasses, changing buses several times. Eszter thought she was overdoing it. She didn't know Zsolt. Anett had told her plenty.

Eszter insisted there wasn't as much danger as Anett believed. If Zsolt didn't even know she existed, they were safe. Why didn't Anett just move in and stay with Dani?

Anett said she didn't want to risk it. Alone, she could focus better on earning money.

Which was true.

But she never spoke of the nightmares.

* * *

Mici néni raised her glass to the two men, smiling. She was proud of them. Both of them. They'd pulled it off.

"Congratulations," she said with real warmth, watching them clink glasses with her in perfect sync.

They made a good team. Off the clock too. They didn't need half-words—they understood each other without speaking. A tiny facial twitch, the faint lift of an eyebrow, an odd emphasis: any small gesture that meant nothing to outsiders was enough for each to know exactly what the other wanted.

"If only everything went this smoothly!" Viktor quoted a classic, tossing back the plum brandy.

Dénes sighed. He hated these movie references—even when he actually recognized them, like now. Still, he had to admit they were better, if only by a hair, than the old lady's proverbs. And things *had* worked out exactly as written. No wonder: he'd written this chapter himself.

The job was his brainchild. He'd laid it out step by step, everyone's role mapped with precision. The hardest part, at least in his view, had fallen to his aunt. Even though Mici néni hadn't appeared on stage, the whole thing stood or fell on her performance. And she'd been flawless.

Viktor too. He'd played the nonexistent Gergő Horváth—cheerfully parting with his grandfather's junk—so convincingly that even Dénes would have bought it. He told him so.

"In other words, you deserve an Oscar," he finished, then waited for the punchline to land.

It did. Mici néni burst out laughing first—*Oszkár*, that was good—then Viktor joined in, his cheeks reddening.

"Thanks," he said, pleased, but after a beat went on, "only I learned everything from you. So really you're praising yourself. And if you ask me, that's pretty arrogant."

Mici néni smiled again and exchanged a look with her nephew.

"Well, there you have it," Dénes sighed in mock regret. "You make one polite, encouraging remark—not necessarily heartfelt—and what do you get? They dump it right back in your face."

"Dénes!" his aunt snapped. Vulgar talk irritated her to no end.

"Pardon," he replied in a thick French accent, rolling the *r* in his throat. Mici néni waved him off.

"As an appraiser you weren't bad either," Viktor said then, easy enough—but added, "that much."

He didn't mean the jab. Not really. In truth, he admired Dénes's performance—just as he admired how he'd constructed the whole operation, which, allegedly—and that was the neat part—had grown out of a cheap flyer.

Dénes had spotted Oszkár Balogh's ad on a telephone pole and, as he reported a few days later, instantly smelled potential. He began shadowing the man at a respectful distance, disguised just enough to stay safe, and quickly worked out his routine. By the time he told the story to the others, he already had a plan.

It hinged partly on their future "client's" colleague, Fischer Szilárd, whom Oszkár—Dénes on his heels—had recently visited to admire his latest acquisitions. Including three original Ács Antal paintings.

The fourth, Dénes decided (and later said aloud), would have to be painted by Mici néni. She hadn't jumped at the commission. She hadn't held a brush in years, she protested—and even then it had only been hobby dabbling, painting nonsense for her own amusement.

Her nephew wore her down. More precisely, he talked through every last objection. His main argument: if she did this, it would finally give meaning to that year and a half she'd spent in prison.

That was where she'd learned to paint. State-funded instruction, no less. She could've chosen basket-weaving or box-folding, but she'd signed up for the basic art course instead. A good choice. That was where her gift came out—especially for copying. She'd cashed in on this skill a few times after her release, but she'd never forged a truly valuable painting. Never planned to either.

Then Dénes appeared with three horse portraits blown up from a catalog, saying they needed one more that looked exactly like them—only different. And she shouldn't worry: the job wasn't dangerous.

He walked them through the whole scheme.

They bought it on the spot.

Mici néni sat down at the easel again.

And now here they were, four million forints richer.

"You're brave, kid," Dénes replied to the jab. "Or rather—reckless."

"I like living dangerously," said the former Gergő Horváth, inwardly groaning at the even weaker-than-usual wordplay, which he was sure Dénes had deployed purely to torture him.

"Just watch you don't end up with a real monocle under that eye."

Viktor grinned, ready with a comeback—when Mici néni

steered things back where she wanted them.

"I hope you cleaned up every trace," she said, half scolding, eyeing them like two naughty schoolboys.

"Of course," her nephew reassured her. "We left the place sparkling. Right?"

"I doubt it's been that clean in thirty years," Viktor said. Mici néni nodded.

"Good. With a shameless character like that, you never know how he'll react once he realizes he's been had. By the way—he didn't suspect anything?"

The man who'd played Gergő shook his head.

"He was more worried I'd start suspecting *him*."

"Which you did," Mici néni said with satisfaction. "Right at the last moment. When he thought the jackpot was his."

Always then, Viktor would've retorted—if the other two hadn't drilled that rule into him themselves. In a setup like this, attack really was the best defense. If you wanted to con someone already gearing up to do the same to you, you made things harder for them. Made *them* prove their good intentions, not you.

That was the gist of Dénes's long, mind-numbing psych mini-lecture—minimum twenty minutes, every time. And as he'd pointed out soon enough, the same thing had happened in the park with that Bartha kid. Bartha hadn't been trying to cheat him, true—but he wasn't exactly walking the straight and narrow either. Bribing a public official still counts as a crime.

Which meant his conscience wasn't spotless. So when the fake brother-in-law started fretting, Bartha rushed to calm him. And thanks to Dénes's undiluted repulsiveness, he wanted the whole encounter over as fast as possible—along with the literally sticky smell clinging to his "relative."

Old trick. Still useful.

"In his way *he* got the jackpot too," Viktor said instead. "He's got the painting. Which, by the way, turned out pretty well."

He glanced at Mici néni with real admiration, but she only gave a half-hearted shrug.

"Come on," she muttered. "No way we'd fool an expert for two seconds with that."

"We didn't have to."

"The kid's right," Dénes chimed in, good-humored. "They handed over four million for it. And this is your first painting on the open market..."

He gave Viktor a conspiratorial wink.

"Oh, stop already!" his aunt sighed, but since she clearly wasn't truly offended, he pushed on.

"By the way, if I'd pressed a little, he would've gone to four and a half."

"No, my boy!" Mici néni cut in at once. "You always have to know where the line is."

"You've never said that before," her nephew said innocently.

"Write it down somewhere," Viktor suggested, just as straight-faced. The elderly lady sighed.

"Very funny. But mock all you want, I'm still right. Greed

never leads anywhere good. Ask Oszkár. He's a small fortune poorer thanks to it."

"All right, all right," Dénes leaned closer and patted her hand. "I'm only saying the... private lessons paid off in the end."

"Don't remind me!"

"Why not?" Viktor picked up the baton after his mentor gave him a tiny nod. "If you warmed up a bit, I think next time you could easily tackle that Cézanne they stole from Oxford at the turn of the millennium."

Mici néni couldn't believe her ears, but before she could properly tear into Viktor, Dénes did it for her.

"You're not listening, old man," he said sharply, then lifted one finger and continued, almost syllable by syllable: "You always have to know the limit. Right?"

He looked at his aunt. She stayed silent a moment, ignoring Viktor's poorly hidden grin, then shook her head and finally said:

"It doesn't suit two big, strapping men to mock a poor old woman who couldn't hurt a fly anymore. Of course..." She added slowly, "if there were another woman on the team, the fight would be more balanced."

Both men rolled their eyes. Here she went again. She'd been riding this hobby horse for weeks.

"I thought we'd settled this," Viktor muttered, resigned.

"Just take a look at her," Mici néni pleaded. "For my sake."

"Uh... wait a second." Viktor froze and glanced at Dénes.

The man wore the same expression when he took over.

"You mean," he began cautiously, "you already have someone specific in mind?"

You witch, he thought. *Of course you do.* That's where this whole conversation had been heading. It would've ended up here even if they'd started with the latest breakthroughs in marine biology. His aunt was very good at this: gently, imperceptibly, but effectively steering any topic. A clever and useful trick he himself used all the time, so he *should* have noticed where she was going. But she'd lulled his guard so neatly he never stood a chance. And here they were.

Dénes sighed, studying her as she shrugged, and thought—not for the first time, and not for the last—how much he owed her. Not just because she'd taken him in back then, which couldn't have been easy. At thirty-five, taking in a small child who would overturn the rest of her life and any future plans, which probably hadn't included nonstop, seven-days-a-week duty. Yet that's what she'd done, without exaggeration. People say motherhood is like that... but aunt-hood sure isn't. Mici néni had taken on the job anyway, and he'd never repay her. Not for that, and not for the love with which she'd raised and educated him... and the things she'd taught him herself. Mostly material no regular school touched. Psychology, marketing, a dash of game theory, linguistics (with special attention to accents and dialects), art history, etiquette, basic makeup and cosmetics, the rules of various card games, and a long list of other subjects that never appeared in any national curriculum. Like topic steering. And the topic they had somehow (or as young Dénes used to say: "how-somehow-not") arrived at again was his aunt's latest fixation: expanding the repertoire—and what that required. Expanding the team.

"I noticed her the other day," the old lady went on. "Completely by accident. She was doing the broken-vase trick, and there was something about her... I don't know."

"Potential?" her nephew asked dryly.

"Something like that." Mici néni bobbed her head. "So I followed her home... without her realizing. If you want, you can check her out too."

She gave them such an innocent look, as if she couldn't count to two—but for once, they didn't swallow it.

"Why?" Viktor asked, uneasy. He hadn't given up the fight yet, unlike Dénes.

"So you can see what she's like."

"Isn't that completely irrelevant?" he burst out. "You can't trust women—" He caught himself. "...uh... I mean... younger women."

Too late. Mici néni gave him a look full of pity.

"You really know how to flatter a girl."

"You know what I meant," Viktor muttered, wounded, and glanced at Dénes for backup.

None came. Dénes only pulled his mouth to one side, the way he did when he thought resistance was pointless. And of course he was right. Once Mici néni set her mind on something, you couldn't knock it out with a jackhammer.

"I know what you meant," she said. "And you're wrong. When a woman is loyal to you, she'll give her life for you. Besides, in this profession you sometimes need a pretty face and two firm breasts. Men always look up at that combination. So it's the best, simplest way to redirect attention. Believe me, I know what I'm talking about."

Viktor believed her. Not just because he knew her history, but because he'd seen photos of her youth. And, of course, because of his own past. Pretty face, two good breasts, attention redirected? Check, check, check.

"We're doing so well as just the three of us," he tried one last time; he could feel the battle slipping away.

"Don't count me anymore," Mici néni cut in, flicking her hand. "Just look at me."

"You look great."

"Come off it. I can barely walk. Soon I'll be calling ashes 'Mama.'"

Liar, Viktor thought. *You're tougher than ever.* But fine. Let her have the last word.

Part Two

Chase

He thought that if he slept on it, things would improve a little, the bitter taste would fade—but he was wrong. One night wasn't enough to get over this.

Embarrassment? Humiliation? Scandal? Tragedy?

Oszkár couldn't decide which word fit. Somehow they all did—yet none of them. Maybe there wasn't even a precise term for this. There we go again, back where we started, with this shit. Something he could neither swallow nor spit out. And he feared it would stay that way until he did something to even the score.

It wasn't even about the four million—or not just that. The cash register in his head had gone haywire too: instead of the familiar chiming (which now would've meant roughly ten million forints in pure profit), it took an unexpected turn, started whining, and then simply exploded in his face.

No one had ever screwed over Oszkár Balogh this bad-ly—and now he solemnly vowed that no one ever would again. The thought didn't console him, of course, but he drew some strength from it. Strength for revenge. Because he couldn't let this stand. He had to catch those bastards who'd played him like this. And when he caught them, he'd show no mercy. He'd break their bones one by one, gouge out their eyes, peel off their skin and—

—naturally only after they returned his money. With interest.

He wasn't the forgiving type, not even as a child. He'd al-ways avenged every slight, including pranks meant as friend-ly jabs, and his revenge was invariably crueler than what pro-voked it. His classmates learned quickly: everyone was better off finding a different target. Since then, it hadn't been profit-able to mess with him. Very unprofitable.

And those two rats would soon find that out.

His will to live started returning—but it didn't last long. Be-cause he had no idea how to do this kind of thing. He wasn't some detective wandering around in a trench coat, notebook in hand, flashing a badge now and then like in the movies. Or should he go to the police? No. Absolutely not. What would he tell them—that he'd tried to con some poor gambler and it had backfired? Out of the question. Besides, half the city would find out what happened, and everyone would laugh at him. Maybe even the papers would write about it. *Big Deal Gone Wrong—Ice Cream Licked Back.*

No. The whole thing had to stay secret.

Good thing he hadn't brought anyone but Szilárd in on it. And Szilárd would keep quiet. Of that, Oszkár was certain.

Actually... maybe he could even help.

There was that guy. What was his name? Oszkár couldn't remember—but he did remember how freaked out his friend had been a few years earlier, one summer day, when he got that text from his daughter. The girl (okay, at nineteen she wasn't so little anymore—except to her father) wrote that she was in Thailand with some guy and staying there, but Dad shouldn't worry, everything was happy. Then radio silence.

The girl had probably turned off her phone, thumbing her nose at poor Szilárd, who nearly had a nervous breakdown.

But he got her home in the end. Well—not him. The private investigator he'd hired for the job. The guy was a total pro. Hard as stone. Out there, he'd apparently not only bribed various officials, bartenders, and bellhops—he'd also cracked a few heads before reaching his goal. Including the boyfriend's, who'd just started getting the girl hooked on cocaine so he could talk her into things that hadn't originally been part of the deal. If it was true, her rescuer had arrived at the very last moment.

The girl was back at university now and thought of those two months as just a bad dream.

Because everything had worked out in the end—thanks to that bloodhound. He worked damn expensive, sure, but according to Szilárd, he'd been worth every penny.

Oszkár needed exactly that kind of person.

* * *

She could feel it was a day she should've skipped. It had started badly from the get-go. Not just because of the black cat she'd nearly tripped over as she stepped out the gate (or did it only count as a bad omen—according to superstition, that is—if it ran across your path? Anett suddenly couldn't decide, but she'd practically stumbled over the thing), and not because of this damn rain either, which seemed like it would never stop—but because she'd barely slept the night before. Two hours at most. That was all she'd managed—and they were the worst two hours of the night.

Because she'd spent them in the basement of the Debrecen villa, tied to a chair. Her husband standing in front of her, Dani in his arms, explaining how Mommy had behaved badly and now had to be punished. And then the little boy started crying...

That was when she woke up. To the crying.

Except the tears were flowing from her own eyes.

And this had been going on for more than three months now—okay, not every day, but twice a week for sure. Or more like three.

So now she felt like washed-out shit, and if the mirror she'd put her makeup on in before leaving was to be believed, she looked like it too.

But she needed the money so they could leave the country. Her and Dani. As soon as possible. That was why she couldn't afford to slack off. Yesterday had already been a wash—meaning she hadn't earned a single forint. But finding the location and scoping out the terrain was at least as important in this line of work as the performance itself. You couldn't stage this show just anywhere.

And you couldn't stage it in the same place twice.

So you had to walk the city streets a lot—and Anett walked them.

This place seemed like the perfect choice. Especially the first corner after the tobacco shop, barely three meters from its entrance, where most customers turned left while tearing the cellophane off their freshly bought cigarette pack, barely looking up. She'd observed that at least eight people did this every hour—twice as many around lunchtime. So that was when she took up her position: decoratively wrapped box in hand, right after the corner—but angled so she could see the tobacco shop door reflected in a storefront window across the street, to select the right subject.

And everything went well, like usual—at least until she remembered she'd left her wallet at home, along with the carefully prepared receipt and invoice she'd made the night before to prove the nonexistent Biedermeier vase was today's purchase.

She remembered how, before leaving the apartment, she'd glanced around and sensed something was wrong—just for a moment—but she hadn't paid attention, because she'd been thinking about the umbrella. Specifically which hand to hold it in when she dropped the—

"Are you all right, miss?" an older gentleman asked worriedly, turning reproachfully to the man in the suit. "Now look what you did! She's about to faint, poor thing."

Don't panic, Anett thought furiously. Nobody cares about that stupid receipt. Worst case you say you lost it. Just pull yourself together and say something before they call an ambulance. Come on. One-two.

She sighed, shook her head, and decided that from now on she wouldn't work this dead tired.

"I'm fine," she said finally, smiling.

In this, however, she was wrong.

Because there *was* a problem—a big one—she just didn't know it yet, since it had nothing to do with lack of sleep or the receipt left at home.

Among the onlookers, a bald, short old man in a long gray trench coat had appeared. Pushing aside those in front of him, he stepped closer.

"You didn't buy it for your parents, did you?" he asked quietly. "For their anniversary?"

He pointed with his chin at the box on the ground.

"Yes, I did," Anett replied, surprised. The man seemed familiar from somewhere. "I just said so."

"Except he wasn't here then," a student girl with a backpack spoke up, confused. "He just arrived. I saw him."

"Me too," the suited man muttered, wrinkling his forehead.

"Then how does he know all this?" the older gentleman murmured in amazement.

But Anett already knew the answer. She'd recognized the old man by then—and unfortunately, the recognition was mutual.

"Because," he rumbled, his look ominous, "the young lady played the same game with me last week. On the other side of town."

The street fell silent.

Every eye fixed on Anett.

The looks reflected disbelief at first, then enlightenment as the chain of logic clicked into place. Then shock, slowly giving way to disappointment—until finally hatred and contempt closed the sequence.

It's all over, Anett thought desperately.

But she was wrong again.

Because the worst was still to come.

"You mean..." the suited man stammered, the slowest to grasp the essence of the story.

"I do," the old man replied with disgust, not waiting for the rest.

"The fucking bitch!" the other burst out. "She tried to rob me!"

His hand clenched into a fist.

"She did indeed."

"You paid her?"

"Unfortunately. Yes. Sucker that I am. A hundred thirty-eight thousand forints."

"Fuck! She asked me for the same amount. She said—"

"That she'd show you the receipt? And the invoice?"

"Yeah."

"She would've shown it. If you'd really asked."

And then the worst happened.

Because in the still-drizzling rain, someone else appeared—a grim man in a leather jacket, wearing sunglasses.

"Excuse me, ladies and gentlemen," he said quietly but firmly as he approached. "Police."

He flashed his badge.

"Miss," he said to Anett—who was now genuinely on the verge of fainting—"you are hereby under arrest. You need to come with me now."

One hand clamped onto her arm like a steel vice.

"We've been watching the suspect for three days," he said over his shoulder to the others, "hoping to finally catch her in the act. This way she'll definitely go to prison."

"Excellent!" the older gentleman nodded with satisfaction. "That's where people like this—"

But he didn't finish, because the plainclothes cop cut him off.

"Could I have your name, sir? You were a witness to the incident, if I'm not mistaken."

"You're not. I saw everything that matters. And I'll gladly tell it in court too."

"Excellent. Then I'll record your information. And yours as well," he added, turning to the other two men. "I assume you'll be pressing charges."

"You bet," the old man and the suited man said in unison.

The rest unfolded like a dream.

Another nightmare—this one without her husband, without Dani—but just as paralyzing.

Her vision blurred. Something began roaring in her ears, and what followed—the cop photographing documents with his phone—felt like it was happening to someone else. Then she felt something cold close around her wrist.

Handcuffs, she thought numbly.

Still, she couldn't grasp that this was real. And didn't want to. Because then she'd have to think through what it meant—what it would mean for her son—and she wasn't capable of that yet.

She didn't even notice that the rain had stopped.

* * *

"If you want, I can call him right now," Szilárd said, pulling out his phone.

"You'll vouch for me?" Oszkár raised an eyebrow.

"Yeah. He doesn't take just anyone."

"Thanks."

They were sitting in the back room of the Újlipótváros shop—a small but lavishly furnished office dominated by a beautifully restored black antique desk from around 1910, adorned with exceptional carvings. Mahogany. Szilárd ran his index finger thoughtfully across its surface and examined it up close. Naturally, there wasn't a single speck of dust. Only then did he answer.

"I mean, customers don't just wander in off the street with him."

"Who vouched for you?"

"You won't believe it."

"Tell me."

"But it's a secret."

"Okay. So? Who was it?"

"Gellért."

Oszkár whistled silently.

Gellért Lendvai was famous. His historical novels sold in the hundreds of thousands—which wasn't just outstanding in his genre; everyone envied him for it. Crime writers, romantic novelists, psychologists peddling life wisdom, celebrity barbers—everyone. And not just for the numbers. Readers of all ages devoured his books. Loved them.

Oszkár was no exception. He had all of Lendvai's works at home. Signed. Maybe one day they'd be worth a fortune. There weren't many signed Lendvai books in existence—and there wouldn't be many more. The writer lived reclusively, alone, in a well-guarded villa, and never appeared in public. The mystery only added to his appeal. Journalists had tried for decades to learn anything about him and failed just as consistently. He was as enigmatic now as he'd been thirty years earlier, when his first book came out.

His friends didn't talk either—though there weren't many of those. One of them was Fischer Szilárd. Equally discreet, but for Oszkár—beyond regularly procuring and getting one of the first copies signed straight from the printer—he'd occasionally share a story or two. Strictly between the two of them, of course, under threat of silence.

For instance, about two years earlier, when Lendvai's laptop had been stolen. It contained, among other things, his latest novel, already slated for publication. On the surface it was a trivial case: someone walked up to the car at a red light and reached through the rolled-down window to snatch the notebook from the passenger seat. But it could have caused serious trouble.

Not just because of the novel—though if it had been leaked online or the major twists spoiled, it would've been worth half as much—but because the machine allegedly also held certain letters and photos the writer very much wanted back.

In the end, it *was* recovered—thanks to a substantial finder's fee. At least that's what the rumor said. A few sensation-hungry newspaper articles mentioned the incident, though only in passing. They told the short version. Not very exciting. And not very true.

The reality had been more complicated.

Or two degrees more.

Because the laptop really had been recovered—but that took more than money.

Or rather, someone.

"Don't tell me..." Oszkár began, stunned. Szilárd nodded. Yes. Exactly.

"Shit."

"So what'll it be? Should I call?"

"Yeah."

"I hope he'll take it."

"Why? Might he say no?"

"Of course. But only if he's already on another case. He only handles one at a time."

"And he solves them?"

"Always. Allegedly, anyway. But the fact that he doesn't ask for a single forint until then—that much is certain."

So he works on contingency, Oszkár thought. Even better.

That way, he couldn't lose on the deal.

He'd already lost enough.

*   *   *

She didn't know how long they'd been driving, and she didn't care. She just sat silently in the back seat where the man in the leather jacket had put her, hands still cuffed behind her, staring wide-eyed at the passing streets—yet seeing almost nothing. It wasn't easy, but Anett had decided to shut out the world for as long as possible, turn off her brain, or she'd go crazy.

Fortunately, the man didn't force conversation. He only glanced at her now and then in the rearview mirror, otherwise concentrating on driving. At a red light he sighed, turned around, and removed the handcuffs. When the girl didn't react to that either, he shrugged, then made a call while driving, curtly informing someone they'd arrive in about ten minutes.

The quiet little parking lot they finally pulled into belonged to an elegant apartment building. The cop led Anett through the back door, holding her by the elbow like a gallant escort. They didn't meet anyone on the stairs—though they only went up two floors. At the end of a long corridor, he stopped and opened a door halfway down.

They entered a small foyer with two doors opening off it. The one on the left led to a large, comfortably furnished room that reminded Anett most of an apartment living room—not a police interrogation room, though she'd never actually seen one in person. In the center stood a couch and two comfortable armchairs, with a small coffee table between them. On it waited a plate of cookies, a small pitcher of coffee, and four cups.

All of this reinforced Anett's first impression—but these weren't even the strangest elements of the situation. Nor was the slightly scruffy man in his thirties standing by the window, leaning against the wall and sizing her up with open hostility.

It was the lady in one of the armchairs.

The thin, bird-boned yet energetic-looking woman in her late seventies had freshly permed hair with a silvery-gray sheen. A thousand wrinkles carved her fine-featured face, but her eyes sparkled cheerfully, and a quiet smile played on her lips.

When they entered, she was knitting.

The man in the leather jacket pointed to the couch. Anett

sat down, wrinkling her forehead. For some reason the old lady reminded her of the grandmother she'd lost as a small child—which was strange, because that woman had been more of a mother-hen type, arms always ready for hugs, smacking kisses, and the kind of perpetual good cheer she spread to everyone around her. Anett often thought of her. And now again.

Probably because of the cane.

Her grandmother had always walked with a cane because of her bad knee—and it looked almost exactly like the one now leaning against the armchair, waiting for its owner to reach for it. But the lady didn't do that yet. She simply dropped the knitting needles and yarn into her lap, widened her smile, and looked at Anett.

"Coffee? Cookie?"

"Uh... no thanks."

"And something stronger? For the big scare?" the lady continued sympathetically, then added, "I can call you Anett, can't I?"

The girl shrugged, uneasy.

"That's my name. But... what's going on here?"

Her brain was still dulled—but not just from the forced shutdown she'd imposed on herself. Something didn't add up. She'd had the sense for a while now that reality was slipping slightly, like someone had switched channels without asking while she was watching TV. But she felt it most strongly here. More precisely, when the man in his thirties, silent until now, answered from by the window.

"Job interview!" he said with disgust. Then, as if that explained everything, he added, "Because according to Mici néni, we need exactly a woman like you on the team."

I must be dreaming, Anett thought with relief. A pretty stupid dream—job interview, Mici néni, team (maybe hockey or volleyball, why not?)—but still better than the alternative.

But no. The cat hadn't been a dream. Neither had the rain. Nor the cop. Nor the old man in the trench coat who'd exposed her. So this wasn't a dream either.

Then what?!

"I don't understand a word," she groaned.

The elderly lady sighed.

"I'm not surprised," she muttered, casting a reproachful glance at the younger man. "You rushed ahead a bit."

"Sorry," he muttered, crossing his arms.

"The thing is," the lady turned back to Anett, "we work in the same profession as you, my dear. Just a bit longer. As for me, I started over fifty years ago, under the name Bride Mici. At least that's what the papers called me when—"

I'm off the hook.

That was Anett's first thought, followed by many others. The point was: she wouldn't go to prison after all, and Dani could stay with her. And she owed all this to that strange, mysterious man in the leather jacket standing behind her, watching silently.

Her and the elderly lady, who it now turned out was—

No way.

"The Bride Mici?" she cut in, stunned. "The one who once conned the family's most valuable diamond necklace from Count Szentirmay?"

She'd read about her. In that ancient *Népszabadság*—or maybe *Népszava*—they'd brought out in thick stacks at the library. She'd told them she was a history major writing her thesis on the most famous Hungarian con artists, from World War II to the present. Sitting in that comfortable armchair, she'd learned incredible stories. Bride Mici's had been one of her favorites.

The innocent-looking, beautiful young woman everyone fell in love with—especially middle-aged, well-to-do, gallant gentlemen. They mostly proposed. And Mici, shy and a little afraid, said yes. She didn't like accepting the gifts either, but the happy grooms insisted the rings, necklaces, brooches looked best on her—which was true—so she didn't resist. She thanked them.

And then vanished.

She left behind only a farewell letter explaining, in a story full of novelistic twists, why she'd had to flee the country suddenly and secretly. Most of the men regretted it but understood—and let it go.

All but one.

That man was so in love he went after her. Or rather, his brother did—because he had one. The fake bride hadn't checked. If she had, she would've known he worked for the secret service, and not in just any position.

Everything came out. The false name. The invented background. The "godfather" the men had approached, who turned out to be a retired cabaret actor.

A huge scandal followed. The papers feasted on it for weeks, wringing their hands over socialist morality trampled into the mud and demanding exemplary punishment.

Which never really came.

Most of the victims either didn't press charges or withdrew them. They said the woman the papers called "Bride Mici" possessed a rare mix of charm, grace, and audacity—and that it was hard to stay angry with her.

It showed in the sentence.

"He gave it voluntarily," the former bombshell shrugged, intolerant of imprecision in any area of life. "And it was just one earring. Besides, in the end—so he wouldn't get in trouble—the count got it back. Now it's gathering dust in a Viennese museum."

She paused, then added carefully, "The earring, I mean. And of course he wasn't a real count. That was just his nickname from school. His grandfather was the count. But he wore it proudly..."

"Wow."

That was all Anett could manage.

"By the way, I'm surprised you've heard of me," the elderly lady continued. "You're so young."

"I read everything about the most famous Hungarian con

artists."

"Out of curiosity?"

"Partly. And... for inspiration."

"That's commendable."

"Thank you. By the way—how much did you end up getting?"

"I didn't end up getting anything. Just two years. They let me out six months early."

"For good behavior?"

"Weeeell..." Mici néni pulled her mouth to one side. "That's what they said."

"That's fantastic," Anett sighed. "I mean—" She stopped short. "Because I thought..."

She couldn't finish without being cruel.

The other understood anyway.

"That I'm already dead?" she asked cheerfully. "Not quite yet."

Anett flushed.

"Sorry."

"It's fine," the lady reassured her. "Most of my generation really is already on the other side. And I'm not what I used to be. I only take part in parades very rarely now. Mostly I advise the boys." She nodded toward the man in the leather jacket. "You already know Dénes."

He smiled faintly and inclined his head.

So that was his name.

She owed him her life—or at least the part of it that

mattered. Dani. Her freedom. The chance that things might still work out.

"Yes," Anett turned to him. "And thank you. For saving me."

"My pleasure," he said kindly.

"And you really were like a cop," she added honestly. "No wonder everyone fell for it. Including me."

Dénes shrugged.

"I tried."

"But how did you get there?" she asked suddenly. "You just happened to be passing by, and—"

"Not exactly," he cut in.

"Then?"

"We've been following you for a week," he said. "Viktor and I. Taking turns."

The scruffy man by the window nodded but said nothing.

"Ever since she spotted you," Dénes added, pointing to Mici néni, who immediately took over.

"I was right there when you performed that little... number on Pitypang Street," she said. "And I liked your performance very much."

"Today's wouldn't have impressed anyone," Anett muttered.

But she was pleased. Especially coming from such a source.

"Come now," waved off one of the field's highest authorities. "The broken-vase trick in such a narrowly defined area is downright dangerous."

"I'm definitely laying off it for a while," Anett said quietly.

Or forever, she added to herself.

She wouldn't survive another bust like that. She needed a different way to make money—but what?

Mici néni answered that.

"There are other tricks," she said slowly. "And we can teach them to you, if you want. Along with many other things. For instance, how to react in an emergency—like today."

Anett didn't want to think about it, but the old lady continued.

"And once you've gotten the hang of it, we could try something more serious." She leaned closer, locking eyes with the girl. "Together."

So that was it.

Anett finally understood the feverish phrases from earlier—job interview, team. She just didn't know yet whether she was glad.

"That sounds like an offer," she said carefully.

"Because it is," Mici néni replied.

Anett let out a long breath.

Hell. Purgatory. Heaven. She felt like she'd passed through all three today.

And it was only three-thirty in the afternoon.

* * *

The man listened patiently, then asked a few questions. Oszkár answered as best he could, but even he could feel how little useful information he was providing. He apologized for it, but the other reassured him that for a start, this was plenty.

"But I didn't tell you anything useful," he protested, defeated.

"Come on," the private investigator replied. "The essentials are clear."

"And what are the essentials?"

"That this is a well-oiled team. Probably not their first job."

Oszkár wrinkled his forehead.

"Is that good for us?"

"Of course."

"I'm sorry, but... why?"

"Because they might have a history with the police. I'll look into it."

Oszkár nodded uncertainly, though he couldn't imagine what exactly the other planned to look into on the basis of what he'd said. The skepticism must have shown on his face, because the man continued.

"First, though, I'd like to see that apartment."

"What for?" Oszkár asked, more irritably than he'd meant to.

"In case they left some—"

"They didn't leave anything!" the victimized antique dealer cut in, frustrated. "I already told you—when I realized what had happened, I went straight back. But by then the scum had already cleared out. And cleaned out. There was cleaning-solution smell everywhere. I almost threw up. So if you're looking for fingerprints or a hair, I'm telling you now—it's pointless."

The other didn't react. He just looked at him.

And Oszkár started fidgeting, because for a moment he had the distinct feeling he might get hit.

That wouldn't have ended well. The bloodhound was six-three and weighed maybe two-twenty—lying down, in a series. Possibly even two-sixty. And Oszkár had invited the man here himself. To help him. And now here he was... mouthing off.

"I'm sorry," he said at last, embarrassed. "It's just—when I think about how badly those... fucked me over—"

He let the rest trail off.

"It's fine," the private investigator said, and you could tell he meant it. "You go ahead and get worked up. It's enough if I keep my head."

Oszkár leaned back with relief. He noticed there was a veiled little insult lurking in that phrasing, but decided not to dwell on it—especially since he probably deserved it. Besides, in that mild reprimand he finally sensed the elegance he'd been missing from the man so far.

Bálint Herceg—because that was his name—looked at first glance like a simple muscle-head. With his clothes and haircut, he even leaned into the impression. The jacket two sizes too small, the buzzed hair, the clumsy movements—everything reinforced the moderately primitive bouncer vibe he deliberately projected. And Oszkár had fallen for it.

Szilárd had warned him the first impression would be deceiving.

From that moment on, Oszkár looked at the man differently.

"All right then," he said, now focusing on the hoped-for inner substance rather than the outer shell. "Let's start there."

Herceg nodded.

"Good. I just need to call someone first. So we can get a picture of the guys."

"What do you mean?" Oszkár's voice dropped.

"Literally," Herceg replied—and said no more, pulling out his phone.

* * *

Richárd set down the phone and looked at his boss.

"I don't have good news," he said, rubbing his neck.

Sólyom leaned back. His face went blank.

"Let me guess," he said. "Not for sale."

The secretary nodded. He could've added that, based on the information so far, this had been obvious—but he doubted the billionaire would appreciate the observation.

The sheet music had become Sólyom's obsession. Ever since the latest issue of *Antiques World*—the collectors' bible—had appeared, he'd talked about nothing else. True, he already owned a respectable stack of handwritten scores, including one by John Lennon—but he *needed* this one. The Hungarian-related page from Beethoven's sold-off notebook, on which the Master had jotted down music for *King Stephen* around 1810.

Richárd had never understood why anyone would give a hundred thousand dollars for such nonsense. And that would only be the opening bid at the Connecticut auction. He wouldn't have paid a hundred thousand forints for it. But he kept that opinion to himself. After all, he didn't need to understand everything.

If his boss's hobby was spending fortunes on bullshit, let him.

He considered all those scraps of paper and daubs bullshit—especially that ridiculous torch holder. But the worst was Sólyom's lock-of-hair mania. That, in Richárd's view, bordered on pathology. Who wanted a famous corpse's hair? Was that normal? Of course he knew Sólyom wasn't alone. Supposedly Mozart's locks—blond, as it turned out—had gone under the hammer recently at Sotheby's. So there were other filthy-rich lunatics out there too. That didn't make it more acceptable. At least not to him.

Good thing they didn't collect clipped toenails. Or toilet paper the composer once used—if such a thing even existed back then.

Whatever.

If the boss needed this, let him have it. The important thing was that he paid him too. Which he did—and he wasn't tight-fisted. Not at all. He even handed out bonuses now and then when Richárd earned them.

Usually for something semi-illegal.

Or outright illegal.

Like the time word reached them that a well-known businessman's Balaton house had been robbed. Richárd knew the man was an antiques enthusiast too—not on Sólyom's level, but he did own a rare Horthy letter. Or had. He'd kept it in the summer house, until the burglars made off with it along with cash and jewelry.

Later, one of the stolen necklaces surfaced on the black market. The trail led to a loan shark, who denied everything. They found no evidence, so they let him go. Richárd heard about this through a police contact—along with the man's name and address.

He paid him a discreet visit.

He made an offer.

A handwritten letter from Miklós Horthy was nearly impossible to sell. The buyer couldn't show it to anyone without risking trouble. They reached an agreement quickly.

The transaction happened without Sólyom's knowledge, which made his delight even greater when Richárd casually set the prize on his desk one day. The billionaire expressed his gratitude too—not just in words.

So it paid to please him. Especially in this area: acquisitions.

The factories, mines, construction sites, and whatever else actually produced the money interested Sólyom less and less. His people had been handling those for years, reporting results to Richárd. The last project the billionaire had personally taken an interest in was probably the motel chain along the north shore of Lake Balaton—aptly named Falcon's Nest. Always full. That venture had required class and a certain ruthlessness: a handful of mountaintop guesthouses—hills, really—with panoramic views, each once independent, now in the same hands.

Sólyom's hands.

But that too was years ago. Since then, he'd lost what little interest remained in business—unless it involved some damned antique he wanted for himself.

Which usually worked out.

Except now.

Because the Beethoven score—discovered by chance in an attic during a cleanup, according to *Antiques World*—was only for sale to a museum. One that would put it on display for at least five years. Meaning that no matter how much a private individual—say, not to reach too far, Richárd's boss—offered, he couldn't even bid.

The owner, a Beethoven fanatic, wanted the score to be publicly accessible.

Naturally, the Ministry of Culture pounced. TV channels, newspaper front pages—every available forum blared the same message: since *King Stephen* was involved, the Hungarian people had a right to see it. The state would do everything in its power to acquire the page.

For weeks it poured from every tap.

The minister stood before an elegant but empty vitrine in one of the museum's special rooms—the Giants—staring solemnly into the cameras and swearing he wouldn't rest until the notebook page ended up there.

So Sólyom was right.

The score wasn't for sale.

At least not to him.

* * *

"Is this serious?" Oszkár asked, stunned, when the mouse-faced woman pulled out a graphite pencil.

She didn't answer. She simply opened the large-format notebook on her lap.

"What a technique…" Oszkár muttered, casting a reproachful glance at Bálint, who stood behind the woman, visibly pleased. What exactly he was so pleased about, Oszkár couldn't imagine. He was about to ask when the private investigator cut him off.

"Just wait for the ending," he said mysteriously—still looking like he'd hit the jackpot.

Though the tiny, unkempt, rodent-faced woman reminded Oszkár of many things, the jackpot—whatever that might be—wasn't among them. Bálint swore by her anyway. Swore she was the best in the business.

Well. Oszkár was damn curious to see that.

"Let's start with the younger one," the woman squeaked, and Oszkár nearly burst out laughing in his misery. Her voice sounded like it belonged to the youngest—and stupidest—member of the rodent family in a cartoon. "What were his eyes like?"

The antique dealer sighed and tried to pull himself together, but didn't quite manage.

"Green," he said. Then, catching Bálint's look, he laughed nervously. "Sorry. I mean... average. Nothing special about them."

The woman didn't flinch. She stared at the paper, the pencil hovering barely half a millimeter above it.

"More almond-shaped—or more round?"

"Maybe almond-shaped," Oszkár said uncertainly.

And he went on like that—for the next several dozen questions.

But the uncertainty slowly gave way to amazement. Because throughout the questioning, the woman's hand never stopped moving: drawing, erasing, smudging with the edge of her palm. As they moved from head shape to hair, mouth, nose, a face began to emerge on the paper.

And suddenly, unmistakably, there he was.

The man he'd known as Gergő Horváth.

Holy shit, Oszkár thought, stunned. This woman really is a miracle.

"Was that him?" Bálint asked quietly.

Oszkár nodded.

"Now the fake appraiser," the private investigator said, and the woman turned a page in her notebook without a word. "What was his name again?"

"Halmos," Oszkár said with disgust. "Péter Halmos."

The name struck him oddly, in a completely inappropriate way. It sounded like *Bond. James Bond.*

Except this was probably fake too. The name of the guy in the herringbone jacket.

An hour and a half later, the sketch artist took her leave just as quietly as she'd arrived. Oszkár personally walked her to the door, behaving with such exaggerated courtesy it bordered on excessive. The woman seemed a little flustered—but Oszkár felt it was the very least he owed her, after having insulted her so thoroughly in his thoughts.

Possibly not only in his thoughts.

He couldn't quite remember whether he'd said something aloud too. He hoped not.

"So," Bálint asked once they were alone, "was I right?"

Oszkár stared at the sketches on his desk.

Balogh and Halmos stared back at him.

Or rather—the two vermin who'd introduced themselves before robbing him blind.

His fist clenched.

"Yes," he rasped. "And now what?"

"First, we go to the crime scene. In case we find something after all."

Crime scene, Oszkár thought. Like in the movies. All that was missing was a chalk outline—though his self-respect really had been left there. Most of it, anyway.

But maybe even that would come back.

Because this Bálint, it seemed, really did know his business.

"Should we bring the sketches?" he asked.

"Of course. I'll show them to a few neighbors. If we're lucky, they saw something useful. And if so, I'll recognize them from these if I run into them later."

He paused, then added evenly:

"Or not by chance. Ready?"

* * *

"Damn," Mici néni sighed when she realized the last roll was gone too. She'd bought six on the way to the park and thought that would be enough, since they'd planned a short meeting—but she'd been wrong. The birds were too greedy. Or too hungry. Probably both. Either way, the ammunition had proved insufficient.

She crumpled the paper bag and tossed it into the trash by the bench. Next time she'd bring twice as much, she decided, then turned her face toward the sun and closed her eyes.

The bald old man who sat down beside her also held a small bag—but his was nylon and filled with actual birdseed.

"This is better," he said, scattering a handful in front of him. "Than rolls, I mean."

Mici néni opened her eyes and looked sideways.

"What's in it?" she asked, then glanced at the pigeons pecking around them. "Sunflower seeds?"

The other nodded.

"Among other things. Wheat, barley, yellow and red millet, sorghum, oats, rapeseed."

"Nice."

"Help yourself."

She waved him off.

"They've had enough. Tell me instead."

Her companion smiled and slipped the bag into his pocket.

"Everything went smooth as silk, Mici dear. Like a greased butterfly fart."

"That's what I heard."

"And I enjoyed it."

"I figured you would."

"It really rejuvenated me. Seriously." He paused. "But tell me—who was actually being tested here? The girl, or your nephew?"

"Both," Mici néni said. She'd always preferred simple answers.

And how do you deal with two flies in the simplest way—meaning with the least effort? One swat. True, in this case there'd been a preliminary round (or, as Dénes would say if he knew about it, a *pre-round*), when her old friend had to let himself be conned as an obnoxious mark. But that was just the setup. The story's first act, where her favorite ex-colleague dangled the bait.

And then she'd been the flyswatter too.

Personally.

"It was like the good old days," the old man said, a shiver of pleasure running through him.

He wasn't wearing the long gray trench coat he'd had on over the past few days—just an elegant, if slightly dated, jacket with leather patches on the elbows. Mici néni watched him, smiling, thinking she'd chosen the best man for the job. The best—and the only one still alive who was good for anything.

True, his hair had gone too. But judging by Anett's and her nephew's reports, his talent hadn't faded a bit.

And of course it mattered that he and Dénes had never met.

"If you had to grade them," she asked, "what would you give?"

He stared ahead, considering.

"The girl gets a four. She performed the trick so professionally it ought to be taught. Even cried a little, if I remember right. The audience ate out of her hand. She's got talent."

"I think so too," Mici néni said, satisfied.

"But when the crunch came," he went on, "she froze. Poor thing. Couldn't spit or swallow."

"She'll get the hang of it. We're already working on that."

"You mean..."

"I do."

"Hm. And when will you start..."

"The training? We already have."

"Well then, next time she'll get a five for sure—if you're the one teaching her..."

"Me and Dénes," Mici néni corrected. "By the way—how was *he*?"

"Professional," the old man said at once. "Assuming he really wasn't in on it."

She shook her head.

"I wanted him to have to improvise."

"Then he did it first-rate."

The proud aunt smiled. She knew the boy was clever, but it always pleased her when others confirmed it.

This wasn't the first time she'd thrown her nephew into a hot situation without warning. And it wouldn't be the last. A nasty thing to do, perhaps—but Dénes still needed a few lessons before she could leave him entirely to himself. Lately he'd been getting too independent. Partly good news.

Partly not.

A few stressful situations wouldn't hurt him. Like this very public bust. Dénes could have left the girl on her own—he didn't owe her anything.

But he hadn't.

He'd stepped in.

And that was exactly what Mici néni had counted on.

Because this test hadn't only been useful for evaluating the team's newest member—alongside an old one. It had also bound them together. From now on, Anett would always see her rescuer in Dénes. And for that very reason, Dénes would feel responsible for her.

A working relationship, neatly established.

Especially if neither of them knew the whole thing had been staged.

And for now—thank God.

And Mici néni.

That was exactly how it was.

*   *   *

"Same principle as the broken-vase trick," Dénes said, killing the engine.

"We have to fight?" Anett's voice was flat.

"As loudly as possible." He nodded. "Make it awkward—" He paused. "For them."

That wouldn't be the problem, Anett thought. She just had zero desire for any of it. She'd rather have taken a few days to recover from the epic meltdown she still felt branded by; one night wasn't nearly enough. But Mici néni had talked her out of resting. Said that if she wallowed now—kept replaying that moment of exposure in her head, which she was, helplessly—getting back to peak form would take forever. Better to throw her straight into the deep end the very next day.

The nephew agreed, though he'd used some horse metaphor—or simile; she could never tell. If you get thrown, climb right back on, or you'll never ride again.

Maybe they were right. Didn't make it easier.

And then there was Viktor.

Anett didn't know why, but from the first moment she'd felt it: the team's third member—fourth, if she counted herself now—didn't want her there. He'd looked at her like roadkill at their introduction, and things hadn't improved during the all-night getting-to-know-you session. He barely spoke to her, and when he did, it was curt and edged. The other two tried smoothing things over, treating her like an old friend, even making her laugh once or twice.

Viktor never cracked a smile.

What was his problem? She should ask him. She decided she would—next time.

Then Viktor climbed into the back seat behind them.

"Hey..." He clapped Dénes on the shoulder, then caught Anett's eye in the rearview mirror. "...guys."

How sweet, Anett thought, returning his half-hearted greeting with an equally thin smile. At least he'd managed a plural. Could've been singular—and he wouldn't have meant it.

Whatever. Half a hello was still something.

"Coffee?" Dénes turned around.

Viktor shrugged and jerked his chin toward Anett. "Only if she's buying."

Anett nodded and pulled out her wallet. In the bill compartment, among various denominations, sat five crisp new twenties—fresh from the team captain.

"Deal." She peeled one off, then smoothly snipped a tiny, nearly invisible corner from it and tucked the damaged bill deep back into the wallet. "You can get an orange juice too."

She held out the seemingly pristine note between two fingers. Viktor made a face and pocketed it.

"At the Nexus. And I'm having a beer. Draft Guinness, actually."

"The only drink—" Dénes cut in unexpectedly, "—where the bubbles sink."

"What?!" Viktor looked stricken.

"Like air in the eye of a tornado." His mentor warmed to

the topic, mistaking horror for curiosity. "Only here it's nitrogen that—"

He'd looked this up maybe twenty-five years earlier, the first time he'd encountered it and couldn't understand how it was possible. He'd never liked not understanding things. The world, he'd learned young, was full of mysteries. You ran into inexplicable stuff constantly—but if you dug in a little, most things gave up their secrets.

Most people didn't bother. They lived their lives clueless about everyday mysteries: why geese fly in formation; why clocks in shop windows always show 10:10 (easy); why a duck's quack doesn't echo (still unsolved); why with twenty-three people in a room there's a fifty-percent chance two share a birthday (most people *really* didn't get that one)... or why Guinness bubbles sink.

Dénes was pleased that at least this last one seemed to interest others. He took a breath to explain.

Then stopped.

He'd just registered the dominant expressions in his audience: blank incomprehension—and careful pity.

These things were genuinely interesting. Well. Their loss.

"Never mind." He waved it off, a little wounded, and steered back to the point. "Anyway, they only have Soproni there. But at the Baltazár you might get lucky."

"I'll be judging there?"

"We'll work it so you are."

"Thanks. Can't wait to watch you pull off a..."

"Parade?" Viktor laughed.

"Yeah. By the way, you could finally tell the old lady that word went out of fashion a century ago."

"She'd say that's exactly when she did too."

"Hold on," Anett cut in. "What's this Nexus-and-Baltazár thing?"

Dénes looked at her, surprised. "Restaurants. Beer halls, really. Not much food."

She frowned. "Okay, but what does that have to do with us?"

"Just that we're hitting all of them today."

Anett groaned. "And we're doing this... thing at every one?"

"Of course. What did you think?"

Not this, she almost said, but swallowed it. She wasn't even sure she could pull off the big scene once convincingly—let alone repeatedly.

"How many times?" Her voice came out tired.

"Seven minimum." Dénes sounded cheerful. After a beat he added, "But if there's time, we'll go for eight."

"Wonderful," Anett muttered.

He patted her hand, smiling. "Because you need eight, I assume—"

Another weak pun. He didn't wait for a reaction.

"Anyway, it'll get easier each time. Don't worry. Right, Viktor?"

He checked the rearview mirror.

"By the end," came the voice from the back seat, encouraging on the surface, "you'll be so slick you won't want to stop."

Anett heard the grin.

"Glad you're having fun." She bristled—then realized, to her surprise, that she didn't actually mind. "Of course. That's what matters most."

"Well, it's definitely top three," Dénes said, considering. Then he turned back to her. "But seriously—this is how it works. You drill it until it's muscle memory."

"That's what your aunt said too," Anett muttered. Then she caught the other thing that had been nagging at her. "And you're really going to score me?"

"Strictly."

"Ready to start?"

Anett sighed and shrugged.

"The parade?" she said. "Let's go."

* * *

He'd seen the apartment empty twice before. First when he'd packed everything up, thinking he'd caught God's coattails; then when he came back after realizing he was screwed—or, if he *had* caught them, that the divine foot attached had kicked him so hard he'd never recover. Still, even now it surprised him how small it looked without furniture. You'd think the opposite—that bare walls would make the place feel bigger.

Instead, it felt cramped.

And quiet.

"Fuck," Oszkár hissed, grinding his teeth.

Christ, I'm losing it, he thought. Not a good sign—talking out loud in an empty room. At least there were no witnesses. Though Bálint could walk in any second. He'd pull himself together by then.

He took several deep breaths, closed his eyes, tried to picture the endless ocean, the sparkling blue sky above it—but instead of a gentle breeze, the fake appraiser's voice filled his head:

Let's make it an even four. Final offer.

"You okay?" The private investigator sounded genuinely concerned as he stepped in.

Oszkár was hopping on one foot, shaking his hand like he'd slammed it into something solid.

"Fine." His voice came out tight. "Just—" He waved it off. "Never mind. What did you find?"

Bálint nodded and pulled out his notebook.

"Well, first: an old man named Tamás Horváth really did live here."

What a revelation, Oszkár thought sourly, tucking his throbbing fingers under his arm. He could've told him that.

"And he really did die a few weeks ago."

They didn't bury him alive? What a relief. I was starting to think—

"But he didn't have a son."

Son? Why would he have a son?

That worm had been the grandson—or claimed to be. The filthy... whatever he was. Clearly Bálint, professional as he'd seemed at first, wasn't going to earn his five million. If that was even the agreed sum. Oh—right. Since the story used Horváth as the heir's name too, it had to be the paternal grandfather, which meant—

Good thing he hadn't said any of that out loud this time. He'd have made a fool of himself again. The pain wasn't helping his thinking, either. Who knew the wall would be so goddamn hard?

One-Armed Bandit in a Cast.

Or: The Wall Strikes Back.

"...just a daughter who lives in Szeged," the investigator continued. "She went home right after the funeral. Well—not right after." He corrected himself. "First she rented out the apartment."

"To him?" Oszkár asked.

Bálint held up the sketch of the fake heir.

Oszkár cleared his throat. "Furnished?"

His voice was flat. He tested his fingers carefully. Maybe none were broken.

Bálint shook his head.

"Empty. What you saw, he brought in. With a moving company."

"Set dressing."

Bálint nodded.

"I'm guessing he shopped flea markets. All that horse stuff. Arranged it around the bait painting."

"Which was deliberately in shadow," Oszkár said sharply. "So you couldn't examine it properly."

Not that it would've helped much. He'd never really understood paintings, even up close.

"Or photograph it," the investigator added, raising a finger. "Unless you used flash."

"Too obvious."

"I know. And so did they. That's why they set it up this way."

"Motherfuckers."

"But my favorite is the photo. From Helvéczy Castle. And that clever little story about the nonexistent friendship."

He said it with something like admiration—like a connoisseur praising a difficult recipe.

"You liked that?" Oszkár bristled.

"They executed it well," Bálint replied carefully.

"Are you trying to comfort me?"

"No. Just reconstructing events. Trying to understand the perpetrators. From what I can see, a detail-minded crew. They really didn't leave any traces."

Then his client smiled.

It was sudden. And oddly genuine.

He'd drifted to the window—and spotted something.

Something he hadn't noticed last time. Though it must have been there then too.

Got you, he thought, even forgetting the throb in his fingers.

"Except one," he said, pleased.

*   *   *

Viktor had watched the performance twice already—two and a half times, technically—but the third run gave him just as much pleasure. Nothing special had happened yet, apart from Dénes walking in ten minutes earlier and ordering sparkling water from the redheaded waiter, who pulled a barely concealed grimace but, to his credit, didn't ask, "That's it?" He didn't need to; it was written all over his face. Still, nobody's pulse would've climbed.

Except Viktor's, sitting at a back table in the café, nursing an apple juice.

True, he had an advantage—he knew exactly what was coming. Or rather, he knew fuck-all exactly. Just the broad strokes. That was the whole point. Nothing ever happened the same way twice. Dénes had been drilling this into his head for three years—the way Mici néni had drilled it into Dénes's for thirty-three.

And it was true. Always something different, even if only slightly. Sometimes very different. Same with theater. Or a rock concert, a stand-up set, Bartók's Second Piano Concerto—anything performed from a score or script. No two performances identical, even when it's literally written down what you're supposed to do, say, sing.

Viktor often thought of their late neighbor, old man Koller, who'd seemed at least a hundred when Viktor was a kid. Claimed he'd seen Hofi nine times and said every night—late night, really—there were a few brand-new jokes that only existed there and then. Responses to something: an audience member sneezing, a dropped wallet, a lightbulb burning out. That was the magic of live performance, the old man concluded—though he never added that it was also the danger. What if you froze? Reacted badly? Or reacted well, but too late?

That neighbor was in Viktor's head now, watching Dénes sip his sparkling water and signal the waiter that he'd pay—there were two of them—but not because of Hofi. Because of the thrill this mundane, boring-looking moment triggered.

Because if it was true—and why wouldn't it be?—old man Koller must've felt this same pleasant anticipation, along with hundreds of thousands of fellow Hungarians, when the Golden Team started passing the ball around their own half, looking bored and uncreative. Nothing special about it either, beyond the passes being so precise they could've been computer-generated. Sometimes it even looked like they were killing time—unless you knew what was coming.

The Hungarians knew. The other team would get fed up, try to intercept, and our boys would explode forward with feints and passes in a beautiful attack that ended in a goal people would talk about for years.

The old man remembered some of those decades later—along with that tense, tingling before-the-goal feeling: those minutes of passing that looked monotonous to the clueless, practiced a thousand times to perfection. Because the home crowd's coming roar was already inside it. The other team just didn't know yet. That was the Hungarian way. Unfortunately, foreigners eventually learned it too—and we, in parallel, forgot even the basics, which is why today (and the old man never forgave this) they call the technique Brazilian style.

Viktor felt that same Koller-style advance-goal joy when his mentor received the bill in an elegant leather folder and replaced it with the damaged twenty. Last time they'd had no luck—the Baltazár waiter, despite the missing piece being a millimeter-and-a-half triangle, spotted it and refused the bill, forcing them to abort before things even started, right when Viktor had been enjoying his draft Guinness with its sinking bubbles, like in hurricanes...

Or was it tornadoes? He'd ask—assuming he wanted to sit through another meteorological lecture. A few months back he'd already made that mistake over the difference between *shower* and *downpour*. Which weren't the same, apparently. Probably like hurricane versus tornado. Useful knowledge, sure. Might come in handy someday. Like if you get caught in a storm in the Sahara or the middle of the ocean, beer in hand.

Better not ask.

Back to the Baltazár waiter—rare to see eyes that sharp. No problem this time. The blond waiter smoothly took the folder, and since the customer didn't shout after him to keep the change, you filthy animal, he neatly swapped the twenty for nineteen in change at the register, so the second, more exciting act could begin.

Starring Anett Kertész.

She entered the café two minutes after Dénes left. When she scanned the room for a table, her gaze swept over Viktor without flickering—earning her first good mark. At this location, anyway. At the previous six (Baltazár would've been seven, but they never went in), she'd already racked up plenty. Actually, all of them. Viktor had given her maximum points every time.

And realized Mici néni was right again.

The men in the room changed the moment Anett appeared. They straightened, tucked in shirts, adjusted their chairs until they faced her. Voices got louder. Energy rose.

In that state you could get them to do a lot—things they wouldn't have done twenty minutes earlier. It wasn't just vision that got hazy; thinking did too. Like alcohol. Vigilance slackened, reflexes dulled, coordination tanked—and somehow the whole species got stupider.

Isn't that the perfect mark?

Exactly. And the old lady knew it. Viktor knew it too. Knew very well what effect a beautiful woman had on a man.

Shame that knowledge had cost him nearly a hundred and eighty million—and his illusions about women. And life. Broke his heart too.

Since then he'd been careful. Maybe too careful. For three years he hadn't trusted a single woman, especially not a beautiful one—so he was triply suspicious of Anett. The team had its rhythm, functioned perfectly. Then a new player gets added, disrupting the harmony. Excuse him for not liking it.

He'd said so to Mici néni. She shut him down. Same with the nephew, who now seemed fully converted.

Neither suspected that long-term Viktor would be the one to upset the system. Least of all Viktor himself.

From the first moment he'd decided to stay alert. From now on, Mici néni would be the only exception to his don't-trust-women rule—though she barely counted, more a surrogate mother. Not that he needed anything else. Or if he did, there were professionals.

He paid his respects weekly—sometimes twice—at a discreet downtown massage salon, where he received services ninety-nine percent of men only dreamed about.

Had to pay? Please. He'd paid that last lying bitch he'd wanted to marry. Literally gave her everything. For nothing.

Bad deal.

The massage salon, though—good deal. Clean equation. Something for something.

While running his inner report card for the hundredth time (*D, son, sit down*), he watched Anett order a cappuccino with a charming smile from the blond waiter, who brightened like he'd found life's purpose. Shame she'd have to ask the redhead for the bill. Harder job. But she'd manage. Viktor was increasingly certain.

He'd missed the first three performances—this morning Dénes had watched while Viktor played the paying customer who had to leave early to clear the field—but then they'd switched. This was his third time seeing the cage match.

This guy wouldn't fall for fluttering eyelashes or a frightened look. Even that world-class cleavage would be wasted—though so far no waiter had managed to look away within a polite timeframe.

Until now, no big scene had been necessary. She'd solved it cleanly every time. Viktor couldn't help being impressed. The admiration carried bitterness—what happened to the waiters had happened to him once too—but he pushed the thought aside.

Now she was on his team. Except in a way, so was the mark. Which meant old tricks wouldn't work.

He was curious what Anett would do.

She scrolled her phone. Then checked her watch and clapped a hand to her mouth, suddenly flustered.

"Excuse me—" she called, shy but urgent, as the redhead set down another beer. "Could I get my check?"

"Right away." Grudging.

The girl smiled when she got the leather folder, slipped in a two-thousand.

"Out of fifteen hundred, please."

Charming.

The redhead twisted his mouth and hurried off.

Poor bastard, Viktor thought, taking a sip. He doesn't know yet how dearly he'll pay for not liking the girl. Not his fault—he doesn't like any girls. Viktor, on the other hand...

"Thanks," the waiter returned, setting down a five-hundred and turning away.

"Thank—" Anett began, then stopped, staring at the folder.

"Problem?" He paused.

"Yes!" Her voice cracked, sharp enough to turn heads. "Big problem."

No flower-girl routine. No tears.

"Do I look that stupid?" she demanded.

"But—what's wrong?"

Anett laughed, bitter and bright. "You're trying to rip me off."

"Me?!"

"Yes. You."

The blond waiter rushed over.

"What happened?"

"No idea," the redhead muttered.

"Then I'll explain," Anett said, turning to the blond. "Your colleague shorted me eighteen thousand."

"What?!" the redhead roared.

"I paid with a twenty," she hissed. "And this"—she indicated the five-hundred—"is not it."

"That wasn't a twenty!"

"The hell it wasn't!" She yanked open her wallet. "I just pulled a hundred grand. Five twenties—four still here."

She held them up. A tiny scrap fluttered to the floor.

Anett smiled, pinched it between her fingers.

"Better yet—here's the corner of the fifth one."

Silence.

"Let's check the register," the blond said quickly. "If her twenty's there—easy to recognize."

Good instinct, Viktor thought cheerfully. People always trust their eyes more than—

More than they should.

They returned with apologies—and Dénes's twenty, missing exactly the piece Anett held.

She accepted the apology with a sour nod and left, corrected change in her wallet.

* * *

The headline screamed in massive type: *THE MINISTER TOLD THE TRUTH!*

Sólyom, sprawled across the Volvo's back seat, shook his head and picked up the paper.

"Well, well." His voice carried a lazy mockery as he flipped to the article.

"Why not?" Richárd shrugged. "He's allowed, occasionally."

His boss smiled. Pretty good line. And accurate.

The politician had actually kept his promise: Beethoven's handwritten score now belonged to the Hungarian state. For a hundred seventy-five thousand dollars, the ministry had acquired the most valuable page from the Master's notebook at the Connecticut auction. In a few days it would be flown home, straight to the Giants Museum, where—in two weeks—the most ambitious exhibition yet of the composer's life work would open. The main attraction was the score the minister now held up proudly on the cover of this month's *Musical Life*, photographed minutes after the auction.

"That's the thing," the billionaire said, scanning the article. "The wording really does imply he lies the rest of the time."

"He does." His secretary nodded.

"But that wasn't the goal—calling attention to it. This is a puff piece."

"Then the journalist wasn't very clever." Richárd shrugged.

"The headline, sure. But the article's actually good. Not the ass-kissing interview—that part's awful. But what he writes about Beethoven..."

"That's beyond me."

"Not me. And I can see this..." Sólyom flipped to the end. "Pongrácz gets it too. Devotes a whole page to tempo. Know what that is?"

"How fast they play a piece?" Richárd sighed, already bracing himself.

"Exactly. And it matters. A lot. Ever heard *Clair de Lune* in Debussy's own performance?"

"Uh... doesn't ring a bell."

"Some say it's practically unlistenable. Know why? Because he plays it too fast. Even though he wrote it. Just ignored his own rhythm and tempo markings. What do you make of that?"

"Fascinating." The secretary arranged interest on his face.

"Toscanini conducted *Boléro* way faster than Ravel wrote it too."

"Really? Wow. Didn't know that either."

The billionaire missed the irony—his employee hid it well enough to deny it later if needed.

"Beethoven, though," Sólyom went on, "always insisted on his speed specifications. For the Ninth he wrote such precise metronome numbers you'd have to be an idiot to get them wrong. Most people still butcher it. To this day."

Richárd, just for fun, nearly asked which Ninth they were talking about—but shelved the joke and went safer.

"Seriously?"

His boss nodded.

"Incredible, right? Bernstein—no slouch—conducted it in seventy-eight minutes at that famous concert in reunified Berlin. They even changed the lyrics, imagine. Solti with the Chicago Symphony clocked seventy-six and a half."

"And how long should it be?" Richárd asked, now genuinely curious.

"According to the score? About an hour. Give or take two or three minutes."

His secretary stared.

"Wow."

"Strange, right?"

"That's a huge difference."

"Massive."

"But why drag it out so much?"

The billionaire snorted.

"Because they like it better that way. They just override Beethoven."

"They're allowed to do that?" Richárd frowned.

Sólyom sighed and looked out the window.

"Well... no law against it, so yes. I just don't think it's right. Or shouldn't be. It's like someone rewriting *Romeo and Juliet*. Also not illegal—and they're more careful with that one—but in this fucked-up liberal world nothing's off limits."

He stared irritably through the glass.

* * *

Oszkár had to dig deep into his memory to recall the last time he'd felt this excited—then it hit him.

When he'd seen that damned horse portrait.

Hard to admit, but that had been one of the happiest moments of his life. Pathetic, he knew—especially considering what came after—but he couldn't deny it: he'd felt pure euphoria, the best kind. Everything had unfolded like a fairy tale. Or a movie, really—that Roald Dahl story everyone remembers even if they've never seen the film. The one where the hero finds gold in shit. True, the happy ending doesn't land there either, which only made the parallel to his own life more painfully apt.

Though his story wasn't over yet. His favorite sequence was just beginning.

Still strange, though. Less than a week since those two filthy rats humiliated him, yet it felt like a century had passed.

And now he'd caught them—at least one. The one Bálint had already dug into. Thanks to him. To Oszkár. Or more precisely, thanks to that half-empty—no, be optimistic, half-full—coffee cup he'd noticed yesterday behind the curtain.

Both of them had touched it, leaving what looked like perfect fingerprints even to his untrained eye—especially after the private investigator coaxed them out with powder. And the fake appraiser had even drunk from it before setting it on the windowsill—because the liquid was too hot. Burned that lying, deceitful mouth.

Oszkár hoped it hurt.

Of course, what he had in store would hurt worse.

Because the man—unlike his accomplice, and to his misfortune—was in the police database. Just not under the name Péter Halmos. His real name stared up from the cover of the file in front of Oszkár. According to this, the scumbag's honest name was Dénes Szalay—*honest* being a complete anachronism here. Anyway. That was what the filth was called.

Oszkár hadn't touched the document yet. He was still admiring it, the way he used to stare at Christmas presents as a child—partly to brace himself, partly to savor those few seconds of delicious anticipation before tearing into the wrapping.

"Not exactly how I pictured baby Jesus as a kid," he said cheerfully to the private investigator across from him. "But still..."

"Borderline case?" the other man rumbled.

Oszkár laughed. "Let's say I'm not complaining."

"That's something."

Then Oszkár drew a steady breath and reached for the file. Bálint watched him from across the table.

"Lucky he's in the registry," the ex-cop said as Oszkár began reading. "Makes anyone findable in seconds."

"But as I see..." the antique dealer hummed, turning a page, "he's only in here because he punched a cop on his eighteenth birthday. One who tried to ID him. Actually..." He paused. "He just punched back."

"That's enough," Bálint said. "More than enough. Back then he was lucky to walk off with a suspended sentence."

"My point being, they didn't catch him for fraud. Though that seems to be his thing now."

The ex-cop nodded.

"They didn't know that about him before," he said. "We do, though."

"True."

"And now I'll be on his trail. Personally." Bálint's voice stayed matter-of-fact. "Until I serve him up to you with his legs tied, lemon in his mouth. Like I promised."

Oszkár shook his head, amused.

"Sounds good. But what's the next step? Because so far we've just... identified the guy."

The private investigator smiled—a smile with more threat than warmth.

"I stick to him," he said. "Find out everything. Where he lives, where he goes at night, who his friends are..."

"I hope that includes the other scumbag."

"It will. Don't worry. I'll track him down too. And at their next move—whatever it is—I'll be there, documenting every moment."

"We'll get fresher pictures of him too?"

Oszkár stared at the three-by-four-centimeter photo clipped to the file: a bland-faced, cocky punk staring back.

"Of course. Plenty. Him and his buddy. And if I have my way, some that can put them behind bars. If you want."

The antique dealer considered that—and liked it. Then he dove back into the file.

"Dénes Szalay," he murmured. "Born '75... parents died... raised by his aunt..." He frowned, leaned closer, then looked up, confused. "But what's this star next to the old lady?"

Bálint leaned back, casual as ever.

"Just a reference," he said. "Means she has a file too."

He paused—then grinned and pulled a much thicker dossier from his bag, like a magician producing the final trick.

"And it's way more interesting."

* * *

"So..." Dénes began, pressing his fingertips together, his forehead creasing. "You've got an eighteen-month-old son with a Debrecen mobster who's hunting you because he thinks you stole the kid, and if that's true, he won't rest until he gets him back. So you've been running for four months and feel the noose tightening—which we can take literally, given his methods. That about right?"

He looked at Anett on the couch.

She stared back, stunned.

Viktor understood. He knew exactly what it felt like when his mentor compressed your whole life into one monstrous, overstuffed sentence. Goddamn frustrating.

"Uh..." the girl managed. "Four and a half months."

Precision always pleased Mici néni. She smiled. Her nephew caught the same point; their eyes flicked together.

"Pardon," Dénes said, unbothered.

"He did this to me too," Viktor leaned toward the girl in consolation. "When we met."

"He interrogated you for hours just to play it back in thirty seconds?" she asked. "Compressed?"

"Yep." Viktor nodded. "Except he didn't need to interrogate me. I told him everything voluntarily."

"Everything," his mentor corrected. "Forty minutes without breathing."

"I was a little drunk."

"And desperate."

"Not a little."

Anett watched the back-and-forth, bewildered. She understood they were doing it for her—trying to loosen the knot in her stomach. The knot that had formed when, after going over the puzzle performances, they'd suddenly asked her to talk about her husband.

She'd come expecting analysis of the returning-twenty series, especially her part in it—handling those seven waiters. Seven. She'd first thought, *That's it?* It had felt like far more, their faces blurring together—might as well have been seventy.

But that was the point. Run it on autopilot, as Viktor put it—crudely phrased but accurate. And it had worked. Thirty minutes of praise from three different directions, and she felt like she could play the role in her sleep. Bring on the next one.

Classic trick. Just turbocharged by Mici néni and company.

But before they moved on, the old woman had said she wanted Anett to tell the story of her marriage. Last time she'd given only a few sentences—which might have been enough normally—except they'd done some research on her husband since then. Not just online. Her nephew had acquired a fairly detailed file through an old police contact.

And it contained disturbing things.

"Do I have to?" Anett had asked sourly.

Then she'd begun—with a sigh heavy enough to bend the table. The interruptions had stretched it to nearly half an hour.

And now this man had just compressed it into twenty seconds.

"Anyway..." the girl said reluctantly. "You extracted the essence pretty efficiently."

Viktor silently agreed. Yes, Dénes was good at that. Extracting essence. Useful skill—irritating as hell sometimes. Viktor could talk about that. Maybe someday.

He looked at his mentor, who inhaled to respond, but his aunt beat him to it.

"You know," she leaned toward the girl, "we're not digging

into your past out of curiosity."

"Sure." The reply was uncertain.

"I once made the mistake of not checking someone's family background, and things ended badly. If I had, I'd never have learned what women's prison is like on the inside. So since then, I check anything that might matter later."

"And if you've got a powerful enemy—" Dénes picked up the thread.

"—from the underworld no less—" his aunt continued, handing it back.

"—who's hunting you—"

"—that's pretty important," the nephew concluded. "Because whoever's chasing you is now chasing us too."

Anett dropped her head.

"Oh." Her voice was quiet. "I didn't even think of that. That I'm putting you all in danger."

"Come now, sweetie." Mici néni patted her knee. "That's not what this is about."

"Then what?" Anett went still.

"That we're a team. Which means when there's trouble, we solve it together."

Mici néni gave Anett a warm smile.

"Besides, you didn't come here to foist yourself on us," Viktor added—less prickly these days. "If I remember right."

"I can't expect you—" Anett burst out, agitated, "—to take a huge risk for me."

"Leave that to us." Dénes waved it off, shifting to the

practical. "But running isn't a solution. Going to Transylvania and hiding the rest of your life."

The girl snorted. "Then what should I do?"

"Don't know yet." He shrugged. "We'll think about it. But first, we need every detail. About Zsolt, Dani, your life together..."

"I just told you everything." Anett bristled.

"That was warm-up," he said. "Now, if you don't mind, start over. From the beginning."

Anett rolled her eyes. "Are you serious?"

Dénes nodded, almost apologetic.

"And don't skip anything. Not even the small stuff. Actually—especially the small stuff."

"Okay." Anett sighed, resigned. "Then chapter one. How we met. Ready?"

"Go ahead."

"So..." She drew a breath. "When they fired me from the salon where I'd worked for two years, I got depressed. I went to a nicer bar and ordered a vodka-orange. I was drinking it when this guy in his forties came over and started talking. But funny—" she smiled despite herself, "—he said sometimes you drop into someone's life exactly when they need cheering up, encouragement. And sometimes that job falls to you, for whatever reason. Like now, with him and me. But he was honest: the fact that he found me *relatively* attractive made it a little easier."

"That *relatively attractive*," she added. "That was my favorite."

"Not bad," Dénes said, after a beat.

"Right?" Anett let out a breath.

"Bit bold," Mici néni muttered—then, after a moment, "but still workable."

"And serviceable," the nephew added.

"Sliding Doors," Viktor said.

They all stared at him.

He sighed, then added—as if that explained everything—"with Gwyneth Paltrow."

When this produced even less understanding—if anything, they now looked at him like he'd just had a stroke and started speaking Swahili—he realized he'd have to spell it out.

"It's a movie," he said, resigned. "*Sliding Doors*. That's the title. Gwyneth Paltrow's in it."

"And?" Anett asked, tension creeping into her voice.

"And the male lead says the same thing to her," Viktor went on. "When he's trying to pick her up. I mean—he's not just trying. It works."

"You're kidding," Anett groaned. "You're telling me he lifted that line from a movie?"

Viktor nodded, then—seeing the look on her face—hurried to add, "But from a good movie."

Anett wasn't comforted.

"Jesus," she said bleakly. "That's just... pathetic."

"Why?" Dénes cut in. "If it worked—and judging by the evidence—"

"Because then it's all fake," Anett snapped. "I thought it was his. Something he came up with, for me, right there. And now it turns out he was just quoting some crap."

"It's not crap," Viktor said, raising a hand. "I told you. I can't remember the IMDb score off the top of my head, but I'm pretty sure—"

"Don't worry about them," Mici néni said, leaning closer to Anett. "Men don't understand this sort of thing. How humiliating it is to realize a man is courting us out of a book. Or a movie," she added quickly, before someone corrected her. "If it isn't inspiration—*our* inspiration—speaking through them, if they're just regurgitating something memorized in advance, like an actor, then the whole thing collapses. The personal part disappears. What makes the moment unrepeatable."

"Exactly," Anett said, nodding. "It becomes imitation. Routine. At this point I wouldn't be surprised if he used the same line on every woman he met."

"I hate to break it to you, sweetheart," Mici néni said gently, "but that's almost certainly the case."

"So what?" Dénes asked, genuinely curious. "No offense—I may sound insensitive—"

"You are," his aunt assured him, thinking that despite all those psychology books, a few key volumes were still missing from his education.

"—but I don't see why it's such a problem if someone approaches a woman with a well-crafted line that actually works and that she likes."

"Because then it's a lie," Anett said quietly. "If they're not his own words."

"Like what?" Dénes asked. "Hi, you look great—can I buy you a drink?"

Anett pulled a face, then looked at Viktor, who immediately grinned and pretended he was seeing her for the first time.

"Sorry," he said, frowning theatrically, "but you look really familiar. Haven't we met before?"

"Well then," Dénes jumped in without missing a beat, "what's a girl this beautiful doing in a place this ugly?"

"Hi—are you waiting for this bus too?"

"These aren't exactly original either," Anett protested, laughing despite herself—but they were already on a roll.

"Have you noticed how close we're standing?"

"Want to dance? You match my tie."

"Sorry, have you seen three penguins around here? About this tall."

Anett burst out laughing.

"All right. Fine. I could've done worse. Is that what you wanted to hear?"

"That," they said in unison, clapping their hands together.

Mici néni sighed and turned to Anett.

"See this?" she said, shaking her head. "Two grown men—middle-aged, even—and they behave like—"

"Hey!" Viktor objected. "I'm not middle-aged yet."

"And what about me?" Dénes asked, mildly offended.

"You're past even that," Anett shot back grinning.

* * *

"Blows my mind," Oszkár muttered as he read. "And she raised him?"

"He wasn't even five when he came to her," Bálint replied.

"Tough..." Oszkár twisted his mouth. "But I've never been moved by the hard-childhood routine."

"Me neither," the private investigator said at once—and clearly meant it.

"By the way—" his client continued, studying the grainy black-and-white photo, "—she wasn't a bad-looking woman. Even by today's standards. There's a little..."

He stared ahead, forehead creasing.

"Audrey Hepburn?" Bálint ventured.

Oszkár blinked. "Yes. You see it too?"

"Absolutely. Same type. Sweet. Innocent. Naïve. And beautiful."

"That's exactly what her fiancés thought. All eight of them."

"Six withdrew their complaints."

"Yes, I see." Oszkár hummed. "Wonder why. Afraid of scandal?"

"That played a role."

"What else?"

"They were crazy about her."

"Even after it came out she was a con artist and had been lying to them the whole time?"

"Yes. Even then."

"How do you figure?"

"From this." Bálint produced several photocopied sheets.

"Well now." Oszkár leaned forward, energized. "That bag of yours is like Santa's sack. Just keeps delivering."

"I try to earn my money."

"I can see that. And I've never been happier to pay out five million in my life. But go on—what else did you bring me?"

"Some old newspaper articles. I did a little digging."

The antique dealer spread the copies before him and dove in hungrily. Bálint watched for a moment, then glanced around and picked up a magazine from the desk. Its cover showed a yellowed sheet of music. He flipped to the article.

"Holy shit." He stared. "Over sixty grand for one... piece of paper?"

Oszkár looked up. "I know someone who'd pay double."

"Guy normal?"

He smiled faintly. "Wouldn't say that. But he's loaded. And he loves Beethoven. Good article, though."

He returned to the report in his hand.

Bride Mici Strikes Again.

"Made quite a stir," the investigator said, skimming. "She was the hot topic for months. Supposedly they wanted to make a movie about it. Only the Party wouldn't allow it."

"Can't say I'm surprised," Oszkár muttered, moving to the next article. "In a socialist society this kind of thing doesn't happen. Maybe in America. And if it does—" he tapped the page, "—you make an example."

"They did." Bálint shrugged. "She went to prison. Though

plenty of people upstairs complained she only got two years."

"Yes... I see." Oszkár moved on. "But after her release she claimed she'd learned her lesson. Said she'd go straight. You think she meant it?"

"She lived on translation work for the next twenty-eight years," Bálint said. "So I'd say yes. Or at least mostly. Might've stepped away because of the kid. She was thirty-five when she took him in."

Oszkár grunted. "The appraiser? From the pawnshop?"

The investigator nodded. "She's been raising him since he was four and a half."

"Nice little pair," Oszkár murmured.

He bit his lower lip, thinking—then looked up.

"Wonder what the old lady taught him."

* * *

"Jesus!" Anett cried. "Do you know what this is?"

She stared at the brand-new device she'd just pulled from its case. The packaging had been wrapped with ceremonial care, like a proper gift—complete with an elegant little bow—but the girl, now sporting short blond hair, tore through it all to get to the prize.

"A fancy phone," Mici néni said with a shrug, already peering at the menu. The girl's excitement left her cold—which fit her role in this parade perfectly: the sour, old-school grandma paired with the spoiled darling of the new world.

The "grandkid" snorted.

"Nooo," she said, rolling her eyes. "This isn't just a fancy phone."

The tattooed-forearm waiter beside them suppressed a smile—a good sign, since the whole act was for him. Anett pressed on.

"This is a brand-new iPhone 13. OLED display. Four thousand gigabytes of memory. And the camera software can recognize *four* people in a single photo."

The elderly woman—head wrapped in a scarf, eyes hidden behind oversized sixties movie-star sunglasses—twisted her mouth.

"How... practical," she said, withering.

The girl stared at her in disbelief.

"Oh, Grandma," she sighed. "You can't even imagine what a beauty like this can do."

"No," the technologically illiterate fossil snapped, her face souring. "But if it's good for phone calls, it can't be that bad. Because that's what *I* use these... things for."

She turned sharply to the waiter.

"What about you, young man?"

"Same," he said instantly.

Mici néni nodded, satisfied—until he kept going.

"Plus music, movies, email, games. Sometimes studying. And it's got GPS, bus schedules—"

"Still not worth hundreds of thousands," the old woman cut in, ending the discussion with a slash of her hand. "But there's no talking to my son. Especially about his one and only spoiled daughter."

"That would be me," Anett said brightly, raising her hand like she was in school.

The waiter grinned.

"Almost guessed."

*   *   *

Well, buddy, you won't be in such a good mood much longer.

The private investigator snapped a close-up of the grinning waiter—who, by closing time, wouldn't have much to smile about.

He sat in a van directly across from the restaurant, and because the two women had chosen a window booth, he had a perfect view of their every move. With this telephoto lens, he could document the whole con. Complete cast. Start to finish. Soon the two men would show up to perform the second act with an outwardly flawless but worthless fake phone—maybe worth a grand—the kind they'd been distributing by the half-dozen lately. And then he'd have them all.

More precisely, Oszkár would have them.

And he'd get five million.

Bálint Herceg hated lawbreaking—and happily busted every lawbreaker. At least until six years ago, when he left the police force. That was when he realized not everything was black and white. That realization cost his father his life: a man who had also broken the law, and on whom the state came down with full force. Punishment, fines, an occupational ban—and if he hadn't chosen another, permanent solution, prison might have been next. As it was, he managed to die without a record, but in ruins, physically and mentally.

First, to avoid bigger trouble and pay off the debts that would otherwise have passed to his sons, the old man sold his house. The house he'd built with his own hands over thirty years, on one of the most beautiful spots in the settlement—a tree-covered hilltop. That was the final drop of cyanide in his cup. The poison had begun earlier, when a six-person party checked in early that season.

After his wife died and the boys moved to Pest, the old man remodeled the place and—partly to supplement his pension, partly out of loneliness—joined the rising wave of rural tourism. A good idea, financially and otherwise—even though he never earned what he could have. But that was his own fault. He wasn't a businessman; it quickly became clear that money wasn't the point at all. He missed company the way others miss bread. So he befriended his lodgers. Some became regulars, practically family. He pampered them, cooked for them, and poured his homemade plum brandy—charging such ridiculous prices that guests sometimes rounded up on their own and still got a deal.

Everyone was happy. The old man especially. He proudly said he "spread by word of mouth," meaning he barely had to advertise. Returning guests brought friends; he ran full all summer.

That's how the three young couples arrived for a long

weekend, citing an old guest. "Young" only relatively—the thirty-to-forty range—but according to his father they were about that age, and already not thirsty when they rolled in with their minibus around three. Hungry, though. Very hungry. In slightly slurred speech they asked the host to make a big batch of his legendary red-wine beef stew for dinner. And if he still had any of that supposedly world-champion brandy left, they'd take about five liters. Which they'd naturally consume in his company, if he had time, though they didn't want to impose.

He never turned down such a kind invitation, he'd protested happily. He prepared one of the best stews of his life by exactly eight p.m., then sat down with the guests, carrying the five-liter demijohn.

It must have been around eleven when, in the middle of one of his favorite fishing stories, the laughter stopped. Just cut off—he told his son later—like someone snapping a string. One moment they were toasting and roaring with laughter; the next, the room was a crypt. Then, in the frozen silence, all six reached into their pockets at once and pulled out tax authority badges.

The slightly drunk old man struggled to grasp what was happening. Words like *invoice, receipt, tax stamp* drifted toward him; at first he only furrowed his brow, though a stabbing pain spread across his chest. When the picture finally clicked—that a jealous neighbor or a competitor had probably reported him—blood rushed to his head. He began cursing the leader of the group, but he didn't lay a finger on anyone. He swore this to his son, who believed him—knowing his father, the gentlest man alive.

The tax officials later testified otherwise. After he hired a lawyer and protested the charges, they all claimed he'd shoved their boss, scuffled with him, and in the heat of the argument grabbed at least a twenty-centimeter kitchen knife and come at him waving it, issuing life-threatening warnings. Only their collective restraint, they said, had prevented disaster. Death even—which, through another participant, eventually happened anyway.

Since the boss was an official person and the alleged assault occurred during an official proceeding, the elder Bálint Herceg had—as his lawyer put it—about as much chance as Szálasi at his main trial. So after hearing the team leader's private offer—essentially a catastrophically unfavorable settlement—he took the deal. Sold the house. Paid the debts. Then, lacking any will to live, swallowed two boxes of heart medication and died quietly—slightly over-fulfilling his part of the bargain.

His son could never forgive the state, the system, the whole fucking world for how they treated his father. Maybe the old man hadn't given receipts; maybe he sold untaxed alcohol—fine, he'd sign off on that. But sending a damned commando after him, wrecking everything he'd built, pushing him to his death—that crossed every line. No wonder the poor man eventually died from it, with some... assistance.

And Bálint couldn't do anything. Despite being a cop, he wasn't allowed near the case. But thanks to a few old friends, he learned what he needed: who was behind it all. He even visited the man—now a wealthy entrepreneur and the new owner of his father's house. The entrepreneur shrugged.

"That's life," he said. "If someone breaks the law, they get caught."

His father's death he dismissed as tough luck.

At that point Bálint pulled the service weapon from his side and shoved it into the man's face. No use. The man stayed calm. Knew the cop wouldn't shoot.

And he really didn't want to—except his finger twitched.

That was tough luck too.

After the incident he obviously couldn't stay on the force. But he didn't mind. The sight of the entrepreneur staring in disbelief while blood streamed from his ear was worth any price—especially since the bullet had lodged in the wall instead of the skull. He wasn't a murderer. Just someone who'd had a nervous breakdown, according to the medical expert opinion—arranged by a colleague through an old friend moved by the case. No serious proceedings followed.

He shifted to the private sector. More lucrative anyway, especially if you knew your business and didn't cling too tightly to the letter of the law. If you had to bribe someone—or rough them up, bug their apartment or car, even plant cameras—well, Herceg had gotten over such things quickly after the funeral. And since he was a pro, clients passed him along hand to hand.

He, too, spread by word of mouth.

God rest the elder Bálint Herceg's soul.

* * *

Well, babe, I was just thinking about you, the tattooed-forearm waiter almost said—you and your tits—but caught himself in time. Don't scare off the chick. Let her talk. Let her explain who she even is.

"I was just there with my grandmother," the girl continued on the phone. "Like... twenty-five minutes ago."

Her voice sounded desperate. Or confused. Which made sense—it was always awkward when a woman called the guy she liked and he didn't remember her. At least not right away.

"Ohhh..." He finally granted mercy. "The phone girl?"

"Yes." She sighed with relief, then hurried on. "I found your number online—I mean, the restaurant's. And I hoped you'd answer. Actually, that's why I'm calling..." She added, flustered in a way the tattooed waiter liked, because he liked when a woman was a bit ditzy—though ultimately they all were. "About the, uh... phone."

What?!

"Because—" the bombshell sighed, frustrated, "—I just opened the box and, imagine, damn... it's not in there."

So she didn't want a date. What a shame. He'd really gotten into it. Still—maybe there was hope.

"Must've fallen out somewhere," he said smoothly. "Could

you check around the table? Or if it slipped behind the seat?"

"Uh... sure," the waiter said, adjusting his glasses. *If it's there, she'll come back for it—happy, grateful, expressive in many ways, for instance...*

"Thanks!"

You can thank me in person later.

"No problem."

But until then he'd behave like a gentleman. Because that's what he was: a gallant gentleman rushing to a lady's aid.

Speaking of rushing...

The waiter, phone at his ear, stepped out from behind the bar and glanced toward the window booth, where two new customers had just arrived. Businessmen types, jackets and ties. One of them—mid-thirties, hair slicked back like he'd stepped out of a black-and-white film—was examining a designer phone.

"Think you're in luck," the gentleman said into the receiver, adding silently, *and me too.* "But hold on a sec." He headed toward the table.

"Look at this—" the slicked-back one said as the waiter reached them, "—it's not even unwrapped."

"Show me." His companion—mid-forties, trendy circle beard—reached out. "Really," he muttered, turning it over. "What a lucky bastard you are."

They ignored the waiter hovering beside them, so he cleared his throat.

"Excuse me, gentlemen," he began politely. "That phone

was left by the previous customer. She just called about it."
He held up the restaurant phone with one hand and gestured with the other. "May I have it?"

The older man didn't respond the way he should have. Instead he chewed his lip, thinking.

"No," he said at last—decisively.

The waiter blinked. "What do you mean, no?"

He must have heard wrong. Impossible that someone in this situation would refuse to cooperate—

"I mean, buddy," the circle-beard said, "that's not how this works. Because this thing—" he studied the phone—"is worth, like... two hundred grand."

"More like three," the younger one said. "This is an iPhone 13."

"And brand new," the older added, upping the stakes. "Film still on it. So sorry, buddy, but we're not handing over something this expensive to just anyone... on say-so. We found it."

The bespectacled waiter stared. *Say-so? Is this guy normal?*

"Actually, I found it," the slicked-back one corrected. "So hand it over."

Circle-beard shrugged and passed the device back. The younger man examined it again.

"Really nice piece," he said. "But no name on it." He pressed the side button repeatedly; nothing. "Can't turn it on to figure out whose it is."

"But I'm telling you—" the waiter began.

"You can say anything, old man," the circle-beard cut in. "I can say it's mine. Bought it yesterday. What do you say to that?"

He stared challengingly.

The waiter opened his mouth, but indignation blocked his throat.

"Just that..." he finally managed, "the girl who lost it is right here on the line, and—"

"Then ask her," the older man said.

The waiter frowned, losing the thread. "Uh... what?"

"How much she'll pay for it." The circle-beard's patience thinned. "Finder's fee. Without one, we'll just sell this shit to some Arab at one of the ring-road phone shops. Right?"

He glanced at slicked-back, who nodded meekly.

The waiter's world collapsed.

"Well..." he muttered, disappointed in humanity. "I can ask." He raised the phone. "Okay, I'm back," he told the girl. "And I've got good news and bad news."

"You found it?" she asked, excited.

"Yes, that's the good news, but the thing is—"

"Thank God," she breathed. "Dad would've killed me if—"

"Wait," he cut in, nervous. "It's not that simple."

"What's wrong?"

"The guys who found it... they want money for it."

He shot the two suits a reproachful look. They showed zero remorse.

"You mean a reward?" the girl asked, surprised.

"Yes. Otherwise they won't give it back."

"The bastards!" she burst out. "They can't hear us, right?"

"Only half," he reassured her—meaning: they couldn't hear her. "But what should I tell them?"

A big, resigned sigh.

"That... okay. I mean, what can I do, right?"

"Not much."

"And how much do they want?"

"I don't kn—"

"Would fifty thousand be enough?"

His face stayed blank—though he wanted to grin.

"I think so," he said, bored-sounding. Good thing she wasn't on speaker.

"If they really push, you can go to eighty."

Also not heard by the thieves. Perfect.

"Okay," he said, nodding.

"I'm still better off than buying a new one for three-twenty," she muttered. Then her voice tightened. "Only problem is I can't come now. I've got class until three-thirty and definitely can't get free before five. Could you until then..."

She didn't finish, but he understood—and didn't mind. Loan her the money. Score points. Profit. Maybe more than points. He'd come out ahead no matter what.

"Sure I can," he said, suddenly convinced it would be the best evening of his life.

"You're so cool!" she gushed. "And I'll pay you back at five, I swear. Then I'll buy you a beer. And a Jäger."

"Sounds good." Especially if you come up to see my nonexistent stamp collection. Without panties...

"See you soon," she said. "And thanks. Really."

"No problem. Bye."

He hung up and turned back to circle-beard.

"Well?" the man asked. "How much is she putting up?"

"She said thirty thousand," the waiter lied carefully.

"Make it forty," the man shot back. "Plus lunch. Deal?"

The would-be Don Juan sighed. He'd get eighty from the girl—tell her he'd fought the bastards down from a hundred—plus beer, Jäger, and, if all went well, her body. Beautiful day.

"Then I'd have to add ten from my own pocket," he said unhappily, sticking to his story.

"Plus two beef stews," circle-beard added. "And a beer each."

The waiter shook his head—then nodded.

"Fine. Deal."

And so it was.

* * *

"What's wrong?" Mici néni's voice was kind.

The girl shrugged. "Nothing."

"Come on. I can see something's weighing on you."

They were on first-name terms in real life now too. It had come easily to both of them. Maybe, Anett thought, they shared something—or at least something similar. The rapport was unmistakable. They'd run through that grandma-granddaughter duet eight times straight, barely acting. So the girl appointed Mici néni an honorary substitute grandmother, and she accepted the role without hesitation.

"I just don't understand what this is all for." Anett's shrug was awkward. She set down her cup.

"You mean this phone parade?"

"Yeah. It's cool and everything, but each run takes about two hours on average—"

She stopped. The elderly woman raised an eyebrow.

"And?"

"And we make thirty, forty grand from it." The dissatisfaction in the girl's voice was clear. She waited a beat, then added, "Split four ways."

Mici néni sipped her tea and nodded.

"Not a great hourly rate, that's for sure."

"I don't think so either."

"But the money's not the point."

"Then what is?"

"Getting in sync."

Anett shook her head, mulled it over, then sighed.

"So this is... what... team-building? Bride Mici style?"

"Like you said. It's important we know each other. Not just us knowing you, but you knowing us. And only in the field do you learn what to expect from people going forward."

"Okay," Anett muttered, resigned. Then she remembered something she'd been curious about. "By the way—what's his problem with them?"

The other woman frowned. "Meaning...?"

"Meaning Dénes. With waiters. Why does he hate them

so much? I'm only asking because we keep conning waiters, and—"

"Don't worry, none of them will die from it." Mici néni waved it off. "You've seen for yourself—they're only out a few tens of thousands."

"Right, but... he's not exactly fond of them, is he?"

"He's not," Mici néni admitted reluctantly. "But only because he knows their tricks."

"How?"

"After graduation he worked three months at a restaurant on Lake Balaton. Dishwasher. But he met a lot of waiters too and... got disillusioned. If you ask him, he'll talk for hours about the vile tricks they use to scam even the most innocent customers. So you're worrying unnecessarily. These guys steal everything back, many times over."

"Uh-huh." Anett nodded—then noticed the woman watching her closely. "What?" she asked, uncomfortable.

"The money doesn't bother you." Mici néni looked straight at her, then poured more tea into the girl's cup. "And it's not loyalty to waiters either. Right? It's your husband. And what Dénes said about him. That running won't help."

Anett let out a bitter breath.

"Well... it wasn't exactly encouraging."

"But it is," the old woman said. "Believe me, he'll figure something out. Or maybe he already has."

"Something that'll get me free of Zsolt?" The girl's voice was defeated. They didn't know her husband. You couldn't just get rid of that man—couldn't get rid of him at all.

"He won't use force," Mici néni said, trying to pump some hope into her.

"Then how? With brains?" Anett shot back, mocking—then immediately regretted it. She knew Mici néni only wanted to help, like her nephew did, so she continued quickly. "It's just that my husband doesn't respond to logical arguments."

"These ones will work," her honorary grandmother said. Or tried to say convincingly.

But it didn't stick. The girl trusted Dénes's abilities, but not miracles. And getting Zsolt Bereczki off her back would take a miracle—a major one.

"Whatever they end up being," Mici néni added thoughtfully, since she didn't know what her nephew was planning—if he was planning anything at all—so she had no details about those "arguments" either.

The girl wasn't convinced, obviously, but this time she stayed quiet. She had nothing new to add beyond fundamental skepticism about any rescue operation. She knew perfectly well what Zsolt Bereczki was capable of when he wanted something.

And he wanted the kid desperately.

Never mind that he already had two from his ex-wives—one a dancer, one a manicurist—he needed Dani too. Because three boys ("I rarely miss," he liked telling his buddies) from three different women—that was something. A dynasty. And he was the head.

So he'd never give up the dynasty's youngest member. Not that he cared about him any more than the other two. For the first few months he'd doted on each of them, then quickly tired of it. Occasionally the fatherly mood struck, and he'd visit, spend a few hours with them and their mothers—whom he supported generously—then vanish again for weeks. He did the same with Dani. Enjoyed playing with him here and there, or taking them to the zoo, the playground—but never for more than two or three days. Then it was back to the nightly—or, if busy, every-two-or-three-nights—single-kiss routine.

That didn't mean he didn't claim the boy. His blood ran in him; therefore, his property. And his wife—also his property—had stolen him.

You couldn't steal from Zsolt Bereczki without consequences.

Impossible he'd ever let it go. He wouldn't rest until he got back what was his.

The boy.

Dénes had asked a lot about Dani. In detail. Even asked to see photos—from infancy on—and had Anett walk him through everything: the birth, the vaccinations, the star-shaped birthmark, every time the boy had been sick. Then he had her retell the giraffe story. He even pressed her for details about the half-brothers, the other two Bereczki boys, though she didn't know much—one around twelve, the other maybe seven.

And though she didn't understand why it all mattered so much, she talked. What mother wouldn't? About her only son. Or about her own mother—because Dénes questioned her about that too. Especially the last years at home. Aunt Luca and her boy. No use insisting her husband didn't know them, had no connection. Dénes waved it off, said *she* had a connection, and he was curious about everything that had happened to her, so go on.

And the girl—who appreciated being listened to, truly listened to—did.

* * *

Good photos. Everyone recognizable—with a little imagination.

"Bride Mici at work," Oszkár said, satisfied, when he reached the picture of the kerchiefed old woman explaining something to the bespectacled waiter. "If that's really her."

"The waiter could identify her anytime in a confrontation. If it comes to that."

"He said so?"

The investigator nodded.

"Got his statement too. Pretty detailed. And, shall we say, absolutely incriminating for the ladies."

"Good. Though I'm more interested in these guys."

He began examining the shots of the two men. Some showed both scumbags together; others featured only the circle-beard, Dénes—which Oszkár flipped through without interest.

"And what do we know—" he began, stopping at a portrait of the slicked-back fake heir examining a phone, "—about my friend Gergő?"

Bálint checked his notes.

"For instance, that his name is Viktor Vadász. Economics degree. Speaks English and French at an advanced level, intermediate German and Russian. Got this from the Golding Bank website—he worked there after graduation. Five years later he was about to become branch manager when something happened: a 'mutual agreement' to terminate employment. Supposedly a hundred-and-eighty-million-forint loan issue in the background—not entirely clean—that he arranged for a lady acquaintance who was, shall we say, prettier than necessary."

"Cherchez la femme," Oszkár muttered, exhausting half his French.

"According to my source, the case stayed out of court only because someone paid the debt immediately. Not clear who, but Vadász's apartment, vacation home, and car all became bank property."

"What a gentleman," the antique dealer said, mocking.

"More like what a sucker," Bálint corrected. "Or both."

Oszkár frowned.

"You mean the woman conned him?"

"Opinions differ. Either way, word got around that he was either not talented enough or not trustworthy enough. And since neither looks good on a reference letter, banking doors closed to him for life."

His client liked this even better.

"Well, well." He smiled. "God doesn't strike with a stick."

"After that, he had to leave banking anyway."

"And switched to fraud?"

"Yes. Though on paper he's in shipping now. Same as his partner. Same company." Bálint stared into the distance for a moment, then added casually, "By the way, I'm not sure bankers aren't the biggest frauds."

"Takes one to know one," Oszkár said, then picked up another photo. "And her?"

The investigator checked his papers again.

"That's Anett Kertész. From Debrecen. Former waitress, hairdresser, shop clerk—then became wife and mother. Her husband, who she ran from, is a local underworld figure. Zsolt Bereczki."

"Never heard of him."

"In that region he's considered serious."

"And why'd the girl run from him?"

"Don't know. Maybe they fought. But she's been hiding since. Under a false name."

"Then how'd you find her?"

"Followed her home. Then when she went to the store, I broke in and looked around."

"Oh!" Oszkár looked impressed. "How simple."

Bálint shrugged.

"Five minutes total. Especially since her driver's license with her real name was lying on the table. The rest was child's play."

"Speaking of child—" Oszkár said. "What about him? You said she became wife and mother."

"Yes, but I don't know anything about him. The kid, I mean. Just that his name is Dani. And he's definitely not living with the mother."

"Uh-huh." The antique dealer nodded, already bored—children didn't interest him, and Anett only as far as she related to "the two birds." "So the girl came to Pest and fell in with bad company."

"Something like that," Bálint said. "Now she's the fourth member of the crew."

Oszkár studied the photos, thoughtful.

"And you're saying—" he began slowly, "—that with these... I can put all of them behind bars?"

"Easily." Bálint said it decisively, though the slight hitch in his voice made it clear he'd like to qualify the word but didn't know where to start.

"There's something else, right?" Oszkár asked.

"Not really." Discomfort flickered across Bálint's face. "After all, my job was just to track them down—"

"Just?" the antique dealer cut in, appreciative. "I wouldn't have known where to start. And you figured out who they were in a few days, practically from nothing."

"You found the glass."

"Because someone dragged me back to that fucking apartment by the ear." Oszkár waved it off. "Thanks for the recognition, but you ran this whole show. Still—" he added, shaking his head, "—feels good that I had a tiny part. And even that I owe you. And that you hunted down the whole gang one by one. So—" he concluded, half-watching his phone while typing something, "—best advice of my life was when my friend Szilárd recommended you. Best decision was taking it."

"Glad you're satisfied with my work," the detective rumbled.

"So satisfied, friend," Oszkár said, grinning, "that I've already transferred the five million we agreed on."

At that moment Bálint's phone chirped.

"Yes, I see," he said after checking the message. "Thank you."

"Thank *you*," Oszkár replied warmly. He waited a beat. "And now that we're past the business part—would you tell me what you wanted to say earlier? Between friends."

The investigator sighed, then began cautiously.

"Just that... revenge is nice. And you're entitled to it. They deserve to have their guts stomped out."

"But?" Oszkár prompted, knowing that was just the preamble.

"But putting them away won't get your money back. In fact, if we add my five million—"

"Then we're at nine million two-forty. I know," Oszkár cut in cheerfully. "Except there's another version."

"They buy their freedom and pay?"

The antique dealer smiled.

"Like you said. And I think they'll pay—with interest. And I'm not calculating the standard bank rate."

"Figured as much," Bálint said, grinning too. Then, carefully: "But wouldn't it be even smarter... how shall I put it... to find a solution where the goat gets fed too—"

"What are you thinking?" Oszkár raised an eyebrow.

"Well..." the ex-cop began, then stopped—remembering not to start sentences with *well*—but continued anyway. "Just that this is an exceptionally skilled crew. I've seen con artists in my day, especially on the force, but these four... easily the best."

"And?" Oszkár asked tensely.

"And that could be exploited."

"Meaning...?"

"Meaning their expertise."

The antique dealer stared ahead, the thought taking shape.

"So I profit from it too," he said, liking the idea more with every second.

The investigator nodded.

"And not exclusively financially. Though that too. But if there's something you care about... something you need handled that's... dicey... criminal... dangerous... and you don't have the stomach for it..." He paused. "Well, I wouldn't let their talent go to waste if I were you. I'd exploit it."

Oszkár didn't answer. While the other spoke, he glanced at the photo magazine on the table—and something occurred to him. His mouth went dry in a good way. Because if the plan forming in his head worked, not only would that rusted cash register start chiming again, he'd finally give someone such a surprise that even those damned painted eyebrows would go gray.

And the papers, when they wrote the story, would need a new headline:

The Swindlers' Last Con. Or: The Mark Strikes Back

* * *

Few people knew that the overweight, heavily mustached man named Karcsi—sitting motionless in a camping chair amid the chaos, a greasy wide-brimmed hat pulled low over his eyes—could get you anything, if you paid right. Most saw only a fat flea-market hustler, which he was—but one of the best.

Now he looked asleep, no small feat in this din, seeming not to hear the other vendors hawking their wares. He didn't bother with the browsers either, those picking through the junk piled on his table—only because he knew they were unserious. No intention of actually buying anything (he always sensed that), and no real interest either. So he sat with half-closed lids, breathing steadily, while around him life proceeded with haggling, bickering, select insults, and all the essential operations of flea markets—sounds dear to his ears.

Then another browser arrived.

The man in his mid-forties, in jeans, moved differently

from the rest—though Karcsi only realized why when he peered out from under his hat. He recognized one of his favorite clients, the kind who sometimes surprised him with odd requests. Last time, for instance, he'd wanted anything horse-related. Pictures, photos, decorative objects, vases, ashtrays—it didn't matter, as long as it had a horse on it. And he'd only needed it for a few days, so he'd gotten the full selection at half price, then returned it all three days later, intact. Great deal. If only there were more like that.

"Dénes, my boy!" the junk dealer said, pleased. "Expected you yesterday."

"I know," the other replied. "But I had some business at the Black Raven."

"That some whorehouse?"

"No. A salon where... they fulfill special requests too."

"Aha." Karcsi grinned. "So a pervert whorehouse. Though—" he added, thoughtful, "—I do the same thing. Meaning I fulfill special requests. Like this."

He jerked his chin skyward—and beyond, since the merchandise he meant was somewhere behind him.

"Can I see it?" Dénes asked, excited.

Karcsi nodded.

"Hell yes. Come on, it's back here in the warehouse."

He heaved himself up and led the way behind the stall, where a battered, dent-riddled camper at least thirty years old waited. That was the "warehouse."

"Ta-da..." The proud owner opened the door and stepped

aside so the customer could inspect the cargo that had taken him more than a month to obtain.

Dénes moved closer and, after running his eyes over the merchandise, nodded with satisfaction.

"Perfect."

"What you had in mind?" the junk dealer asked. He liked being praised when he'd earned it, so he fished for another compliment. The other understood and didn't hold back.

"Exactly what I had in mind. Where'd you get it?"

Karcsi smiled.

"A rural community center."

"I searched the whole city," Dénes said, shaking his head. "Scoured the internet too. Nothing."

The hatted man felt like he was being buttered up—or worse, buttering someone up, which, if you thought about it, was disgusting in every detail. He decided to drop the metaphor.

"Should've come straight to me."

Dénes smiled.

"Yeah, would've saved a lot of time. But we're still on schedule—"

He suddenly hissed and grabbed his shoulder.

"What's wrong?" Karcsi asked, concerned.

"Nothing. Just a little wound. Sometimes something shoots through it like hell. But it's not serious. Can I pay by card?"

Karcsi laughed, flashing twenty-four-carat dental work—which in his case was literal, since the gold in his mouth could've bought an upper-mid-range car.

"Sure," he said between laughs. "And you'll get a VAT invoice and a stamp on the contract too."

"Don't need a stamp." Dénes shook his head—already regretting the joke, unprepared for the sight of that gold grill—then paused, as if reconsidering. "Let's do it smart instead."

He pulled out the prepared two hundred eighty thousand forints. Karcsi stuffed it into his fanny pack without counting.

"Come back anytime!"

"I will, don't worry. Did I mention you're the best?"

"Not enough, Dénes, my man."

* * *

"Uh... the thing is... this month... maybe the weather... so... traffic wasn't what it usually is, and..."

He kept going. The bullshit. Even though he knew Zsolt Bereczki didn't like people wasting his time. Because time is money; therefore, if someone steals your time... But the man making excuses—unimaginatively, at that—hadn't bothered to think this simple syllogism through. He just kept hunting for reasons why the club had been doing so badly lately.

And this despite the fact that a few weeks earlier they'd brought in three new girls, straight from Ukraine, where lately you could get many things cheaper—especially live merchandise. They'd upgraded the stage tech too, put new wallpaper in the private rooms. All of it had cost a fortune. Still, the nightclub's revenue dropped.

Not because of weather, though, like this idiot thought—if you could call what happened in that head "thinking"—but because of a guy named Vuk. Serbian for wolf, oddly enough, giving the finger to one of the best cartoons ever made. Though the bastard was unfortunately cunning enough anyway, plus ruthless and brutal—a lousy combination when the person in question was your worst enemy. Trying to push you out. And doing it damn cleverly.

This latest move, for instance, was pure genius. Not force, but brains.

Force he'd tried already, and failed—Zsolt had repelled and retaliated against every attack. Except the first one, which he hadn't seen coming and couldn't prevent. But they'd gotten lucky—Dani's stomach had hurt that night, so he'd slept with his mother. Meaning the grenade that landed in the kid's room harmed no one in the end.

Anett left the next day, though. With the boy.

Nearly five months ago.

During those five months, the Serbian army shrank by seven heads, so Vuk finally surrendered and offered peace. A ceasefire, more precisely. Zsolt accepted.

Apparently the news hadn't reached that bitch yet, wherever she was, or she'd have come back already. If she had half a brain. She should know her husband would track her down eventually—and it wouldn't go well.

But that was another matter. What mattered now was that for three days something had been burning like hell between his legs, especially when pissing, despite the antibiotics. And several other men felt the same—connected not just by belonging to Debrecen's cream, but by all having recently paid respects at the Exotic Chickens, availing themselves of one of the new girls' services. As he had too, as usual. All three of them. Sometimes together.

Turned out the girls carried in their blood a bacterium called *Neisseria gonorrhoeae*—the one that gave you the clap, with really damn unpleasant symptoms.

Not that it was that simple. The screening tests every three days showed nothing. The Exotic always made sure the workers stayed healthy—if not for their sake, then for business. The point was reliability, and the doctor examined them regularly. At least he'd seemed reliable. Three years with the club, never a problem.

Not reliable enough, apparently.

Vuk probably gave him more. Or blackmailed him with something. They'd never know—last week the good doctor fell from an eighth-floor balcony, so he couldn't be asked what exactly had happened. But since the girls swore they'd been fine when they arrived, Zsolt, though he couldn't prove it (since the only witness's earthly remains had to be collected with a teaspoon from roughly a hundred square meters), still guessed what had likely occurred: someone persuaded the doctor to infect them during a blood draw, then falsify their results as long as possible. Which, given the disease's incubation period, could've been two visits max—but plenty.

Didn't take much imagination to figure out who that some-one was. The only one who profited from the business. While the Exotic's traffic declined, the Orient Sexpress—in the Serbs' sphere—grew. News spreads fast. Faster than the clap.

And *this* guy comes at him with *weather*! How can someone be that stupid?

Zsolt asked exactly that.

The accountant paled. Thought of a headless corpse. Didn't want to end that way.

"Sorry..." he stammered. "I only see the numbers... and based on those..."

He stopped because Zsolt's phone chirped. Zsolt reached into his pocket reluctantly, tapped the screen, and looked. Whatever he saw pleased him—he suddenly smiled.

"Finally."

He returned magnanimously to the original topic.

"I'm not mad. After all, you can't help anything. Keep look-ing at your numbers."

He patted the pale man's shoulder and walked off.

The accountant exhaled, wiped his forehead, and thought that whoever had sent Zsolt Bereczki that zoo photo—kid ad-miring the giraffes with his mom—he was damn grateful to them.

*   *   *

The steak was a degree bloodier than average, but Dénes liked it exactly that way. He'd just cut himself another bite when a wrestler-built man stopped beside him and, without a word, sat down in the opposite seat.

Dénes frowned and looked around. Most booths in the restaurant were empty, so he quickly dismissed the idea that the guy had chosen his table for lack of space. Still strange. More than strange. Ballsy. You don't just—

Then the man set a large envelope in front of him.

"I'd like you to look at these." He leaned back like someone who had completed his assigned task.

Dénes stared at the man. Then at the envelope. His face—until now showing only mild surprise—slowly shifted into the look of someone trying, desperately, to produce a reasonable explanation for an unreasonable situation. Unsuccessfully.

"Excuse me—" he began carefully, "—but would you mind telling me—"

"We'd save a lot of time and energy," the man cut in, rude and absolute, "if you didn't ask anything and just did what I said. And that goes for the future too."

Something in his voice brooked no argument. His whole manner did.

Dénes shrugged, as if to say *What harm could come from looking in the stupid envelope?* At least they could get this over with and discover it was all a misunderstanding—Concrete Face had simply confused him with someone else. Then he could eat.

So he sighed, reached for the envelope, pulled out a stack of photos—

—and came face to face with himself.

In an elegant suit. Circle beard. Sitting at a window table in another restaurant, examining what looked like a valuable phone. In the next photo, slicked-back Viktor was explaining something to a bespectacled, tattooed waiter who looked pretty sour. Not like Anett in the third picture—smiling brightly as she poured water for a grumpy Mici néni.

If they'd arranged the photos chronologically, the story they told would have been even clearer—though it was already unmistakable. What he held was basically a photo essay. A comic book without the comics.

"With the waiters' testimony—because I talked to the others too—this is minimum five years," Concrete Face said. "And for your aunt, Mr. Szalay, probably her last five. Because the other guy didn't mix up anybody."

"What do you want from me?" Dénes asked. His voice was flat. He pushed his plate away like someone who'd instantly lost his appetite.

The uninvited guest grinned.

"Your services. And your talent. Plus your body and soul. Did I leave anything out?"

It was obvious that Dénes had nothing sensible to say—but he didn't need to.

He wasn't the one being addressed.

"Just that," said a new voice from behind the man, "all of this applies to your friend as well. The one I know as Gergő Horváth—but who, at Golding Bank, if I'm not mistaken, embezzled a hundred and eighty million under the name Viktor Vadász."

The voice belonged to someone who had apparently been sitting in the neighboring booth the entire time, listening. He stood and stepped over to them.

"Yes," he said with a smile. "That's me. The unfortunate owner of a fake Antal Ács painting."

Part Three

Ultimatum

What a production, the security guard thought. He wanted to spit—except you don't spit in a museum. Not even when no one's around. And you're never truly alone here anyway. Not in the special gallery. Cameras watched every angle. Santa was probably watching him right now from downstairs, eyes glued to the screens, just waiting for him to screw up.

Csaba straightened and arranged his face like he was waiting for the Holy Crown itself—orb, scepter, the works—not just a sheet of music. Okay, not just any sheet music. If he'd heard right, they'd paid seventy million for it—flown in by armored Mercedes, four motorcycle cops escorting it from the airport. Still felt over the top.

The door opened. The director entered, the press chief behind him, and with them a hulking guy in a suit carrying a briefcase—handcuffed to his wrist. *Christ*, Csaba thought as he fell in with them. These people really don't mess around.

The small procession crossed the gallery, skirting the gorgeous piano, Beethoven's life-sized bust, the vitrines of personal effects. They stopped at the glass-topped display case in the center of the room. The big guy braced the briefcase on his forearm, spun the combination lock, then turned toward the others and opened it. They leaned in. Their faces took on the reverence of men gazing into the Ark of the Covenant.

Csaba stood behind the guy in the suit, couldn't see a thing—and didn't much care. He'd be guarding it from now on; he'd have plenty of time to stare at it. Still, the moment sparked a line from his favorite movie, and he had to bite his tongue to keep from asking, *We happy, Vincent?* He nearly cracked up, especially when he noticed the director actually did look a little like Travolta. He pulled his face back into museum-neutral. Nobody noticed. Hopefully not even Santa downstairs, glued to the monitors, waiting to nail him for something.

"Beautiful," the director breathed. He pulled on cotton gloves, a surgeon preparing for the big cut, creating a sterile little world before reaching into the case.

He lifted Beethoven's handwritten score with exacting care. Csaba half-expected him to call for suction—but the press chief was already holding the broad, hinged lid of the case. No free hands left to mop his brow. The operation continued in taut silence. Finally the page found its home: the geometric center of the display, set deep in red velvet.

The director exhaled and leaned back. He nodded. The press chief lowered the glass top.

Operation successful.

* * *

Sólyom studied his visitor. The man was taking in the furnishings with something like reverence. Everyone did that on their first visit here. Or their second. Or their hundred and twenty-sixth. The desk, the Gulácsy above it, the bookshelves, the carpet—then the panorama rolling out behind everything. It stopped your breath. Sometimes even his.

So he let the man have his moment while he wondered what the hell he wanted. Supposedly not something to discuss over the phone.

"Beautiful," Oszkár said at last. "May I sit?"

"Make yourself at home."

The antique dealer chose a delicate-looking chair that proved sturdier than it appeared.

"I imagine you're curious," he began, choosing each word carefully, "why I was so... mysterious."

Sólyom shrugged. "If I had to guess, you want to sell me something."

"Bingo."

The billionaire sighed. "What are you trying to unload this time?"

Oszkár reached into his bag and pulled out the latest issue

of *Antiques World.* "This." He set the magazine on the desk. He had several copies. He'd already given one to a man named Dénes Szalay that day—along with instructions the man hadn't appreciated. Either of them. Too bad.

Sólyom stared at the Beethoven score on the cover, then looked up.

"Interested?" Oszkár asked with a smile.

"You know I am." Sólyom's surprise sounded genuine. "But you also know—if you read the article—that the goddamn museum already grabbed it with the government's help. They'll never sell it."

"No," Oszkár agreed. He let a beat pass. "The question is—how would you feel if it somehow... came to me? Theoretically."

Well now, Sólyom thought. This is getting interesting.

"I'd say," he answered slowly—and for once regretted not having his hearing aid in, because this conversation, contrary to expectations, required focus—"*theoretically* that I've misjudged you."

"Fine. But would you buy it?"

"Of course." No hesitation.

"For how much?"

Sólyom picked up a pen and turned it between his fingers. "Well." He angled his head so his almost-decent right ear could catch the reply, as if inspiration might drift in from the churning clouds outside. "At auction, I'd have gone... say... two hundred fifty thousand dollars."

"Try three," Oszkár shot back. "Knowing you. Beethoven. Original. Handwritten."

"Okay." Sólyom cut him off, irritated. "Let's say three. But that"—he added quickly—"would have been a legal purchase. What you're talking about—if I'm reading this right—isn't."

"I'm not talking about anything." The antique dealer lifted his hands. "This is just a... you know... thought experiment."

"Uh-huh."

"So. How much would it be worth to you if—"

"If I had to keep it in a safe forever and couldn't show it to anyone?" Sólyom finished for him.

Oszkár nodded.

Sólyom sighed and stared into the middle distance. "Maybe half."

"One hundred fifty thousand dollars." Oszkár savored it. "A bit over sixty million forints."

"Thereabouts."

"What about seventy? Make it round."

Sólyom pulled a face. "Fine. I hate haggling."

"I know." The dealer's grin widened. He'd never thank Bálint enough for planting this bug in his ear. Because that bug—if everything worked—would bring in seventy million. Plus the satisfaction that might restore his self-worth. Especially against this pompous, fascist asshole he'd finally managed to surprise. "But that's not all."

"You don't just want money for it." Sólyom sensed trouble.

"Not just money." Oszkár let the moment breathe.

"Tell me." Sólyom's sigh turned sour.

And he told him—exactly what the billionaire had feared. The kind of thing that had only one answer.

"Out of the question."

The antique dealer shrugged. "Then no deal." He rose with a look of genuine regret and started for the door.

"You can't be serious." The host stammered. "You'd walk away from seventy million forints?"

"I'll find another buyer, don't worry. As an old friend—and a great Beethoven enthusiast—I thought I'd ask you first."

"That was good of you," Sólyom choked out.

"But I was hoping you'd return the... courtesy. Not with money—I can get that elsewhere. A friendly gesture, though. That would mean something. Like this one."

The billionaire stared past him. If the man was bluffing, he was doing it damn well. But why would he? Just to make a fool of him for a few minutes? There was no profit in that. Sooner or later it would come out he only had two lousy threes—unless he had two more. Sólyom doubted it. But the only way to be sure was to call.

"All right!" The word burst out, frustrated. "Then we have a deal?"

"We do?" Oszkár brightened. He didn't mind that the other man didn't return the smile. Quite the opposite.

"Yes, we do." Zero enthusiasm. "But only once I have the score in my hand."

"You will. Don't worry."

"And how exactly do you plan to acquire it?"

"I don't. But I know someone who'll probably try."

"And this person... owes you?"

"Let's just say he owes me one."

* * *

Mici néni sat frozen, staring at the knitting needles that had slipped into her lap. She was trying to digest what she'd heard. It wasn't going well—for her or for anyone else.

"And this is really... I mean... realistic?" Anett asked, pale. "That he'd send us to prison?"

Dénes let out a breath. "If the marks testify, yes."

"Victims," Viktor corrected, then winced. "More precisely, *injured parties*. That's what they'll call them in court."

"Unless we do what the antique dealer asks." Mici néni spoke quietly.

Her nephew nodded.

"And what exactly is that?" Anett's forehead creased.

"We have to steal this." Dénes pulled a folded magazine from his jacket and held up the cover. "A sheet of music torn from a notebook Beethoven used in 1810. He jotted ideas in it—including the first version of a piece commissioned by Hungary. King Stephen. A few bars, anyway. After the old man died, nobody knows what happened to the notebook. They tore it apart and sold the pages to collectors. This is one of the last pieces. The Hungarian state paid a hundred seventy-five thousand dollars for it at an American auction and agreed to put it on public display for five years. If I'm right, it's arriving at the museum right now with a police escort. They open the exhibition tomorrow morning."

Silence.

They looked at one another.

Viktor slowly shook his head. "Too big a bite for us. And we have no idea how."

"Because we're not thieves!" Mici néni slapped the armrest.

"According to Oszkár Balogh, we are," Dénes said. "He claims we stole four million forints from him."

"Then his memory's faulty." His aunt straightened. "That money—if I recall—he gave willingly. Nobody put a gun to his head."

"But he's putting one to ours now." Dénes's voice darkened. "And if we say no, he'll pull the trigger. Four times. So I don't think we have much choice."

The elderly woman huffed. "Of course we don't." Her voice dropped. "I just hate being jerked around on a string."

"So you're in?"

Instead of answering, Mici néni shrugged. It was enough.

Dénes turned to Viktor, the question plain on his face.

Viktor met his gaze, then sighed. "That bastard backed us into a corner."

"Meaning?"

"Meaning..." He hesitated, then nodded. "Let's try it."

Anett—who had just been thinking this was the second bust she'd been dragged into in a short time—suddenly realized all eyes were on her.

"Um... what am I supposed to say?" She twisted her hands. "That asshole photographed me too."

Dénes shook his head. "You can still pass. We'll do it without you. Or at least... we'll try. And besides, you weren't in on the Antal Ács thing, so nobody would blame you if—"

"I know." She cut him off. "But I'm staying."

Especially after, she added silently, the man had saved her life the other day—not literally, maybe, but close enough. If they'd arrested him, they would have taken Dani from her, and then life wouldn't have been worth much. And his aunt had practically adopted her—treated her not just as a team member but as family, a substitute granddaughter, after the last parade.

"Good," Dénes said. "Because he wants to meet you too."

"Who?"

"Our client. Tomorrow morning. At the grand opening. He wants all of us there."

"Why?"

Dénes shrugged. "To show us what the score is: he's the boss, we do what he says. And... he'd like to see the gang together. His word."

Anett snorted. "Bastard."

Dénes spread his hands—then remembered something else. "Oh—and I haven't even told you the best part."

All eyes turned to him.

"Don't spare us," Viktor groaned, bracing himself for

another shovelful onto the already massive pile of shit. He wasn't wrong.

"He gave us a week," Dénes said. "If we don't get the score by then, he goes to the police."

"And we go to prison," Viktor muttered, then flicked a hand. "Of course. Either way, that's how it ends."

He wasn't an optimist

* * *

"And the kid?" Zsolt Bereczki's voice was tight.

The guy with the earring—who had spent nearly every day of the past five months parked by the giraffe enclosure, filming with his phone's pro camera—gave a small shrug.

"He... uh... didn't come with her." He stalled, and when his boss kept looking at him without a word, the silence did the work. He swallowed and pushed on. "Because I was following your wife."

"And?!"

"And after the zoo they went to a playground, where Anett met up with a girlfriend—"

"What girlfriend?" Zsolt cut in.

"I don't know." The gorilla eased out his phone. "But I got a picture. Recognize her?"

His boss glanced at it.

"No. Continue."

"So they met up, and Dani stayed with her—the woman, I mean. Your wife came home. Here." He jerked his chin toward the building across the street. "Then about ten minutes later she called a cab and left with a small gym bag... somewhere."

"Where?"

The guy with the earring felt it bear down on him. None of it was his fault—but he still had to make his boss see that. Not simple.

"Well, they headed that way." He forced the words out, tilting his chin toward the nearest intersection. "Then they turned off toward the bridge. But from there—" his voice thinned; here came the hard part "—in that goddamn rush-hour traffic, it was impossible to stay on them. They used the bus lane, of course..."

"You didn't?!" Zsolt cut in. The tone was mild. Which meant danger.

"Of course I did." The reply shot out. "But a cop pulled me over and wrote me up. By the time we were done, the taxi was gone."

He paused. Regret flickered—story over. Still, maybe pointing out the upside would help.

"Which sucks, but... it's not that bad. Now we know the address. We just wait. She'll turn up sooner or later. Her and the kid both."

Zsolt stared straight ahead, unreadable. The man with the earring watched him anyway—felt a bead of sweat crawl down from his temple.

"I think she went to the gym," a voice from the back seat offered. "Or a pool."

"You think that because of the gym bag?" Zsolt asked. Contempt coated the words as he glanced in the rearview mirror at the hundred-and-forty-kilo former wrestler.

The man shrugged, offended but not invested. He barely cared—as long as he didn't have to stake out that cemetery again. Months on that assignment had been torture. After a few days, he'd been tempted to climb into the grave himself. The boredom had felt lethal.

"Just a theory," he muttered, leaning back.

"You did good," Zsolt said suddenly to the guy with the earring.

The man exhaled and wiped his face.

"Thanks." Relief softened his voice. "So now what? What's the plan?"

His boss considered it.

"You two wait here." He made the call. "If she shows up, ring me immediately."

"Why—where will you be?"

"Getting a hotel room. Somewhere nearby."

"For how long?"

Zsolt didn't look back.

"Until I get my son back."

*   *   *

At least two hundred people crowded the gallery. Musicians, critics, businessmen, journalists, politicians, and a mob of Beethoven devotees. Plus three TV crews with cameras, cables, reflectors—Csaba already felt sick, and the ceremony hadn't even started.

The director and press secretary huddled with the minister and an influential-looking weasel with white-dyed hair—too bad he'd left his eyebrows black; gave him something demonic. The man carried himself like the others worked for him. They acted like they did. *Who the hell is this guy?* Csaba wondered idly. Some famous conductor or something. He kept scanning the room, glancing now and then at the elegant display case in the center, still draped.

Oszkár watched the case too, then let his gaze drift to the con artists. Pleased to see all four had come. So they'd taken the threat seriously—not surprising, because he'd meant every word. The old woman stood beside the piano, leaning on a cane, arm linked with that Anett girl. When he smiled at them from across the room, both women looked like they'd bitten into lemons. Still, they nodded politely—just to be safe. After all, technically they worked for him now. *Hehe.* Even if unwillingly.

But he wasn't here for them. He wanted the two good fellows.

The younger one—press card dangling from his neck—snapped away with a digital camera, looking far more groomed than when he'd offered him beer in the Eighth District. The other—the fake appraiser—wore a thin mustache today and ugly, thick-framed glasses. He stood by a pillar, studying the composer's bust with great interest. And the cameras mounted in the room's two most strategic corners.

So when Oszkár finally drifted toward him through the crowd, the man didn't look cheerful.

"You see it too, don't you?" he murmured, adjusting his glasses.

The antique dealer glanced around with mild curiosity, pretending not to know.

"See what?"

Dénes swallowed and leaned closer. "That what you're asking is impossible."

"Well... it certainly doesn't look simple." Oszkár nodded sympathetically—then added, hopeful, "But you'll figure something out. Because I see"—he went on with relish—"the whole family's here."

He jerked his chin at Mici néni, whom Anett had just left to make another circuit around the still-covered score. The gesture took in Viktor across the room, his camera clicking nonstop.

"Yes." Dénes went pale. "But they're saying it too—impossible to steal anything from here."

"You'll have to anyway." The antique dealer's voice cooled. "Otherwise you can spend your time folding paper bags."

"Couldn't we just—" Shame crept into Dénes's face; he felt how pathetic this sounded. "—give back the four million... with interest... you could ask for double..."

"No, my friend." His client cut him off, contemptuous. "I need the score. From you specifically."

To forestall further debate, he moved off—especially since he saw the minister and museum director, after apologetic handshakes with Sólyom, heading toward the improvised podium.

Dénes watched him go, jaw tight, then joined Mici néni, who stood alone.

Neither noticed the man in the blue bow tie on the opposite side of the pillar, apparently absorbed in reading Beethoven's biography posted in three languages.

He couldn't have cared less about that.

The conversation he'd just overheard—that was another matter.

Shushing rippled through the crowd. The buzz softened as everyone turned toward the platform. The director tapped his microphone.

"That him?" Mici néni asked quietly, glancing toward Oszkár's back. After her nephew nodded, she pulled a face. "Slappable sort of mug."

"Dear friends!" The amplified voice rang out. "Today is a great day for all of us who love music… and love Beethoven, whose life was Music itself, capital M."

The guard stationed by the entrance pulled a face—pleased to see the knockout beside him making her own. When their eyes met, both knew the other wasn't impressed by the rhetorical masterpiece.

"Total bullshit speech," the security guard muttered out of the corner of his mouth. "Capital B."

The girl clapped a hand over her mouth to stifle a laugh, then elbowed him lightly in the ribs, like they'd known each other forever.

"Idiot." Her look carried mock reproach.

But clearly she wasn't angry. In fact, Csaba thought the joke had landed well—so he instantly worked on the next one.

"Good thing the poor bastard can't hear this," he whispered a moment later, shaking his head. "Not that he'd hear it anyway..." He leaned toward her ear and delivered the punchline. "He was deaf."

Anett laughed, then glanced around apologetically; nobody cared.

"Stop it," she whispered, though her voice warmed. She waved off the increasingly proud, self-appointed stand-up comic, convinced his material beat whatever the guy on the platform was saying:

"...This is proven by that magnificent cantata he wrote for us Hungarians. We're about to hear several bars from it. Which bars exactly... you'll never guess..."

Polite laughter. Because the speaker looked hopefully in his direction, even Sólyom pulled his mouth into a brief smile. Let the poor bastard enjoy himself.

Then his secretary slipped in behind him and, knowing his boss barely heard anything with his left ear, leaned close to the right and whispered at length. The billionaire listened, eyebrows lifting, and gave a small approving nod. Clever boy, he thought—almost forgave him that terrible blue bow tie.

"But first—" the museum director resumed, "—let me thank the minister, who five months ago, when this beautiful piece turned up in a Viennese attic, made a very public promise to acquire it for the museum. And behold"—he raised his hands in vaguely biblical fashion—"the promise has been kept."

"Amen," the security guard muttered, making sure Anett could hear—otherwise, what was the point.

The director and minister each grabbed a corner of the cloth covering the display case. With a synchronized pull they whisked it away, revealing the decade's most famous sheet of music.

"And now—" the speaker called once the applause faded, "let the music speak!"

Beethoven's *King Stephen* poured from the speakers—the passage whose handwritten notes, penned by the composer himself, had now become public treasure.

* * *

Where the hell was that woman?

Zsolt threw his phone onto the bed. He'd gotten several calls over the past few hours—but not the one that mattered. He'd staked out this shithole hotel all night, convinced yesterday would finally put an end to the Anett situation. Nearly five months now. He was sick of it.

He'd played the reunion out in his head more times than he could count. One day—when she least expected it—he'd appear out of nowhere, stop right in front of her, hands in his pockets like he just happened to be passing by.

Hey baby. Long time no see. What's up?

She'd shit herself on the spot. As she should. Every reason to. She had to know what she'd done couldn't go unpunished.

And now—nothing. It was already past noon. Even if she'd spent the night at some guy's place (the whore), she should've been home by now. Unless she'd gone straight to work—if, after years of comfort and luxury, she was suddenly willing to work again. Zsolt seriously doubted it.

Or maybe she'd spotted one of the idiots. Like last time.

His men had tracked her down once already. Found an address through a rental contract. Solid lead—or so it seemed. Anett never showed. She'd definitely lived there for at least three weeks. Somehow she'd caught wind of it and vanished again. Zsolt really hoped this wouldn't be case number three—that this disappearance had some boring, explainable reason.

He'd ask her.

Or ask his son.

Right. The kid still barely talked. Didn't know many words beyond *mama* and the giraffe he insisted on calling a seagull. Still, he was the youngest member of the Bereczki clan. And Zsolt could barely remember his face anymore.

Of course, all babies looked the same for the first few years. Meaning they were cute—when they weren't screaming their heads off. That always got on his nerves. He'd never understood how his exes (soon to be three of them) tolerated it. He would've smacked them long ago—the screaming brats, not their mothers. Though sometimes them too.

Still, right after a diaper change they could be all right. You sat them on your lap for a few minutes, and they even smelled good—like pastries. Not like that rotten-dog-carcass-puked-on-by-rotten-eggs stench they gave off before cleanup. Best not to share airspace then. Luckily they got potty-trained fast.

Though until they were well past the annoying stage, you still couldn't do much with them. He'd never tolerated the cooing and baby talk. Thought that kind of shit was faggy. And nobody had ever called *him* that—he'd have broken the neck of anyone who tried—and nobody ever would.

His oldest boy, Robi—that was different.

The kid was finally hitting the age where you could have a real conversation with him. Do real father–son things. Stop tiptoeing around feelings and start talking about how the world actually worked.

Last week, for instance, they'd gone to the Exotica together. Zsolt figured it was time the boy learned a few things without fairy tales or women filling his head with nonsense. With the help of a twenty-two-year-old blonde bombshell from Slovakia, he'd made sure Robi stopped being so damn hesitant about everything.

Too bad the little idiot had cried afterward.

You could tell his mother had raised him.

But Zsolt would make a man out of him. In this world, only those who took what was theirs got ahead. And really—what better lesson could there be than learning early that pleasure, like everything else, was something you paid for and moved on from?

Exactly.

Besides, his own father had never bothered with that sort of thing. Hell, the loser couldn't even support the family. From sixteen on, Zsolt had had to take the household in hand himself. And now look where he was.

One of Debrecen's most powerful men.

No high school diploma. Some people had brought that up early on. But only once. They learned fast it wasn't a healthy topic. Zsolt Bereczki was sensitive about it.

Just as sensitive as when someone betrayed him.

Like his wife. Number three. *Numero* three. Not *numbera*—of those there'd been about three hundred, give or take a few dozen; he'd never bothered counting—but his official, legally wedded wife. Who, like her predecessors, had sworn eternal loyalty.

Then took off.

That alone was unforgivable.

There were things a man could do that a woman absolutely couldn't. Because it was completely different when *he* left someone—like when he'd left the mothers of his older kids. That was the natural order. Men got tired of women. Men were built that way. Not exactly PC, but facts were facts.

One egg a month versus several hundred million sperm.

And his exes had no complaints. None. Both were grateful.

He'd taken care of them even after he threw them out. Bought each an apartment after the divorces. Transferred a million and a half forints to their accounts on the first of every month. They could live comfortably without working. Focus on the kids.

He visited regularly. Spent a few hours with them. Bought birthday presents. Arranged entertainment when needed.

So yes—he was a damn good father. Especially to Robi. But the middle one couldn't complain either.

The youngest, though—that was Dani. And his mother had taken him without notice.

Without permission.

The kid would've gotten the same deal as the others. Apartment. Allowance. Security. Anett too.

But she didn't want it.

And she was going to regret that.

Real soon.

Once she finally showed up.

* * *

While the footage played, Viktor the cameraman offered running commentary.

"Right, so what jumps out immediately—two cameras. Both trained on that goddamn sheet of music. Plus a fire alarm with its suppression system, motion sensors that probably only work at night..."

He trailed off. All those movies came to mind—the *Ocean's*

trilogy, for instance—the same setup every time: a crew of professional thieves sitting around, spinning complicated plans to steal some heavily guarded, absurdly valuable item.

Just like them now.

Except they weren't thieves, and they didn't have the first fucking clue how to do this. Which was a shame. And they didn't have any of those clever little gadgets that disabled security systems or laser whatevers—unless this cheap digital camera from the score-presentation ceremony counted. The kind that would've earned a contemptuous smile even in the Balmazújváros elementary school media club.

As for the crew, he mused, his mood lifting a notch: right now *he* was Brad Pitt. Dénes, obviously, was George Clooney—the age fit.

Small comfort, but better than nothing.

A bit sour, a bit yellow—but it's ours.

Viktor realized the pause had stretched too long. He cleared his throat and continued, as if he'd merely been waiting for the right moment in the footage.

"And here's my favorite—the armed security guard." He froze the frame. "Luckily Anett already made friends with him. What's his name again?"

"Some kind of Csaba." The woman shrugged vaguely, her mind elsewhere.

"You have his number?"

"Of course. He got mine too."

"Perfect."

"I hope," Anett muttered darkly, "I don't have to sleep with him."

"We'll let you know," Dénes said, straight-faced.

"Hilarious." She snorted—mostly for form.

The security guard didn't worry her. He was the type she could handle anytime. Unlike Zsolt. Whom she never could.

"And this right here—" the fake cameraman froze the frame again, "—the world's most expensive scrap of paper. I mean—" he added, correcting himself, "—of the ones I've seen in person."

"Should've thrown it in the trash!" Mici néni burst out. She'd been silent until now. "Beethoven, I mean. While he was alive. We wouldn't have all this trouble."

"If my aunt had wheels—" Dénes sighed, then clapped a hand over his mouth as if something had just occurred to him. "Oh wait. That's you. Sorry."

"You're in such a good mood." The old woman shook her head. "Though you have no reason to be."

"Well, not much, that's for sure." Viktor shrugged. He didn't understand why his mentor wasn't as deflated as he and the two women beside him.

What they'd suspected was becoming harder and harder to deny: that score couldn't be stolen.

Which meant they'd all spend the next few years behind bars.

And here he was, cracking jokes.

"Why?" Dénes asked, sounding mildly wounded. "Would it

be better if I cried?" He paused. "Anyway, we shouldn't give up before we even start. We haven't begun the... planning."

"What planning?!" Mici néni exploded. "It's completely obvious we're unfit for this kind of thing."

"Not so sure about that." Her nephew's protest lacked conviction.

"Then tell us what to do," Viktor challenged.

"First of all—" Dénes began, thinking aloud, "—we need to get the museum floor plan somehow. And the evacuation plan for fire emergencies..." He frowned. "There *is* one, right?"

So much for George Clooney, Viktor thought.

"How should I know? But I'll have it by tomorrow."

Danny Ocean's caricature turned to Anett.

"You need to go on a date with that meathead. At night, preferably. Inside. Scout the terrain."

Anett rolled her eyes.

"And if he tries to climb on me during this 'scouting'?"

"He won't."

"Promise?"

"Promise. Nobody wants to make a scene at work—least of all a security guard who's already bent the rules once by letting someone in at night. If he even lets you in."

Anett flicked her hand dismissively.

"Leave that to me."

*   *   *

Nobody could have executed this assignment more professionally, Richárd thought with satisfaction. His boss was probably thinking the same. Which meant extra money—a lot of extra money—maybe the most yet.

Still, no reason to get ahead of himself.

"So Balogh's mysterious client walked those two women home," Sólyom mused, stroking his eyebrow. "The old one and the younger one. Then what?"

"Then someone else joined them."

Richárd angled his phone toward the billionaire.

"Familiar," the man muttered, brow creasing as he spread two fingers to zoom in on the face on the screen.

"Because he was at the opening too," Richárd supplied. "Camera in hand."

"Ah." Something clicked. "And what were the four of them up to?"

"No idea." Richárd shrugged, a hint of regret creeping in. "But it took a while. They split up an hour ago. More precisely, the two men went home then."

"And you didn't happen to follow one of them?" Sólyom asked, already reading the answer on his secretary's face.

"I did."

"I hope it wasn't him." The billionaire gestured at the phone, still displaying the fake cameraman.

"No." Richárd smiled. "The other one. The man Oszkár was whispering with. I think he's the boss."

"Good." Sólyom nodded, pleased. "What did you learn

about him?"

"His address," Richárd said, letting the beat land. "First round. Then, when he checked his mailbox, I figured I'd check it too."

Sólyom leaned forward, excitement making him forget his hearing aid was still in. He tilted his head.

"So what's our friend's name?"

"If I'm right," Richárd said, "Dénes Szalay."

* * *

"Kept getting kicked to voicemail." The security guard's complaint came out as a grumble, though inside he was celebrating. He'd never had a girlfriend this hot.

Deep down, he suspected he didn't have one now either—the *girl*, as he kept thinking of her, hadn't come back to the museum for him. She'd come for that stupid piece of sheet music. And the fact that after calling all evening—eight texts included—he still hadn't gotten a response... well.

Hope dies last.

"I'm an idiot. Sorry." Anett sighed and pulled an adorable little grimace. "I accidentally gave you my old number."

"That explains it." Csaba nodded, relieved.

He didn't believe a word of it. But the fact that she'd invented a lie—made the effort—might actually be a good sign.

The knockout glanced at the tourist group packed tight around the score.

"Always this mobbed?" She looked troubled and tucked the

notebook she'd been clutching under her arm back into her bag.

"Yeah." His tone slipped sour. "People go nuts over that thing."

"Can't blame them." Anett sighed again. "After all, Beethoven wrote it with his own hand."

Csaba, assuming this was another joke like last time at the opening, was about to grin—then he took a closer look at her.

Right. Back then, the jokes had all been his. Anett had only laughed.

And music history had always been a closed book to him. Like most subjects. All of them, really. So instead of blowing his chance, he tested the waters.

"You... uh... work in music too?"

"Capital M?" She smiled, invoking the director's favorite cliché. "No. I study graphology."

Csaba nodded as if he knew what that was.

Privately, he figured it was some kind of medical thing—pharmaceutical, maybe—and tried to work out what pills had to do with a deaf composer. No clue. Better to wait for her to keep talking.

Which she did.

"I'm writing my thesis on him. Beethoven, I mean. Specifically his handwriting."

Oh.

Right.

Csaba mentally slapped his forehead. That crime show last

week—some expert had read a blackmail letter and figured out the writer had been molested by his uncle... or something like that. He didn't remember the details, but at least now he had a rough idea. Not pharmaceuticals.

"That's why I'd love to finally see that page," Anett went on. "Up close. At my own pace. But it looks like it's impossible to get anywhere near it."

She shrugged, deflated.

"Can't you work from a photo?" Csaba asked, hoping he wasn't saying something stupid.

Anett shook her head.

"A lot of things only show up on the original. How hard he pressed the pen or pencil. That sort of thing."

"Got it." Csaba nodded—then something occurred to him. "How long would an examination like that take?"

"About... half an hour, roughly. Why?"

"Just that... if you want... I could bring you in one evening. After closing."

Her mouth fell open. She stared at him as if he'd just offered her a kidney.

"Seriously?"

"Yeah. But you'd only have twenty minutes. After that the gallery locks automatically. Nobody in or out."

"Twenty minutes is plenty." Her voice flooded with gratitude, then softened with embarrassment. "But it's kind of urgent."

Csaba shrugged.

"Let's do it tonight, then. Yeah?"

"Okay!"

"Meet me at the staff entrance at quarter to seven."

* * *

Zsolt Bereczki was pissed, which never meant anything good. The guy with the earring started talking fast.

"The apartment's rented by a woman named Anna Horváth—five years now—but the landlord hasn't seen her in four months."

"How's that possible?"

"Says she paid six months' rent and utilities upfront, so they don't really deal with each other. This Anna's about thirty. Average-looking. Maybe finished eighth grade. Came from some little village near Marosvásárhely a few years back to try her luck."

"From the look of this neighborhood—" Zsolt cast a contemptuous glance out the window, "—that luck didn't pan out."

The ex-wrestler in the back laughed on cue. When the others didn't even twitch, he cut it short and stared at the floor.

"Still better than back home," the guy with the earring said quietly.

"Doing what?"

"Cleaning."

Zsolt snorted.

"Must be ugly." He didn't bother disguising the logic. He couldn't imagine a woman—unless she was a total beast—spending eight hours a day on her knees scrubbing floors when she could spend ninety minutes doing something else. Also on her knees.

"How do they know each other?"

"Her and Anett? No idea. The landlord doesn't know either. I showed him your wife's picture, but he says he's never seen her."

Zsolt stared into the middle distance.

"They could've met anywhere," he muttered at last. Then he turned to the man in the passenger seat. "Where's this woman now?"

"Supposedly visits her parents a lot."

"In Transylvania?"

"Yeah. Want me to send someone to find her?"

Zsolt exhaled, thinking it through.

"If neither of them shows up in two days, yes." He decided. "Until then, we look around inside. Maybe we'll learn something."

"Okay. When?"

"Tonight. When it's quiet." He paused. "Meanwhile, track down that other bitch for me—the one my wife handed Dani off to at the playground."

"I'll try." The guy with the earring swallowed. He had no idea how to track someone down from a single photo.

His boss noticed.

"Oh, come on!" Zsolt snapped. "There are tons of facial-recognition programs. You've used one before, right?"

The man didn't answer.

He didn't need to. The silence said everything.

"Fine." Zsolt's voice went flat. "I'll do it myself."

* * *

Richárd would have preferred better news, but he couldn't change the facts.

"So, nothing?" Sólyom looked up from behind his desk. "Aside from the aunt doing a few years for fraud thirty-some years ago?"

The secretary spread his hands and sighed.

"I'm sorry." He meant it—but to his surprise, Sólyom looked satisfied.

"Don't be." He grinned, leaned back, and examined his fingernails. "The important part came through."

Richárd frowned. Nothing had come through. His police contact had confirmed that, aside from a juvenile scuffle, Dénes Szalay had never appeared on the authorities' radar.

His confusion must have shown, because his boss sighed and went on.

"Come on. You heard him yourself—our friend wants to steal that score. Right? On Oszkár Balogh's commission. And for a job that delicate, he'd never hire an amateur. Follow me?"

"Not really," Richárd admitted, choosing his words carefully. He felt exceptionally stupid, which didn't happen often.

But this was over his head. There had to be logic to it—he just couldn't see it yet.

Unlike Sólyom.

The billionaire was famous for turning the most hopeless situations into profit. Because, as he liked to say, you could always look at things from a different angle. More than that—sometimes you *had* to look at them from a different angle, and suddenly everything shifted. Few people could do that. Changing perspective required knowledge, talent, courage, and a whole chain of other qualities all at once—qualities most people didn't possess, even individually.

"Let me help you." Sólyom's voice brightened. "If this man makes his living this way and still isn't in any database, he probably knows what he's doing. Right?"

"Right." Richárd nodded, annoyed with himself for not thinking of it sooner. It *was* logical. If a high-end antique dealer wanted to steal something from a heavily guarded museum, he'd look for someone with experience. And if that person had never been caught, he must be very good at his job.

But his boss wasn't finished.

"And if someone's a professional," Sólyom said, smiling, "you can always have a rational conversation with them."

* * *

By ten that night, Anett had reached the end of her report.

"Twenty minutes past closing, they really do pull down the shutter—literally," she said, shivering as she recalled what had happened an hour and a half earlier.

The grate connected to the glass lid of the score's display

table had slammed down with a deafening crash, stopping barely ten centimeters from her nose.

Csaba had told her to stand right there and just watch. So she had.

After the security guard had kindly let her spend exactly nineteen and a half minutes close to the manuscript, studying and photographing every square centimeter the way Dénes had asked, she'd done exactly as instructed. Even when the guy suddenly started counting backward—ten, nine, eight, seven—she hadn't suspected a thing. She'd only felt a strange, anticipatory thrill.

Then at zero she'd nearly had a heart attack—jumped back in terror, straight into Csaba's waiting arms. He'd apologized afterward for not warning her, but the giggling threaded through his mea culpa undermined the whole gesture.

"Also, it's loud as hell and scary as shit," Anett added flatly.

Then she laid out the rest of what she'd learned.

"Plus, the motion sensor kicks in at the same time. From that point on, getting into the special exhibition room—at least through the door—is impossible."

"You mean," Mici néni cut in, "he can't go in either? Your... suitor?"

Viktor snorted. Both women shot him reproachful looks.

"Sorry," he said. "Just... haven't heard that word in a while."

"Because you had no upbringing," the old woman muttered. Then she turned back to Anett, who gave a small, apologetic shrug.

"The security system's wired directly to the police station," Anett said. "He has nothing to do with it."

"So he can't even turn it off?" the former bride asked, deflated.

Anett shook her head.

"Damn it!"

"And there's no other way in," Viktor added, picking up the thread. He'd spent the entire day in various libraries, tracking down everything he could—floor plans, evacuation diagrams, detailed descriptions of security protocols for state facilities. "The windows have bars. Solid cast iron. Four centimeters thick."

"Then we go in through the door after all," Dénes said suddenly.

The others turned to him, stunned.

Before anyone could protest or ask what he meant, he went on.

"Just not at night. During the day. When everyone's there."

"What's that supposed to mean?" his aunt asked, frowning.

"Exactly what it sounds like," he said. "The plan's changed. From now on, we do what we're good at. Especially you."

* * *

"What's taking you so damn long?" Zsolt hissed.

He watched the guy with the earring kneeling at the door, working the tried-and-tested skeleton key to relock the entrance to the tiny Józsefváros apartment facing the courtyard.

"Almost done. Relax." The man's mutter was tight.

Then came the click—the bolt sliding home.

Two minutes later they were in the car, staring out at the empty street, waiting for their hearts to slow. For different reasons, but both pounding.

One of them was wired from the break-in itself—burglary, or, as the penal code put it, unlawful entry. If they got caught, they wouldn't be walking away.

The other had found a document.

Middle drawer of the nightstand, tucked between rattles, pacifiers, and a stack of official papers. If what that document suggested was true, everything changed. But Zsolt Bereczki still couldn't quite wrap his head around what *everything* meant.

Soon enough, he would.

The noose was tightening around his wife and Dani. The boy was probably still with that mysterious woman—except she wasn't so mysterious anymore. An illegally acquired facial-recognition program had delivered a ninety-seven-point-five percent match in ten seconds flat, cross-referencing the playground photo with a Facebook profile.

Now Zsolt had her name.

A little digging—barely worth calling work—gave him her address too.

Tomorrow he'd pay her a visit.

Ask a few questions.

"You find anything interesting?" The slab of muscle in the

back seat leaned forward. He'd stayed in the car the whole time, playing lookout, phone in hand, ready to warn them if trouble came close.

"Yeah." Zsolt's voice went cold. "More than interesting."

He didn't elaborate.

*   *   *

"Do what?!" The craftsman stared at him. He must have heard wrong.

He hadn't. Dénes repeated it, word for word.

"Scalp it."

The specialist pushed his cap back and looked again at the piece. A dealer named Karcsi had tracked it down after weeks of searching—found it in some community-center library. A beautiful object. And this man wanted to destroy it.

"You're not serious." His voice hovered between hope and disbelief. The customer did not look like someone who joked.

"I am." Dénes sounded almost apologetic. Then he added, "And I'll tell you exactly how I want it done. It won't be simple."

He pulled out paper and pen and began to draw as he explained.

The craftsman felt a flicker of professional awe. This really wouldn't be simple. The operation would require an incredibly precise, delicate hand. What it was *for*, though, he still couldn't figure out.

Not that it mattered, he decided.

If the customer wanted it, he'd deliver. For good money.

And money clearly wouldn't be an issue here—one glance at the man told him that.

It wasn't.

The client didn't blink when he named the figure, didn't hesitate when told half was due upfront. He only asked whether the deadline was doable.

When the craftsman said yes—adding a few expert observations and a convincing list of tools—Dénes actually thanked him, visibly relieved, and reached for his wallet.

Meanwhile, he was thinking he'd gladly pay more.

If there were a few critical details the entire plan stood or fell on, this was definitely one of them.

* * *

The old woman was on edge. She'd done this kind of work before, but the stakes had never been this high.

One mistake now and they'd all end up in prison. She would end up there literally—and unlike last time, when she'd done eighteen months standing on her head, that was then. Now, at her age, a cell would be her last address before the morgue and the cemetery.

Mici néni wanted to die at home. Unlike the poet Petőfi, she had no quarrel with the idea of dying in bed, surrounded by pillows. In fact, that *was* the plan. Exactly the plan.

But first she had to do her part.

Precisely.

So she steadied herself—the way she had so many times

over the years—and focused on the task at hand. If there were a few critical details the entire plan stood or fell on, this was definitely one of them.

*   *   *

"It's for my grandmother," Anett said. Then she added, "The doctor says she won't be able to make longer trips on her own anymore."

"Poor thing." The employee tried to arrange her face into something sympathetic, failed, and switched to enthusiasm. "But this will make her so much more comfortable, believe me."

Anett sighed, nodded, and scanned the row of wheelchairs on display. She needed something substantial, with a large padded backrest—just as Dénes had specified.

Her eyes settled on a model that looked right. She moved toward it. The saleswoman followed, perking up—this one was from the pricier range.

"Do you think she'd like this one?" Anett asked, letting just the right note of uncertainty into her voice.

"Definitely." The saleswoman didn't hesitate, launching into a detailed recitation of features.

Anett appeared to listen. She even asked a few relevant questions. But her thoughts kept drifting to Dani.

Tonight she'd finally see him again. After three long days. This whole cursed manuscript business had left no time to visit. And if the job went south, three years might pass before she could hold him again.

If they didn't take him away permanently.

And she still had to swing by the apartment this afternoon to—

Focus, she told herself. Focus on the task.

She pulled herself back into the medical supply store, let herself be talked into the wheelchair she'd already chosen anyway, then asked a few questions about another product.

If there were a few critical details the entire plan stood or fell on, this was definitely one of them.

*   *   *

Viktor had never set foot in a gun shop before. Not that this one resembled the armory in *Falling Down,* where Michael Douglas browses grenade launchers and machine guns. Still, he spotted a few dangerous-looking items and gave them a wide berth.

What he needed was different. Sure, it had seen combat too—just with less permanent results than, say, an AK-47. The clerk's mouth tightened when Viktor made his request. He led him to a back shelf with something close to contempt.

Now Viktor stood there, squinting at the fine print on the boxes, a little lost. He finally picked the two most promising models and grabbed five of each.

That afternoon he'd head to one of the forests around Buda, find an empty clearing, and test them out. Like the Jackal preparing to assassinate De Gaulle—who'd nearly pulled it off—*sighting in* his weapon with a watermelon. In the bleached Bruce Willis remake, dangerous-profession-choosing, future–*School of Rock* Jack Black had played the melon's role, if Viktor remembered correctly. Brilliantly.

This was a dangerous job they were prepping for. Way outside their wheelhouse. But if they did it right—and caught a little luck—it might actually work. They'd dodge prison. Better yet, they'd make money.

Thanks to Dénes, who'd come up with yet another meticulously crafted plan—one that, in Viktor's opinion, relied far too heavily on blind luck, but was still brilliant. Something that never would have occurred to him, despite the fact that he'd spent the past few days beating his head against the wall trying to figure out how to pull off this goddamn manuscript heist.

The results had been dismal. Pathetic.

He'd kept his ideas to himself. Better for everyone.

He could just picture his mentor's reaction to the suggestion that one of them hide behind a curtain before closing, then spend the night inching along with slow, careful precision. Never mind.

Though even that was better than the Reagan-and-Nixon-mask-wearing, gun-toting duo version—dead on arrival. Or, as Dénes would put it, a *Point Break* situation. If he'd seen the movie. And actually remembered it. An unlikely combination.

So Viktor kept his mouth shut, sparing himself the well-deserved but still stinging comments. Now that he knew the plan Dénes had worked out, staying quiet seemed even wiser.

He added a third type to his basket—might be better than the other two.

No room for mistakes now. If there were a few critical details the entire plan stood or fell on, this was definitely one of them.

*   *   *

When the woman—he knew her name now, and her address—appeared at the end of the street, Zsolt smiled.

Not with joy.

Even if this brought him closer to Anett—who still hadn't gone home since they'd found her apartment—the whole thing might amount to nothing. Still, the feeling of finally closing a case that had dragged on for five months gave him a certain satisfaction. And this pretty little bombshell, late twenties, would help him put a period at the end.

She was nearing the café entrance by her building. A lucky break—the place was well positioned. From the window, you could see the entire street. So when the girl—who looked far better in person than in the playground photo his guy had snapped—turned the corner, they spotted her immediately.

It gave Zsolt time to work out his approach. What he'd say when he buzzed her apartment.

He couldn't tell her the truth. That he was the father of the little boy named Dani she'd been watching. Anett could've filled her head with any kind of bullshit—how Zsolt was some Jack the Ripper who beat them, drank, forced them to run. If he started with reality, the woman might start screaming.

Not that she wouldn't scream anyway if she refused to answer his questions.

Still, he needed a cover story.

Then it hit him.

Just tweak the truth.

He could have gone to the police, right? Filed a report: wife takes the child from his usual place of residence without consent, violates his share of joint custody—basically kidnaps their own kid. Nine out of ten men would do exactly that.

The fact that he was number ten didn't matter right now.

Because what would happen if he did go that route? Child services and juvenile authorities would launch proceedings against Anett. Start looking for Dani.

He just had to decide which role to play.

Cop—or child-protective-services bureaucrat?

Zsolt went with the latter.

His smile widened.

Then, a second later, it occurred to him that the bitch might've shown her photos of him. In that case, the whole thing was blown.

Whatever.

He shrugged.

Then it would be the screaming version.

* * *

"So tomorrow?" Oszkár's voice pitched higher. "Excellent."

They sat in the back room of the antique shop, on opposite sides of an IKEA table. No one who cared about patina ever made it back here anyway. This was the dealer's private domain, and cheap but functional suited him just fine.

Dénes didn't count—Oszkár had filed him under *staff* a while back. Him and his crew. Or *gang*, as he'd called them last time, which had made the man's face twitch for a second.

So—*gang*, then.

You don't give much weight to employee opinions, right?

Right, Oszkár answered himself.

That was when the man had called Oszkár's disposable, untraceable mobile. Said he was in the neighborhood. Wanted to stop by and report developments. The antique dealer had politely shooed the browsing customers out, flipped the *Open* sign to *Closed* without actually locking the door, then retreated to the office to wait—and picture how he'd spend the seventy million forints he'd be richer by if the man pulled off the impossible.

He still considered it impossible.

But Bálint's professional assessment had convinced him otherwise. The ex-cop knew his business. And if these four were as good as the investigator claimed, why not test them? He could only win.

When the bell over the entrance jingled, Oszkár straightened.

"In here."

Then he glanced around, faintly anxious—he didn't usually let anyone back here.

Anyone who mattered, anyway.

Dénes walked in without knocking, looking uncomfortable. Oszkár understood. Even appreciated it. To make the hierarchy unmistakable, he didn't greet the man—just pointed silently to the opposite chair and waited.

CEO to security guard.

So the security guard started talking.

He laid out their plan. Dangerous, sure. But since they didn't want the old woman receiving last rites in a prison hospital, they'd decided to try tomorrow morning.

If they lived that long, he added dryly.

Which sounded excellent.

"Happy, aren't you?" Dénes muttered. Then added, "Lucky you."

Damn right, Oszkár thought, genuinely.

He leaned closer, curious.

"So how are you going to do it?" His voice dropped.

The would-be thief shook his head.

"Our business. Yours is to be at the scene. Three, four hours after the action, we disappear from the city."

Oszkár smiled.

"But first," he said softly, "you hand me something. Right?"

Dénes's mouth twisted.

"Yeah. Unless something goes sideways." He paused.

"When the show's over, meet me at the Thermostat. Little bar, a few blocks from the museum. Hope you can find it."

"Don't worry," Oszkár said. "I'll be there."

*   *   *

"Hey, baby. What's up?" Zsolt Bereczki smiled, hands in his pockets. Twenty minutes earlier the ex-wrestler had called with the news that the little bird had finally returned to her cage. As planned, Zsolt added, with studied indifference, "Been a while."

He shoved the death-pale woman aside and stepped into the apartment. The guy with the earring followed, closed the door, then leaned against the wall with his arms crossed.

Anett swallowed. This had already happened in her dreams—more than once—and it never ended well. Unless her own terrified scream counted, the one that jolted her awake, heart hammering, just before the first blow landed.

"Well... Zsolt..." She could barely form the words. She stopped herself from adding *what are you doing here?*

"Where is he?" His voice came out hard. Direct.

The morning interrogation had gone nowhere. The woman knew nothing about Dani—only that she'd watched him two or three times for a few hours, the way she did with other kids. Professional babysitter; that was how she made her living. Clear enough from her online ads, which she'd shown readily to the child-services official.

As for Anett, she'd said, a little nervous, she didn't really know her either. So many mothers—they all blurred together. But she was glad there were so many; glad they kept passing her number around. It meant steady work. Supposedly another playground mom had recommended her to Anett, but which one, she couldn't say.

In the end, she'd asked—worried—whether she was going to get in trouble for any of this. She'd had no idea the boy's family situation was complicated. That the mother had taken him illegally. She had just—

But Zsolt had assured her this was all on Anett.

The aforementioned Anett sank into a chair instead of answering.

"We'll come back to that." Zsolt nodded, as if accepting her silence. Which couldn't have been further from the truth. But he had something else on his mind first. He shifted course. "First I want you to tell me something."

He moved to the nightstand, pulled open the middle drawer, reached in without looking, and took out a piece of paper.

The girl closed her eyes. She knew what was coming.

She was right.

Zsolt tossed the document into her lap and jabbed a finger at it.

"This what I think it is?"

The paper contained the results of an anonymous DNA test. Based on oral swabs from a mother, a child, and the alleged father, it established a definitive match.

The girl didn't answer. Her face did it for her.

Zsolt nodded once.

"And who's the lucky guy?" His voice was rough.

Anett tried to make herself smaller.

"His name is András..." she began carefully.

Before she could finish, her husband roared:

"I knew it! That bitch Lujza's son from the nursing home, right?"

"Luca..." the girl corrected automatically.

That was when the first slap landed.

*　*　*

Sólyom ended the call, thoughtful.

He couldn't imagine why Oszkár wanted him at the museum the next day, but he'd promised he'd be there. The antique dealer's voice had carried a note of mystery—as if he were about to hand over the world's best birthday present.

And maybe he was.

Which meant it could only be about the Beethoven manuscript.

Except that, as Sólyom had already confirmed, it was unfortunately impossible to steal. Unless this mysterious Dénes Szalay fellow was a magician. And since magicians didn't exist, they were right back where they'd started. He stroked his eyebrow, irritated.

Still.

He could spare a morning.

Worst case, nothing happened. He simply got to see the

marvel again in person—the piece that belonged, he was certain, in his secret private collection downstairs. And if there was even a thousandth of a percent chance it might end up there, he could mobilize his people.

That was what he paid them for.

"Well?" his secretary asked. He'd put the call on speaker; she'd heard every word.

"Let's make the rounds," Sólyom said with a shrug.

She pulled out her phone.

* * *

They stared at each other in silence, hatred crackling between them.

Anett thought this was worse than her dreams. In those, the pain had never been real—unlike what she felt now. The bleeding from the blows had stopped, at least. Still, she was afraid that if she started talking, the cut at the corner of her mouth would split open again and she'd need another tissue.

Small comfort watching Zsolt lick his knuckles—she'd gouged them with her canine—but then she remembered he'd probably take that fury out on the man who could walk through the door any second.

Because Anett had called him here.

Not willingly—Zsolt had gripped her hair with one hand, her throat with the other while she made the call, monitoring every word—but still. She'd put an innocent man's head in a noose.

When the buzzer sounded, she went pale.

Before she could move, the guy with the earring was already at the door. He yanked it open and dragged the visitor inside without a word.

"What the—"

The stunned man got that far before a massive blow to his solar plexus folded him in half.

The bodyguard shut the door and shoved him toward the center of the room. Momentum carried him to the floor.

Anett rushed over, crouched beside him, panicked.

"András!" Her voice came out strangled. She looked toward the corner. "Don't hurt him. Please!"

She started crying.

Zsolt stepped out from behind the wardrobe where he'd been waiting. He gestured toward the couch.

"Sit," he said. Rough. "And don't talk unless I ask you something."

The man obeyed, searching for Anett's eyes.

He didn't find them. She kept her head down, face buried in her palms, sobbing.

"So..." Zsolt Bereczki positioned himself in front of the trembling man once he'd taken his seat. "You're the one who fucked my wife."

The guy swallowed hard and began to stammer, words tumbling over each other. Anett had been in a really bad place back then. She kept complaining her husband was sleeping around, which destroyed her emotionally—

(And you took advantage, right?) Zsolt cut in with disgust, but waved for him to continue.

He'd tried to comfort her. To cheer her up. Then there'd been a moment. When things developed. When—

"When you pulled off her panties," Zsolt finished.

Meanwhile, he wondered how the hell his wife could've chosen such a broke, spineless excuse for a man when she had him.

"You pulled off plenty of women's panties!" Anett's voice cut in suddenly. She raised her face, bitter.

"I'm allowed," her husband snapped, furious. Then he turned back to the visitor. "And how was it? At least tell me you enjoyed it."

The man froze. Both yes and no felt fatal—correctly—so he tried to dodge.

"I... don't really remember..."

"Why? Had a stroke during it? Amnesia?"

The other man tried to swallow, but his mouth was dry. It just worked uselessly.

"It was so long ago..."

"Not that long!" Zsolt barked.

"Besides..." the man pressed on desperately, "it only happened once..."

"Looks like once was enough." Zsolt's voice turned bitter.

Then something occurred to him.

He frowned, turned to Anett. "But you—if you only slept with him once, how did you know Dani was his? We were doing it sometimes multiple times a day. And you can't pinpoint conception. Yet you got a DNA test."

"The birthmark," Anett said quietly.

Zsolt froze.

Just for a second.

Then he stepped in front of the increasingly pale man and tore at his cheap shirt with a few violent motions, exposing his bare torso—and the large, reddish, almost perfectly regular five-pointed star blazing on his left shoulder.

"Jesus Christ." Zsolt groaned. "That's disgusting."

"I like it," his wife shot back.

He stared at her.

"Yeah?" His voice dropped into dangerous territory. He pulled a small but terrifying revolver from the holster under his arm. "And this? This doing it for you too?"

Anett stared at the weapon, terror tightening her throat.

"What are you going to do with that?"

Zsolt snorted.

"What do you think?"

"I think nothing," the nearly shirtless man said suddenly, tugging his ruined shirt into place. "Unless you want to go to prison."

Zsolt frowned.

He couldn't understand how this guy—staring straight down death—could speak at all. Most people begged at this point. Or pissed themselves. Sometimes both.

This one sounded calm.

"What are you talking about?" Zsolt asked, surprised.

"The test," the man said. His certainty grew. "I have a copy too. Actually, my lawyer has it."

Zsolt felt something shift.

"So?" Suspicion crept in.

"That one has names on it," the man said. "It shows which sample came from whom. Meaning the police get to you very fast if something happens to me. My lawyer has instructions for that scenario."

Zsolt considered this.

Maybe this guy wasn't such a loser after all.

But something still didn't add up.

"You could've played that card sooner." Distrust thickened his voice.

The other man looked almost embarrassed.

"That wasn't possible."

"Why not?"

"My wife would've lost it," he said quietly. Then, "The kids too."

Zsolt stared at him, horrified.

"You're married?"

Now it clicked.

This worm was a family man. Anett had just been a stray piece of ass.

"I told you—it was a one-time thing," the torn-shirt Casanova rushed to explain. "I didn't think there'd be consequences."

Dani, Zsolt thought bitterly. *As consequences.*

"What if I tell them anyway?" he said. "Just to screw you over?"

"Then everything comes out the same," the man said, spreading his hands. "Because if you force this into the open, the story reaches Debrecen too. Everyone hears it."

That did it.

Zsolt panicked.

Half the city laughing at him. Or worse—pitying him. His reputation shredded. Bad for business.

But if he let it drop, everything stayed as it was.

Besides—Dani wasn't his son. So why cling to him? A bastard. And Anett—the stinking whore who'd supposedly been staying with some *friend* and only came back for some stuffed-horse nonsense—he didn't want anything from her anymore.

Only his pride had taken a hit.

And pride healed. Especially if nobody knew.

"You figured this out pretty well," Zsolt said at last. Reluctant. Almost impressed. "Here's what happens. I go home now and forget both of you exist."

"Dani too?" Anett cut in, hope breaking through her fear.

Zsolt snorted.

"All three of you, then. Fuck it. But you forget me too." He turned to her, hatred flaring. "Tomorrow we file for divorce. You don't ask for anything except the kid. Then you disappear. Both of you. And the names—mine—you change them."

He paused.

"Deal?"

* * *

Richárd sat in the passenger seat of the gray van parked at the end of the street across from the museum, eyes fixed on the main entrance.

He ran through the checklist one last time. Had he handled everything the boss had ordered? If he screwed up now and tanked this already dicey transaction, Sólyom would never forgive him. He'd never forgive himself either. But if it somehow came together, the boss's gratitude wouldn't be small—Sólyom had said so himself, promised he "wouldn't be cheap about it."

Not that he'd been stingy before.

But this was the Beethoven manuscript. For the billionaire, it was the Holy Grail.

Richárd regretted only one thing: that he couldn't be inside. Over the past hour, the entire Szalay quartet had arrived—not all at once, but they were all there now. Plus Oszkár. And beyond them, perhaps a hundred others, including an entire grade from some outer-district music school.

He still didn't understand how anyone could get worked up over a tattered notebook page. But right now he'd give anything to be closer to the action—say, for the next ninety minutes. Because something had to happen in those ninety minutes. Something nobody expected.

Except, perhaps, a third-rate antique dealer.

That was how the boss categorized Oszkár Balogh, and the boss didn't think much of him.

Richárd forced himself to master his curiosity and stay at his assigned observation point, keeping watch on the area and on the twelve men who, like him, worked for Sólyom. Most had arrived in the van he now sat in alone. The rest were spread across two other vehicles.

All in position.

Waiting.

Privately, Richárd considered them unscrupulous thugs. He loathed their type. Still, he had to admit their services were occasionally necessary. Including the *special treatment*.

He hoped that wouldn't be needed today.

He hated violence.

* * *

Viktor's hand found the small device in his pocket, palm-sized. He ran his fingers over it, hoping it would work as well as the one he'd tested yesterday in the forest clearing.

The other two had to work too: the one Mici néni carried—she sat in her wheelchair, but the device was tucked in her bag—and the one Dénes held as he pushed the chair.

For about two more minutes.

Then it would start.

When all three of them stood next to the manuscript.

When his mentor gave the signal.

Anett stood in the far corner of the room, whispering with the security guard. Csaba was concentrating with everything he had on not staring at her chest—not easy, given that the top button of her blouse had somehow come undone. He stood six-three. Looking down meant his gaze landed exactly where it shouldn't.

Which was the whole point.

"Does it show a lot?" Anett asked, voice shy.

"Uh... not really..." Csaba shook his head, flustered. He'd lost the thread of the conversation entirely, but this felt like the safest answer.

Then he remembered—she'd been telling him about an accident. A taxi making an illegal turn, a bus driver slamming the brakes, passengers crashing into one another. She'd hit her mouth on the seat in front of her. Right.

Poor thing.

Her lip had swollen a little. It only made her more attractive, gave her a faintly reckless edge—he kept that thought to himself. And the tiny cut really was barely visible.

So he couldn't have answered better.

"Good," Anett said, relieved.

Her relief—though not about the injury she barely felt anymore—was genuine. Since yesterday, she'd felt free again. For the first time in five months.

If everything went according to plan, she could bring Dani home from Eszter's soon. The constant running was almost over. At least the part connected to Zsolt Bereczki.

One bastard still on their trail.

That bastard stood beside Beethoven's bust, deep in conversation with Sólyom—whom Oszkár considered the *real* bastard.

Because you didn't make billions—no one knew exactly how many, Oszkár estimated between one-fifty and two-fifty—without dirty dealings. Sure, he'd pulled a few underhanded moves himself, and was proud of them. But those were child's play compared to Sólyom's operations, which left dispossessed families, ruined lives, suckers doing long stretches—and sometimes corpses.

The billionaire didn't kill with his own hands. Didn't even order it. He wasn't a mafioso—just a ruthless businessman.

Still. If he hadn't existed, many people would still be alive.

The antique dealer could name three off the top of his head who'd killed themselves because of Sólyom. Two with pills. One—according to the papers—had jumped from—

"Going to tell me why we're here?" Sólyom cut in, impatient. Despite the open windows, he'd begun fanning himself with a brochure.

"I can give you seventy million reasons," Oszkár said, savoring it.

Then he stopped.

He'd spotted the old woman. Her nephew had just wheeled her up to the manuscript display case. She struggled out of the chair—apparently she only needed it for longer distances—then shuffled toward the exhibit, leaning on her cane.

The student group parted politely. Like the Red Sea.

"Really?" the billionaire snorted. "Must need glasses. Because I'm looking at that manuscript still right where it belongs—"

A strange hissing sound cut through the room.

The space filled with impenetrable smoke.

Then the alarm shrieked—sharp, wailing.

Someone shouted *Fire*.

Panic erupted.

The crowd surged toward the exit, trampling bags, bumping shoulders. The smoke erased direction. Chaos rose in screams, collisions, dull thuds.

Those who made it out staggered toward the stairs, coughing, eyes streaming.

An older, gray-bearded security guard stood there, arms spread, blocking their way.

"Nobody's going anywhere!" he shouted.

Some ignored him and pressed on toward the lobby and the street.

The guard chambered a round—loud enough for everyone to hear—and took shooting stance.

"I said everyone stays put!"

Most of the group froze.

"Are you insane?" an older man in a suit demanded, pulling a handkerchief from his mouth. "Can't you see the building's on fire?"

"Don't worry," the guard said calmly as more people stumbled out and the smoke thinned. "You're safe now."

The museum director burst in, his secretary at his heels.

"What happened?" he gasped, pale, staring toward the exhibition room where smoke still rolled—less than thirty seconds old, but terrifying.

"Don't know," the guard—his colleague behind him called him Santa—shrugged. "But it's over."

The director frowned.

Over?

Any disaster felt like it had just begun. The second the alarm sounded, he'd sprinted from his office—never covered those twenty-five meters faster in his life. And this man told him to relax.

"I wish you were right," he muttered, and stepped into the special exhibition room.

The smoke had mostly cleared.

Visitors leaned on one another, coughing, crowding near the windows for air.

And there it was—bad angle, but unmistakable.

The beautifully carved display case.

Csaba stood beside it. Stunned.

"Oh no..." the director whispered, hurrying closer. He murmured a prayer he'd learned as a child.

It didn't work this time either.

Shattered glass covered the floor.

And the deep crimson velvet.

Where a priceless page of manuscript was supposed to be.

Part Four

Endgame

When the secretary heard the alarm, he wanted to jump out of the van—but couldn't. His job was to stay put and manage the situation if needed. Still, he cursed himself for missing "the robbery of the century," as the boss liked to call it.

Which was, let's be honest, an exaggeration. It was just some ratty sheet of music, so "of the century" was pushing it. Even "of the decade" felt generous. Let's stick with "of the year." Or better yet—since nobody had asked him, but Richárd didn't care—one of today's biggest Budapest robberies.

That sounded about right.

Still, he would've liked to see how they pulled it off.

He shared Sólyom's view that the whole music-heist idea was impossible—though the boss had kept himself covered, even hoping, deep down, that he'd miscalculated. That was why he'd sent his most reliable man here.

Him.

And Richárd saw everything—including the five weird figures who suddenly burst out of the museum, faces covered, scattering in different directions. He couldn't tell who they were. Their clothes didn't match the crew, but that meant nothing—they could've changed inside.

He didn't take chances.

He called one of the hired security guys—one of the dirty dozen they'd rented for the day—and told him to tail all five with four colleagues. Until further notice. Then he ended the call.

* * *

The detective sat alone in the first-floor security room, reviewing the footage again. He cursed under his breath.

Same result. A big fat zero.

Nowhere on the tape could he see who had dropped the goddamn smoke bombs they'd found upstairs. Three of them: two near the display case, one farther away—probably kicked there in the chaos. Cheap Chinese manufacture, most likely. You couldn't complain about their effectiveness, though. For twenty-seven seconds after they went off, everything in that room vanished.

Including the perp.

If there was just one. It could've been a multi-person job. Based on what they knew so far—which was still zero—every single visitor could've been involved.

Good thing most of them—ninety-something percent (he couldn't calculate the exact number and didn't want to)—were still on site. Thanks to that older security guard who looked familiar somehow. The man had recognized immediately that a robbery was in progress and had acted like a pro, keeping every suspect on the premises.

Unlike the security system.

The bearded guard had held ninety-two of ninety-seven people.

Because five had left. Four men and one woman. He hadn't been able to stop them. Of course not—he wasn't armed yet. And since they'd fled toward the exit, choking on smoke, all five had covered their faces. Scarves, handkerchiefs, even just their arms.

The three exterior cameras in the lobby caught them, but two couldn't be identified. Even so, the thief was probably among them. Matter of fact, the detective would've bet his badge—big money, too—that the perp worked alone. Dropped the smoke bombs, smashed the vitrine in the chaos, pocketed the goddamn sheet of music, covered their face, and made an English exit.

Hasta la vista, baby.

As for the security cage—pure luck. It malfunctioned. Right then. Sure, suspicious as hell, but the detective didn't believe someone had sabotaged it with a laptop and some flashing, beeping plastic gadget, cutting wires like in dumb

American movies. The red wire or the blue. Bullshit. Mechanical failure was far more likely, even with professional German equipment.

The company specialist would tell them soon enough. The local techs had already shrugged and claimed they'd found no fault anywhere—which, given the scene, felt amateurish. At least the Germans were sending someone who supposedly knew his stuff. Any minute now.

Until then, the detective would try to catch the perp himself.

There was a slim chance—a tiny one—that between the smoke and the crowd, the thief had gotten trapped inside with everyone else. If so, they'd find them. Assuming they still had the score on them.

Before anyone left, everyone would be searched. Not cavity searches, but thorough pat-downs—every centimeter of clothing, every bag, every purse.

He stopped the footage, sighed, and stood. Back to the crime scene, now cordoned off and increasingly crowded with uniforms, forensics, and ministry experts.

His people were ready.

They'd separated the men and women, lined up the understandably impatient visitors in two rows, and waited for his signal. He gave it with a slight nod.

As the pat-downs began, the detective stared at the shattered vitrine that an hour and a half earlier had held a hundred-seventy-five-thousand-dollar sheet of music. Now it was empty.

The evidence techs were still working around it, so he stepped away, toward the two security guards speaking with the director by the window.

"Find anything?" the director asked when he spotted him.

"Nothing yet," the detective said. "We just started. By the way—" He turned to the older guard, who still reminded him annoyingly of someone he couldn't place. "We haven't thanked you for holding them here."

He gestured toward the thinning crowd, where a fragile-looking elderly woman in a wheelchair was being searched. She'd climbed out willingly and tottered aside on her cane while the female officers examined both her and the chair.

"Just doing my job." The gray-bearded guard shrugged, almost military. Then, with regret, "Unfortunately, a few still got away."

"Five," the detective said. "According to the exterior cameras."

"At least those show something," the guard muttered, jerking his chin in a circle. "These probably weren't much use."

"You got that right. Can't see shit through that smoke."

"And the cage? Have they figured out—"

"Not yet. The German guy's on his way. Supposedly knows his stuff."

"You think they were among them, right?" the director said. Dejection crept into his voice. Then he clarified, though no one needed it. "The thief. Among the ones who left."

"Well," the detective said, choosing his words, "I'd bet on it. And once we review the footage from the half hour before the robbery, we'll find them. Everyone's on those tapes. Including the perp. It's just a matter of time."

"I'm afraid we might be chasing shadows," the younger guard said.

His colleague turned on him. "What's that supposed to mean?"

"That they might've stayed," Csaba said, gesturing toward the visitor line.

"Then we'll catch them," the detective said. "If they've got the score on them, we'll find it. I guarantee it. Unless they swallowed it or something."

"What if they had a partner?" Csaba asked.

No one answered.

He nodded toward the open window. "Outside."

The others followed his gaze.

"Oh no..." the director groaned—for the second time that day.

He understood before the others did.

* * *

"A bottle of champagne," Oszkár announced. He'd been seventh in the men's search line, so they'd released him quickly. "Your best. And two glasses."

"Expecting someone?" the Thermostat waiter asked, one eyebrow lifting.

The antique dealer glanced at him. But in his good mood, he didn't ask whether the man had arrived at this insight through the deductive method popularized by Sherlock Holmes or by dumb luck. Nor did he point out what was already on the tip of his tongue—that the waiter had a gift.

"That doesn't begin to describe it, my friend," he said instead, expansive. He set the hard-sided, combination-locked attaché case beside him—worthless for now, but soon to hold a fortune. Then he reconsidered and added, with genuine feeling, "Like the Messiah."

Because he truly stood at salvation's gate.

The seventy million forints he'd receive for the score wouldn't just make him richer; it would launch him to the top of the profession—especially if the other half of the bargain came through. Then he'd really be one of the chosen few.

Even the existence of Sólyom's mysterious private collection was known only to the cream of the trade—or rather, they knew jack shit and relied on hunches and scattered rumors. Concrete proof never surfaced. But that was how legends worked.

Oszkár had first heard about the secret underground room from Szilárd. It supposedly held treasures almost impossible to imagine. Everyone tried anyway, and the fantasies knew no bounds: stolen Picassos, Matisses, Delacroixs, a gorgeous Tintoretto, a Goya. Whispered conversations—not just about paintings but sculptures, tapestries, even a special Fabergé egg. If even half were true—if even a quarter—the Louvre would shut down from lack of interest.

Or shame.

Which was precisely why some connoisseurs dismissed the whole thing as fake.

According to Szilárd—who would've given half his arm to see the collection—that dismissal was part of the plan. Old trick, he'd say: surround the truth with a pile of obvious lies, and the whole thing gets slapped with a guaranteed fake-news label. Better protection than secrecy, which rarely works—and only temporarily. So Sólyom himself seeded the fairy-tale details about the mysterious museum. At least, that was Szilárd's opinion.

Oszkár believed him.

So when he brought up the subject during negotiations with the billionaire, he spoke of the special room as if he knew more than the average collector. Without waiting for the other man to object, he said he wanted to see it. If the deal hadn't involved the Beethoven score, Sólyom would've laughed in his face and had him thrown out—he came close as it was. But the personalized bait proved too sweet. The billionaire nodded, reluctant but compliant.

Which meant it would soon be in Oszkár's hands.

He'd know the dirty secrets. At least some of them. Assuming, of course, they closed the deal first.

For that, all he needed was for Dénes Szalay to arrive and hand over the score he'd stolen an hour and a half ago—in broad daylight, under the noses of a hundred people, one of them his own—from a museum gallery equipped with alarms.

He just had to get it out.

Which, after a thorough search, would be difficult.

But Oszkár trusted the man had thought of that too.

*   *   *

After what the guard had said, the detective no longer believed they'd find anything on anyone—certainly not a sheet of music worth over seventy million forints. So when his uniformed colleagues shook their heads after searching the last visitors, he nodded.

That was that.

He was convinced the masterwork was no longer in the building. The method by which it had probably left, however, was new to him. He'd seen plenty of strange things in his career. This felt like the height of audacity. Maybe because it was so simple, almost obvious—and yet it had taken him this long to see it.

"You can actually imagine"—the director looked at him, still dazed, not fully recovered from Csaba's suggestion—"that someone would commit such... barbarism?"

"Easily," the detective said.

"How is that logical?!"

"Why?" the detective shot back. "Would you have had a better way to get rid of the only evidence after a successful robbery? Especially if that damn cage had worked?"

"Uh... no, but—" the museum's top man faltered. "It's still...

you know..."

"I know," the detective said. "Barbarism."

The director snorted.

These people weren't taking this seriously enough. The scoundrel they were discussing hadn't just robbed the Hungarian state—which in this case meant the Hungarian people, en bloc—but stolen something literally irreplaceable. And if what the security guard thought had happened was true—and now the police did too, if the detective was reading the room correctly—the perp had the gall to do it in such a lowbrow way.

And he didn't mean the theft itself—smashing the glass top of a beautiful rococo table already suggested a lack of upbringing and manners—but what came afterward, if everything checked out.

To simply throw the most valuable page from Beethoven's own handwritten notebook out a window.

That surpassed all imagination.

Or fell beneath it.

* * *

"So far so good," Dénes said, taking a sip of his beer. "But it's not over yet."

Viktor thought of the perfectly functioning smoke bombs, the wheelchair now parked against the wall that had performed its role flawlessly, and the dozen other details that had gone exactly as planned—or better. He shrugged.

"We're past the hard part."

Dénes shook his head. He thought the opposite and would've explained, but his aunt cut in.

"You're wrong, my boy."

"Why?"

"Because this is when you really need to keep your wits about you."

She didn't say out loud that she meant only Dénes—that from here on, at least as far as the story went, he was the sole lead. The others understood without being told. They were done for the day—except for Mici néni's one, or possibly two, small but crucial scenes.

"Sure we can't help with something?" Anett asked. She didn't notice she'd been stirring her coffee with her sore wrist for three minutes, though there was no sugar in it.

The moderately elegant little bistro—where she'd personally reserved the table two days earlier—went by the name Sugar Cube. It sat barely three hundred meters from the museum, and about five hundred from a place called Thermostat, where someone was already waiting eagerly for one of them.

"I have to do this alone." Dénes shook his head, then smiled at her. "Nothing's going to go wrong."

You said the same thing yesterday afternoon, Anett thought.

Back then, both their lives had hung by a thread. Zsolt Bereczki's reactions were unpredictable—yet Dénes had predicted them, down to the gram. Based on Anett's long, meticulous accounts, he'd taken the man apart piece by piece. That was why he'd grilled her for weeks, drilling into details she'd thought insignificant and which turned out to be anything but.

From those details, the story finally assembled itself—the version that, from her husband's point of view, landed like a knockout.

Everything in it checked out—except the essential part.

The man named András, whom Zsolt had been jealous of, really existed, and with reason: Anett really had slept with him. Once. When she was three months pregnant. They'd regretted it immediately and never met again.

Dénes found the man's character useful—after a few adjustments. He slipped into his skin for a few hours. The original lacked sufficient charm (the lesser problem) and, more importantly, the star-shaped birthmark in the middle of his left shoulder.

Dénes's alter ego solved both. The first on his own. The second with help from a tattoo artist nicknamed Satan at the Black Raven salon, who initially suggested henna. Supposedly it lasted weeks and barely smudged if you were careful—at least the expensive kind.

Dénes wanted something permanent.

Satan shrugged and picked up the needle.

It hurt. But the result—whose original a certain individual had once labeled a forbidden symbol of tyranny—proved far more effective than the carefully fabricated DNA test result tucked into the middle dresser drawer, a test they'd never actually performed.

Though Zsolt had already lost his grip pretty thoroughly from that alone.

Together, the two eliminated any remaining doubts—if he still had any. If he had, he would've searched Dénes's pockets, his wallet included, where the appropriate documents sat neatly arranged in their compartments: ID card, address card, health insurance card, driver's license. Shabby forgeries, but convincing at a glance.

They never appeared.

Because by then, Zsolt was no longer curious.

As for what followed the confrontation with the freshly tattooed "birthmark," matching his child's perfectly—just one size larger—that, according to Dénes, was pure psychology. Built on the fact that the man wasn't merely violent and impulsive but also a calculating businessman. Proud. And unwilling to risk his reputation over what amounted to a small matter.

An affair counted as that.

So he chose to write it off as a loss—which he eventually did.

The rescue operation, Anett knew, hadn't started with the tattoo. That was only the dot on the i.

The first step came earlier, when Dénes, after absorbing every detail and weighing the situation, announced they needed to seize control. Specifically, Anett had to reveal herself—apparently by accident—to her pursuers. If Zsolt was still hunting her months later, they'd likely be watching the two most obvious places.

Her mother's grave. Or the giraffes.

Maybe both.

Preferably with Dani, who would promptly disappear again with the help of a professional, anonymous babysitter. The boy would be returned safely to Eszter, out of danger. Anett would remain exposed only long enough to draw the bloodhounds to the apartment, where Viktor had already planted the paternity documents.

Whether Zsolt would risk a break-in to find them was uncertain—but given his impatience, likely enough. Especially if, after a long, deliberately impossible rush-hour chase through the city, Anett vanished again.

Not forever. Just for the few days she spent under Mici néni's hospitality, preparing for the score job.

Zsolt couldn't know whether she'd ever return. So sooner or later, he'd search the apartment. And the never-performed DNA test would fall into his hands.

If not, Dénes said, he'd get everything at once—live, in bulk, on premiere night.

But this way was better. Two installments. Who knew how he'd react if, without warning, he learned that the child he'd hunted for months wasn't his?

According to Anett: very badly.

According to Dénes: exactly as he did.

Fortunately, they'd never know who was right.

"What if something goes wrong?" Anett said, finally stopping her pointless stirring.

"It won't."

"How do you know?"

"Because I—"

"Don't tell me you calculated everything again."

"That's the situation."

She rolled her eyes. Worry lingered there—more than worry, Mici néni thought, and she didn't like it. She hoped she was wrong. If not, it would cause trouble sooner or later.

Especially if Viktor noticed.

Because in the triangle that might—or might not—be forming, Viktor occupied the third, and unhappiest, corner. Which made him a potential hazard.

"And if someone," Zsolt Bereczki's soon-to-be ex-wife said, flaring, "doesn't care about the math and gets nervous and flips the table along with the rules—then what?"

Dénes raised an eyebrow and shrugged. The answer was obvious.

"What do you mean what? Improvise."

She nodded and started massaging her wrist.

"In other words, you have no idea," she said.

"Well—" Dénes paused. He hadn't examined the problem from that angle. "You could put it that way."

He surprised himself a little.

* * *

Csaba didn't understand why the director had suddenly gone so cold toward him. Until now, he'd thought the man actually liked him. They'd talked several times—mostly mornings before opening, sometimes during lunch breaks too—about soccer, cars, food.

Now the man practically looked through him.

Why was he angry? He couldn't be holding him responsible for the robbery. Could he? Csaba had done everything he could in that situation—

Good God.

Had he caught Anett on the footage? And that when the chaos started, Csaba had focused on the girl—specifically her chest—instead of the score? On the bombshell instead of the smoke bombs?

It was true. But only for half a second. All right, a second and a half.

The woman had fainted from terror—or at least staggered—and fallen straight into his arms. He'd caught her without thinking. But when the alarm went off, he'd let go at once, letting her drop to the floor. She'd hit her side hard. Complained about it later while waiting to be searched—her arm too.

Csaba didn't make excuses. He'd been doing his job.

Badly, granted.

His job was—pardon: would have been—to guard the score. Which was now nowhere. In other words, he'd failed.

And even though he'd rushed to the display table almost immediately, trampling through the screaming crowd, the cameras might not have caught that. For half a minute they'd shown nothing but that goddamn smoke. Then only the end result: the empty space where the score had been.

And him standing beside it, stunned.

No.

He shook his head and stood by the window as the realization came. His boss wasn't holding that against him. While they'd waited for the police, the director had even comforted him. Told him not to beat himself up. Said it wasn't his fault. The security system had failed—at the moment the vitrine glass broke, the cage should've dropped.

For once, even Santa had confirmed it.

So what was his problem?

That Csaba had figured out the window theory first? Assuming that was what had happened. Not many explanations fit the facts. And the facts were simple: there had been a score. Now there wasn't.

Which meant it had to be somewhere.

Since they hadn't found it inside, the inevitable conclusion was that it had left the building.

How could it have left?

Two ways. Either someone carried it out the door—probably one of those five unknowns his colleague hadn't managed to detain—or someone threw it out the window. Anyone among the nearly hundred visitors could've done that, while their partner waited below in the dense bushes of the back garden, patiently expecting the roast pigeon to fly into their mouth.

That was the conclusion Csaba reached when he replayed the events. He couldn't understand how the cops had missed it. Or everyone else.

Except him.

Sure, sooner or later a detective would've thought of it. But he'd been faster. The fastest. Maybe that was what bothered the director—that a security guard had beaten them to a strictly theoretical question.

The detective had even praised Csaba in front of everyone. Said his mind was sharp. Told him he should become a cop. Then sent forensics down into the garden to search beneath the window.

That was when the director started acting strange.

Or around then, anyway. Because at first he'd still been friendly—right up until that stupid joke.

Of course.

That had to be it.

Csaba hadn't meant anything bad by it. He'd just wanted to lighten the mood. And the director hadn't even been nearby—or so he'd thought. Turned out the man had been standing two steps behind him, arguing with the baffled specialist from the German security company.

Csaba noticed too late.

The detective and two or three uniforms were still

laughing at his offhand remark, which boiled down to this: the Beethoven score had apparently become *the world's most expensive paper airplane.*

And apparently the director had heard.

No wonder he'd been looking at Csaba with such contempt since then. What he'd said amounted to serious blasphemy. And that was something a priest—especially in his own temple, confronted by a parishioner who usually sat in the front row—had a hard time forgiving.

* * *

While preparing to cross the street, Dénes ran through the gestures one last time—the ones he planned to use during the final act's negotiation scene. He knew they mattered as much as the words. So he'd drilled them thoroughly, then performed the full combination—first for the mirror, then for Mici néni. The audiences, though one was stricter than the other, hadn't booed him offstage at either venue.

Which meant nothing. Live, anything could happen. Even what Anett kept imagining: something going wrong.

But the girl worried too much. Ninety percent of the time—hell, ninety-five—everything went exactly as planned.

A dark-windowed Volvo slowed beside him.

He caught his reflection in the glass, blurred at first. Then it sharpened. Instead of driving on, the car stopped, and his mirrored face began to transform from top to bottom into another. First the hair turned white. Then a high forehead emerged, thick coal-black eyebrows, a slightly hooked, aristocratic nose. For a few surreal seconds they hovered above his own mouth and chin, like a continuation of them.

Then the electric window slid all the way down.

Dénes vanished from the picture, replaced entirely by the upper body of a man sitting alone in the spacious interior, leaning forward.

"Good afternoon, Mr. Szalay," he said. Then, without pause, "Forgive the introduction. I have a business proposition."

He let that sit a beat.

"Antal Sólyom. Perhaps you've heard of me."

Dénes frowned. The billionaire could see he didn't yet understand the situation.

"Uh... sure," Dénes said. Everyone knew that name. "And I'm curious about it—the proposition, I mean. But I can't right now. I've got an important meeting."

"With Oszkár Balogh?" the other man cut in.

Dénes fell silent.

"He can wait," Sólyom said. "I'll be brief. I promise."

He opened the door.

Dénes bit his lower lip, glanced around, saw nothing out of place. He sighed and got in, his face set.

"Fine," he said. "You get five minutes."

"That will be more than enough," Sólyom said. "And to avoid wasting time, I'll get to the point. If you don't mind."

"Go ahead."

Sólyom closed the door, leaned back, and pressed his

fingertips together.

"It's about the Beethoven score. And you'd spare us both time"—he lifted a palm—"by not asking which Beethoven score. You know perfectly well."

"I can guess," Dénes said.

Sólyom continued.

"Mr. Balogh recently offered to sell it to me. Strictly theoretical, of course. We failed to agree on price. You see, our mutual friend has one major flaw. Actually—" He paused. "Several. He knows something about many things, but never enough about any one of them. And then there's the main issue."

He looked at Dénes.

"He lacks proportion. Which is a pity. Proportion matters."

"I know someone who says the same thing," Dénes said.

"Then they must be wise."

"They are."

"Unlike Mr. Balogh. I offered him seventy million forints for something that, even if it came into my possession, could never truly be mine. Legally speaking. That's not tragic—mere possession would bring me pleasure."

His face tightened.

"Not at any price. I have enough money. But he wanted something else. Something I won't give him."

"So you lost interest," Dénes said.

"Nearly."

Dénes caught it. "Nearly?"

"Yes. Because then you came up. Or rather, someone capable

of stealing this treasure from a carefully guarded museum."

"And what makes you think," Dénes asked, "that someone is me?"

"Found out by accident," Sólyom said, dismissing the matter. "But that's irrelevant."

He lifted a small sports bag onto his lap.

"This is what matters."

Dénes didn't ask what was inside. He had a fair idea—and it wasn't a damp towel and used sneakers. More like thick bundles of twenty-thousand-forint notes.

When Sólyom drew the zipper, a small—or rather, large—fortune appeared.

"Nice," Dénes said.

"I agree. And for the record, this is the same seventy million I would've paid Oszkár. I simply decided I'd rather give it to you. In exchange for the score."

He watched Dénes and found exactly what he expected: confusion, edged with desperation. Knowing the cause of both, he wasn't surprised when Dénes shifted in his seat.

"That... sounds good," Dénes said. "Really. And I'd like to give it to you. I swear."

He exhaled, then made a small, abortive gesture with his hand.

"But I can't. Because—"

"Oszkár is blackmailing you," Sólyom said. "I know."

Dénes frowned.

"Then you know I have to refuse."

ENDGAME   269

"Unless," Sólyom said, raising a finger, "I blackmail you as well."

The driver turned into a side street.

"I prefer not to do this," Sólyom said. "But if necessary, I'll make one call. Two plainclothes officers will detain your accomplices. In a pastry shop called Sugar Cube. Right around the corner."

He indicated the direction.

"My information is correct. All three are there now. Unless you've made the mistake of carrying the score on you, one of them has it."

He paused—not to reconsider, but to confirm.

"If we don't reach an agreement, the police will find it this time. Clever hiding won't help. Three suspects are simpler than a hundred. And if complications arise, these officers are not delicate."

He rested his hand on the bag.

"This is insurance. In case seventy million isn't sufficient."

Dénes exhaled.

"If I accept, I go to prison."

"Yes."

"And if I don't?"

"You still do. This"—Sólyom glanced toward the museum—"will carry a longer sentence. And you'll be seventy million forints richer."

He waited.

Dénes stared ahead, twisted his mouth.

"Your five minutes are up," he said.

Then, after a moment, "But you win."

* * *

"Does it hurt much?" Mici néni asked, returning from the bathroom.

Anett was still massaging her wrist.

"I can handle it." She paused, the fall replaying itself. "But I still can't believe that bastard just let me drop."

Really weird. She'd wrapped that Csaba around her finger so tightly she'd assumed he'd be thrilled to finally have her in his arms—even if only via a fainting spell—and wouldn't let go until the show was over. Instead, he caught her, then released her almost immediately and watched her hit the floor. Would've watched, anyway—if anyone could see through the smoke. But Anett knew what happened.

And that wasn't the point.

The point was that the stupid score had mattered more to the guard than her physical safety. Insensitive lug.

"These young men today have no chivalry." Her honorary grandmother shook her head and lowered herself back into the chair beside Viktor, leaning on her cane.

Viktor sighed at the remark.

"I've got chivalry." He paused. "Cost me everything."

Both women knew what he meant: his ex-fiancée, who'd turned out to be interested only in his money—the smaller problem—and had taken it too. The apartment, the car, the vacation house. Straight into the trash.

"You chose the wrong mark, my boy," Mici néni said.

"Won't happen again." Viktor's face said he meant it.

"I hope not with Dénes either," the old woman muttered.

Her mobile rang—literally, since when she'd bought it she'd insisted it sound like a proper phone, ring-ring.

"Speaking of the devil."

She saw her nephew's name and lifted the device.

"Hello?"

Then she listened. For a long time.

Anett and Viktor exchanged looks but stayed quiet, watching as Mici néni's gaze drifted around the bistro before settling on a table by the entrance. Two grim men sat there, observing them over their coffee.

"Yes, I see them."

She listened, eyes still on the table.

"I understand."

A pause.

"Black Volvo. Tinted windows."

She nodded to herself.

"Of course. I'm bringing it now."

She ended the call.

"I'll be right there."

* * *

Richárd stared at the mobile in his hand, wondering where his boss stood in the negotiation—which, if he was honest, was edging closer to extortion. The screen was dark. Silent. But any of the teams could check in at any moment.

They already knew what mattered. More than the police.

The five people who'd left the museum first after the robbery were just regular visitors. The security company's men had ID'd and searched them within two minutes. Found nothing.

Meaning the score was still inside.

It hadn't gone out a window either—another detail the cops didn't have. They hadn't watched the building's perimeter all morning. Or the back garden.

Sólyom had.

Information was power. Used correctly, it was victory. Richárd's boss used it correctly. Otherwise he wouldn't be who he was: one of the country's richest men, who sooner or later—one way or another—got what he wanted.

Dénes Szalay didn't stand a chance.

Richárd felt a brief, almost professional sympathy. Szalay was good. Very good. Few people could've stolen the score this cleanly.

The phone vibrated.

Richárd glanced down at the message from Sugar Cube.

The old woman's on the move.

*　*　*

The champagne still hadn't chilled, but the ice in the bucket was already melting. No wonder, after more than an hour of waiting.

Oszkár was on his third coffee. His pulse had been fast when he arrived—pleasant then, sharpened by anticipation. Now it was anxiety. That they'd caught his people—he still thought of them that way—and that everything had been for nothing. No money. No triumph.

Even though he'd already lived through both in his imagination. Especially the triumph.

Not that seventy million wouldn't be useful too—particularly because he'd paid for it, exceptionally and quite literally. Few moments in his life had devastated him as much as realizing those two had played him and robbed him like some naïve amateur. But the other prize—the professional elevation—was even more tempting.

He pictured Szilárd's face when, strictly in private (because after all, a crime had occurred, and one doesn't advertise such things), he'd recount the events. And then casually mention a few highlights from Sólyom's private collection. Items he'd seen with his own eyes.

For that alone, the whole mess would've been worth it.

But without the score, everything stayed exactly the same.

And he couldn't even call Szalay to ask what was happening.

What if they'd found the stolen goods on him and arrested him? What if, during interrogation—or questioning, that was the word—the phone rang? A cop might answer. And Oszkár would stammer something idiotic about a wrong number.

He could already see the headline:

Apologies, Wrong Number

Score Robbery Ringleader's Pathetic Defense

Of course, there were explanations. They could know each other socially. A party. A casual business inquiry. Szalay might've even wandered into his shop asking about a Zsolnay sculpture.

The problem was that Szalay would have to confirm it. And with a serious charge hanging over his head, why would he? Especially when pinning things on Oszkár might actually serve him. After all, Oszkár had pressured him into the crime.

So no. Better to be careful.

That was why he hadn't called so far. Not from his regular phone, anyway. And from the other one—the supposedly untraceable one—he'd made exactly one call, when Szalay requested the appointment.

If things went south, there was no provable connection between them.

No one knew about their two meetings either—the restaurant, where they'd boxed Dénes in, and yesterday's visit to the office. And if Oszkár denied it—which he would—there was no proof to contradict him.

After turning it over yet again, he realized he was probably panicking for nothing.

Szalay might simply be late. The search was still ongoing. The visitors had been lined up in two long rows. Oszkár himself had been cleared quickly, but there were four of them total, and they likely had to wait for each other.

The girl, if he remembered correctly, had been near the end of the women's line. That alone could take an hour. Maybe two.

In other words, there was no reason to get nervous yet. Nothing was lost.

*   *   *

The driver opened the Volvo's rear door with trained courtesy, bowing slightly as Mici néni approached—slow, but steady.

"Thank you," the old woman said out of habit. Then it occurred to her that if she were Japanese—or Texan (those were the two places that came to mind, both fond of capital punishment)—she'd probably thank the executioner too as he led her into the gas chamber. Or was it lethal injection? She couldn't remember that either. Still, a lady remained a lady, even in hell.

Leaning on her cane, she ducked carefully and peered inside. Two men smiled at her from the spacious interior, with very different degrees of conviction. Dénes's smile, in particular, seemed to lack depth.

"Yes, you're in the right place," he said, sliding over. "Come on."

Mici néni nodded and, with a suppressed groan, settled beside him.

"This is Mr. Antal Sólyom," her nephew said, jerking his chin toward the billionaire opposite. "And this"—he glanced at Mici néni as the door closed—"is my aunt. Mária Hadnagy."

"Madam." Sólyom inclined his head from his seat. "A pleasure to meet you."

"Well," the old woman replied cautiously, "I'm not sure I can say the same."

She looked at Dénes. He let out a long sigh.

"Well..." he muttered, uncertain. "It's... complicated. But we'll talk about that later." He added quickly, reaching for her hand. "Are you sure about this?"

"No," Dénes said bitterly, without changing his posture. "But we don't have another option."

"And what about that Oszkár?"

"We'll... work something out with him."

"We already tried that."

"Yes, but now we can offer more. Much more."

"And if that still isn't enough?"

"Then we're screwed," Dénes snapped, impatience breaking through. He flicked a glance at Sólyom, who was watching the exchange with polite interest and didn't interrupt—he already knew how it would end. "So I hope," Dénes added, more quietly, "that I'll be persuasive enough. But first... please."

Mici néni hesitated, then grimaced and lowered her eyes to the walking stick wedged between her knees. Anett had bought it for her recently at a medical supply store—along with the wheelchair, as a kind of accessory. Both items had been designed for a single purpose, but both happened to excel at others.

The cane's hardened steel handle, for example. Plain. Undecorated. It fit her palm perfectly. Hard enough, too. A clean strike could shatter a museum vitrine.

But that was just a bonus.

The girl had chosen it for another reason.

"Here," Former Bride Mici muttered at last.

Reluctantly, she handed it over. Dénes laid the cane across his lap and, with a quick motion, ran his fingers along the small adjustment holes spaced every two and a half centimeters. Then he twisted.

The cane came apart.

He now held two hollow aluminum tubes—one sliding neatly into the other—and inside them, a tightly rolled sheet of music.

Sólyom watched, openly astonished, as Dénes slipped his pinky finger into the narrow cavity and carefully worked the roll free. Five seconds later, the Beethoven manuscript emerged into daylight.

"Well..." was all the billionaire managed. Only a whisper.

It was rare—unacceptable, really, at his level—to be surprised. He'd suspected a trick. Still, this surpassed it.

"Don't worry," Dénes said, smoothing the rolled sheet across his thighs. "It's fine."

Unable to look away, Sólyom wet the corner of his mouth.

"May I?" His voice came out hoarse.

Dénes shrugged and handed it over with faint, deliberate contempt—like passing a menu to an irritating dinner companion in a bad restaurant.

"It's yours now." He exhaled, then lifted the sports bag from the floor into his lap. "And this is ours, right?"

Sólyom nodded without looking.

What mattered lay in his hands.

And sooner or later—one way or another—he always got what he wanted.

* * *

They hadn't understood the situation before—neither the detectives nor the museum staff—but after the cage dropped, things only got worse.

According to the security company's specialist, this meant the system had worked perfectly. The same was true, he added, three and a half hours earlier when the alarms had sounded.

"Really?" the director asked, his voice strangled. After a pause, through clenched teeth, he added, "Then where's the score?"

"Beats me," the German representative said, frustrated.

Using a beeping plastic remote with red and green lights, he released the gallery entrance again. With a shrug, he went on: one of the wires running under the floor might have been damaged, causing a contact fault—but they'd only know for sure once everything was opened up, which they would do shortly. They'd check the vitrine-side connections as well, assuming the forensics team would finally clear out with their little brushes.

"So an even bigger mess," Csaba muttered from the back.

His eyes met the director's. The man must have been thinking the same thing, because he smiled—for a moment. Csaba breathed easier. It felt like peace had been restored between them.

And he wasn't wrong.

"Wait." The detective spoke up, tearing his gaze from the gadget—familiar from American movies. "This doesn't make sense to me either. If everything works, the cage seals the room the instant the vitrine glass is damaged. Correct?"

He looked at the specialist, who shifted.

"Yes." He hesitated. "Theoretically."

The director snorted, but before he could speak, the detective continued.

"I see." He nodded, almost sympathetically. "Except..." He glanced at the floor, then back up. "As you can see, that's exactly what happened to the glass. It was damaged." A beat. "More than that—it shattered. Into tiny pieces."

Then, flatly: "Practically speaking."

He paused.

"Which suggests to me that everything isn't working after all. Or am I missing something?"

The specialist didn't answer. He didn't mention the underfloor wiring again—just shrugged and spread his hands.

* * *

"A cognac, please!"

The old woman paused at the bar, then—without waiting for a reply—returned to their table, the one she'd left barely half an hour earlier, and practically collapsed into her chair.

"So?" Viktor leaned in. "How did it go?"

"We made seventy million forints," Mici néni said, exhaling. She propped her cane against the seat. "Whether we'll have time to spend it..."

She let the rest trail off and glanced toward the empty table by the entrance.

"They left," Anett said. "About five minutes ago. Someone called them, they asked for the check, and they were gone."

"One less problem," the old woman muttered, scanning for the waiter.

He appeared at once, as if summoned, carrying a crystal snifter.

"Still plenty left," Viktor said. His knee bounced once under the table. "Problems, I mean. But tell us what happened. Details."

"In a minute." Mici néni gave him a look, then turned to the server, who had stopped beside her with practiced calm.

"Hennessy all right?" he asked. "Since the brand didn't come up."

"Perfect." She nodded, grateful. "Thank you."

As he set the glass down, she noted his manners with approval. The team's younger male member across from her—fingers drumming, patience thinning—could learn something from him.

"To your health," Viktor said once the waiter left.

It bought him a second.

Then he pressed again. "But now we really need the story."

Mici néni still hadn't touched the cognac.

* * *

"Finally!" Oszkár groaned with relief, let out a long breath, and leaned back. "Where the devil were you?"

"Just... took care of something," Dénes said, a little hesitantly, as he sat down across from him, clutching the sports bag.

"But there's no problem, right?"

"No. Don't worry."

"Thank God! I thought they'd caught you."

"For now, we got away with it."

The antique dealer nodded. So they'd made it through the pat-down too. Good.

"Then we only have one thing left before you leave, right?" he said, leaning forward with a smile. "Because you said you were leaving the city."

"Yes," Dénes said. "I did say that."

Oszkár frowned. For a moment, something about the other man's emphasis—and, come to think of it, his wording—felt slightly off. Then he shrugged it away. In the end, it didn't matter.

He jerked his chin toward the sports bag he'd been staring at for a while now.

"Bet it's in there," he whispered. The excitement had gone to his throat—his goal now literally within arm's reach.

"We could bet," Dénes said with a shrug, "but you'd lose. If you mean the score."

Oszkár stared at him.

"What else would I mean, you idiot?" he snapped. That earlier feeling returned: the sense that the conversation was starting to slip sideways.

"Then I guessed right," Dénes said pleasantly, leaning into that slip. "But I don't have it."

Without looking, he set the sports bag down beside his chair.

"Then where is it?" Oszkár asked, fixing him with a threatening look.

"In a safe place," Dénes said. The look had no effect; the question remained maddeningly open. "It's just one phone call"—he raised a hand, reassuring—"and they'll bring it here."

Oszkár was not reassured.

Quite the opposite.

"Then call," he hissed. "And fast." He didn't even notice his hand curling into a fist.

Dénes shrugged.

"I thought we'd negotiate first."

"That's out of the question," Oszkár shot back, his voice tight.

"Why?"

"Because I don't negotiate with you! Either you give me that goddamn score within five minutes, or I go to the police."

"Let's go together," Dénes said calmly. Seeing Oszkár falter, he added, almost helpfully, "I've got something they'd be interested in too."

The antique dealer stared at him, pale. He didn't fully understand what was happening, but deep down he sensed that this small sideways slide had turned into something much worse.

And it had.

Dénes took out his phone—but instead of calling one of his accomplices, he tapped the screen a few times and placed the device in the middle of the table.

A short video began to play.

Balogh Oszkár, filmed from very close range. The camera stayed on him all the way to a nonexistent THE END.

"You see it too, right?" came a familiar male voice.

"See what?" Film-Oszkár asked, facing his increasingly stunned present-day self.

"That what you're asking is impossible."

The recording wasn't great, but the setting was easy enough to recognize—especially for anyone familiar with Budapest museums.

"Well... it doesn't look simple," Film-Oszkár said, nodding. Then, brightening, he added, "But you'll figure something out. I can see"—he went on, enjoying himself—"the whole family's here."

He gestured vaguely. The camera showed no one but him, smiling, clearly pleased with his role.

"Yes," the familiar voice said reluctantly. "But they're also saying it's impossible to steal anything from here."

"But you'll have to," Film-Oszkár cut in coldly. "Otherwise you can go—"

"The glasses!" present-day Oszkár burst out, cutting himself off mid-sentence.

"Shh," Dénes said. "It's not over yet." Then, in his normal voice, "This is the important part."

From the phone:

"Couldn't we just give back the four million... with interest... I'd even take double—"

"No," Oszkár Balogh said on screen, cold and unmistakable. "I want the score. From you."

The image went dark.

So did the light in Oszkár's eyes—though that had begun to fade well before the end.

"By the way, I really did use the glasses," Dénes said, slipping the phone into his pocket. "It's incredible what you can buy online these days. Cheap, too. Full HD spy glasses—barely a hundred thirty thousand. Even an idiot can see the value."

Oszkár didn't answer. He stared straight ahead, trying to come to terms with the fact that he'd lost again.

Smart Video Glasses. Hidden Camera Exposes Careless Antique Dealer

It wasn't easy to accept that all his plans had collapsed,

especially right on the edge of victory, but there was nothing to be done. He pulled himself together and saved the self-pity for later.

"And now?" he asked quietly.

Dénes was watching the ice melt in his glass, wondering why restaurant ice was always hollow. He shrugged. "Nothing special. We keep the police out of it. If this footage goes public, you're finished too." He leaned back. "Let's talk about the score."

"What about it?" Oszkár asked cautiously.

"If you still want it, you can still have it," Dénes said. "Fifty million."

Oszkár kept his face still. Years of practice helped. So did his grandfather.

"No one would pay that," he said, twisting his mouth. "Stolen goods are hard to move."

"Forty-five," Dénes cut in. "Cash. Now. That's my last offer." He smiled. "Sound familiar?"

"They call that déjà vu," Oszkár muttered.

"So?" Dénes said. "Do you want it or not?"

"I want it." Twenty-five million was still better than nothing. "I'll go to the bank."

"I'll call my aunt," Dénes said cheerfully. "She has the score. Hurry."

"I'll be back in twenty minutes," Oszkár said, already standing, diplomatic briefcase in hand.

* * *

"So everything went according to plan," Richárd said, settling into the back seat as Sólyom studied the manuscript in his lap.

"Exactly according to plan," Sólyom said. "You deserve credit."

Richárd made a brief attempt at modesty and failed. Sólyom didn't notice.

"I'm glad my work met your standards."

"It will meet them even more tomorrow," Sólyom said. "Check your account."

"You're too generous, sir."

"How did they do it?"

Sólyom explained the walking stick.

"And the alarm?"

"No idea."

"Incredible crew."

"Indeed." A pause. "Did you recall our people?"

"The moment I saw Szalay leave with the bag."

"Good." Then, mildly: "I wonder how they'll manage Oszkár."

"They'll reach an agreement." Richárd sounded bored. "If he gets the seventy, he gets what he wants too—"

He tilted his head.

"Except admission to one of the finest private museums in the world."

* * *

"Sorry," Oszkár said as he returned to his seat. "Have you been waiting long?"

"Not bad." Dénes waved it off and glanced at his aunt. "Right?"

"I'd say," she replied, tired, "that five or six minutes is acceptable for a transaction of this magnitude. But it's been a long day, so if you don't mind—"

"Getting to the point?" her nephew cut in. "I'm in."

"Me too." Oszkár nodded and opened his now genuinely valuable diplomatic case. "Forty-five million forints," he said quietly, sliding out two thick envelopes. "As agreed. What have you brought me?"

"Just this."

Dénes reached for Mici néni's walking stick where it leaned against the wall. He unscrewed the rubber tip and drew out a tightly rolled, slightly worn sheet of paper.

"Abracadabra," he said, smiling at the antique dealer.

"H—"

Oszkár choked, froze, and swallowed the rest. Whatever it had been, it stayed with him. He pushed the envelopes across the table.

"Thank you."

The magician nodded—so that was how his former client now saw him—and handed over the sheet music.

Oszkár took it gingerly, as if he feared it might crumble between his fingers.

"Thank *you*," he said, and meant it. He had never

encountered this level of professionalism.

He pinned one corner against the tablecloth and began coaxing the page flat. It took a few tries. Then it lay open, and he could finally admire the relic—and touch it, which few people on earth could claim.

From Teleki Square to the Pinnacle of the Profession
Or: The King of Junk Dealers

"I hope it didn't get too wrinkled," Mici néni said.

"I'll manage." Oszkár waved it off.

Reassured, the old woman leaned back.

No one on the other side of the table seemed to notice that the paper dated from a good eighty years later than the original.

The heavily worn music notebook—half scribbled over by some unknown child, from which Mici néni had torn the page herself—Dénes had found at an online auction after some research. Nearly identical to Beethoven's paper. Half a centimeter narrower. Not something anyone would notice unless they were already suspicious, as he'd told his aunt.

Work in peace.

She had. Using articles, brochures, and photographs, she copied the composer's notations with all the artistry she could muster, until the page was nearly indistinguishable from the exhibition piece. What helped most were the high-resolution close-ups Anett had taken—every stain, every nick reproduced exactly.

Including on what Oszkár now held in his hands.

And had just paid forty-five million forints to acquire.

In short, Mici néni had done excellent work.

And her nephew—now flipping through the last bundle of twenties under the table—was right again.

"Looks correct," Dénes said when he finished. He slipped the envelopes into the sports bag—now holding exactly one hundred fifteen million forints—then leaned forward. "If I were you, I wouldn't flash a document in public that was stolen from a museum two blocks away less than four hours ago."

Oszkár went pale.

"You're right," he said, grateful. He swept the page back into the case and snapped it shut. "And then... we're finished, I believe."

"Yes." Dénes nodded. He knew that almost nothing was as Oszkár thought—and that he'd find out soon enough. "Which makes this the end of a beautiful friendship, as my friend Viktor would say. *Casablanca.*"

"Except that's the beginning," Oszkár said, smiling. Despite the day's roller coaster, he was convinced he'd come out ahead—twenty-five million in cash, plus more besides. "But—" A thought snagged. "What about the footage?"

"That would land us in as much trouble as you," the cinematographer shrugged. "So don't worry."

"Right."

Oszkár rose. For a moment he considered a handshake, decided against it, and nodded instead.

"See you around."

"God be with you," Mici néni said.

Oszkár gave a curt smile and left.

"I don't think we won his heart," Dénes said, watching him go. Then, with a trace of guilt, "Especially me."

Mici néni pulled her mouth to one side—not amused—and fixed him with a look reserved for a repulsive insect that had just crawled out from under a damp stone.

This puzzled Dénes. They had just pulled off the biggest parade of their lives. He had expected celebration.

When she finally spoke, her voice was calm.

"The poor fool doesn't even know that you'd been leading him by the nose from the very first moment."

She held his gaze.

That, too, was strange—though not nearly as strange as what followed.

"Just as you led us."

Her look was full of accusation, but Dénes averted his eyes in embarrassment. He didn't protest. He knew it would lead nowhere. If his aunt had seen through it, there was no point denying anything.

The waiter arrived to clear the empty glasses.

It gave him a moment to think through his defense.

*　*　*

Csaba only realized he hadn't eaten all day when the cops finally began packing up.

Mission unaccomplished—as his grandfather would've said. No use to anyone. If they'd at least figured out how the

theft had happened, he wouldn't complain, but like this...
they'd just wasted everyone's time. Including his own.

He kept that to himself. Partly because he hated tantrums.
Partly because the lead investigator was actually likable. Even
if he had nothing useful to offer.

"I'm sorry," the man said. "I have no idea what the hell happened."

Honest. Rare.

"So what now?" The director's voice cracked.

"Well... as for the sheet music, I think you can kiss that
goodbye. Unless the thief really was among the people who
left before the lockdown. But I doubt it. We know who all of
them are, and—"

The director let out a bitter sigh.

"Fantastic work. Congratulations."

The cop shrugged, embarrassed. This wasn't exactly a career highlight. He glanced down at Csaba, who was squatting
nearby, stomach growling, muttering as he studied the scene.

Now that the cordoned-off area had finally cleared, something about it bothered him. He couldn't say what. Yet. But if
he stared long enough, he felt the answer would come. Like
when a word you've used a thousand times suddenly won't
surface—sitting right there on your tongue—until it does,
and then you can't imagine how you ever forgot it.

That was what was happening now.

Not a word—a detail. Small. Crucial. Something that fit almost too well.

Csaba closed his eyes and pictured the room from the same angle as yesterday, when everything had still been in place.

He's fallen asleep, the investigator thought, baffled. He'd never seen anyone manage that while squatting.

He bent down to nudge the guard awake before he toppled over and cracked his head—when Csaba's eyes flew open.

"Everything okay?" the investigator asked.

"Yeah." Csaba nodded, still staring ahead. "Just something... off."

The investigator squatted beside him. "Go on."

Csaba explained.

"Let's take a photo," the investigator said when he finished. He nodded toward the vitrine. "Of this. Then pull one from before the theft. Compare them. My kids love those puzzles where you spot the differences between two pictures that look the same."

"Good thinking." Csaba nodded, energized now. "Let's have Santa print out the camera shots—"

He stopped.

The investigator was staring at him.

"What?"

"I knew that guy looked familiar," the cop said, shaking his head. "But I never would've guessed he was Santa Claus himself."

Csaba raised a finger to his lips and glanced around.

"Shhh," he whispered. "If he hears you, we're toast."

"Why?" the investigator asked. "That's a compliment."

"Not to him." Csaba shrugged. "He says it... you know... ages him."

The investigator considered this.

"Well," he muttered, "he might have a point." Then he straightened. "Come on. Let's go talk to him."

* * *

"Sorry," Dénes said, releasing a breath that carried more shame than he'd intended.

He knew the topic wasn't closed. But for now, maybe this would do.

"That private investigator was yours too, wasn't he?" Mici néni asked. Her voice held bitterness. "The one who took the photos. Who found us."

Her nephew shook his head.

"I had to—" He chose his words carefully but got no further.

"Had to what?"

"Get Oszkár to feel," Dénes pressed on, "that he had us in his grip."

"And make us feel it too," his aunt said quietly. "Otherwise we never would've agreed to something this dangerous. And you knew that. That's why you arranged for him to blackmail us."

"Not just for that." Dénes shifted in his chair. "That was only the cherry on top. So I wouldn't have to spend days convincing you—"

Pointlessly, he would've added. Because he doubted either of them would have signed on to a job this far outside their wheelhouse: smoke bombs, pat-downs, moving the entire time under camera coverage. He'd needed to force their hand.

He wisely didn't say that.

Mici néni stared ahead. Despite herself, a grudging respect stirred at her nephew's audacity. She'd always acknowledged any quality honed close to perfection—even when it made her blood boil. Perfection had a way of disarming you.

"So you did it to save time," she said cautiously.

"That too." He shrugged, then sighed. "I know it wasn't a nice move, but—"

"You had to," Mici néni finished. "You've said that already." She added, almost absently, "Though you still need to practice your *mea culpas.*"

"Am I that bad?" Dénes asked, embarrassed.

She nodded.

"Painful to watch. Worse to hear."

"I didn't have time to practice."

"Sometimes there isn't time," she cut in. Then, without softening, returned to the point. "As for the photos—Oszkár used them to blackmail us. Thanks to you."

"Harmless," Dénes said, waving it off.

"What do you mean?"

"I mean they couldn't have caused real trouble. Eating somewhere and talking to a waiter isn't a crime. That's all the photos showed."

"But combined with statements—"

"There were no statements. Not real ones. Just what Bálint and I wrote. And even then, it would've been one server's word against ours. One witness isn't a witness."

She opened her mouth, faltered, then cleared her throat.

"So nobody would actually have gone to prison?"

"Of course not." He looked offended. "The whole thing was just to make the story complete."

"What story?" she asked quietly.

"The manhunt. The mark hires a private investigator who closes in on us, then sets a trap we walk into. Oszkár had to believe he'd caught us."

He kept it at the broad strokes. Left out the planted coffee cup. The staged slip. The detail that Oszkár himself had "discovered" before the investigator did—exactly as planned. Nuance mattered. Who finds what, when. That was something he'd learned from her.

She was shaking her head now.

"Shame I believed it too," Mici néni muttered.

The anger that had boiled fifteen minutes earlier was cooling, giving way to reluctant admiration. She kept that carefully in check.

"That's why it worked," Dénes said. "If Oszkár hadn't believed he had us by the throat, we couldn't have planted the idea. But once he did, it was easy to nudge him toward the thought that revenge would taste better if we worked for him."

"And humiliate us in the process," she said.

"I knew he'd like that," Dénes said. "Especially if the idea came from someone he trusted. Like the investigator who 'caught' us."

"How do you know him?" she asked. "What's his name?"

"Bálint Herceg. I helped him once, after Sólyom got him fired from the police."

"Sólyom?" she interrupted. "Who are you talking about?"

Dénes sighed and recalled the story he'd heard years earlier: Bálint's father, his death, the revenge attempt that nearly ruined the son's life. How Dénes had stepped in, provided documentation, kept him out of prison.

They'd stayed in touch. Had lunch. Talked cases. Clients. Money. But the desire for revenge never left Bálint alone.

So Dénes started thinking too.

Antal Sólyom—whose file Bálint had quietly built—represented the worst kind of man. His hobby of stolen art was only one item on a long list. Dénes built the plan on that. And on Beethoven.

When he saw the minister on TV six months earlier, standing beside the empty vitrine and swearing it wouldn't stay empty, he knew he had the bait.

But first he needed intel. And an antique dealer willing to fence.

That's where Oszkár came in.

"So Sólyom was the target all along," Mici néni said.

"Yes. Though for me it was business." Dénes hesitated. "Financial gain."

"And Oszkár?"

"He was there so Sólyom would have someone to buy from illegally."

"Because Sólyom wouldn't deal with a stranger."

"Exactly."

"But what if Oszkár hadn't wanted revenge?"

"Then we make four million. And we figure something else out for Sólyom. It wasn't personal."

"So you talked poor Oszkár into giving us an assignment we couldn't refuse," Mici néni muttered accusingly—without realizing she was echoing a classic.

"Bálint talked him into it, yes," Dénes said. "He managed to get him to want the score stolen by us."

That took a certain amount of psychology, he reflected. The subject had to feel that the idea genuinely came from him. Bálint had to proceed with great care, subtly steering the antique dealer's scattered thoughts into the proper channel, until they arrived—on their own, as it were—at the suggested eureka moment. And he'd done it well, following expert advice: building the arguments, arranging them in the right order, laying out the available options, and making use of Oszkár's not entirely unfounded inferiority complex where Sólyom was concerned.

In practice, of course, all this was far more difficult than it sounded. You had to adapt to the immediate circumstances, to Oszkár's mood, even to the room's current layout—whether, for instance, there happened to be a picture magazine lying on the table, its cover filled edge to edge with a Beethoven score. That made the private investigator's job slightly easier; if it hadn't been there, he would've had to introduce the topic himself. Not impossible—but this version was better.

"And that's how Oszkár ended up pressing a gun to our heads," Mici néni said, still a little surly. "And you let him."

"Because I knew the gun was loaded with blanks," Dénes said. "So no one was ever in danger."

"You still made fools of us," she said. "You already had the whole plan in your head months ago. Didn't you?"

Her nephew frowned.

"And how exactly do you know that?" he asked cautiously.

Because he'd been so careful—making sure the team reached the realization only gradually, step by step, that a violent break-in simply wasn't feasible. That was why he'd sent them out on a site survey in the first place, from which they'd returned discouraged and disappointed—so they'd be all the more relieved later on by the method that seemed more complicated but was, in fact, less drastic.

A method he had, after long deliberation, come up with nearly three months earlier.

And yet he hadn't told a soul. His aunt had still seen through it.

How, only God knew. And of course the woman herself.

"I'll tell you later," the old lady said mysteriously when she saw how curiosity was practically boring into her nephew's side. She felt it was the least he deserved after everything that had happened. "First make a phone call. That's more important."

She was right.

Dénes nodded and reached for his phone.

* * *

Csaba frowned at the before-and-after photos.

The investigator stepped aside to give him room, but didn't take his eyes off the security guard in the background. This was it. His last shot.

All right, the guard muttered to himself without moving his lips. Let's find the differences. Start with the obvious...

Glass shards scattered across the carpet around the table. Yesterday: clean.

The table's glass top—now in pieces. Yesterday: intact.

Police tape. That hadn't been there either.

And the sheet music. That wasn't there now.

And what else?

What doesn't add up besides these?

Come on, old man. Think.

He leaned in, eyes burning. Something was missing—small, stupid, right in front of him.

Nothing surfaced.

The photos stayed mute.

* * *

"So—" Anett stammered with joy after Viktor ended the call and said everything was okay. "That means—"

"We're going to get Dani," Viktor finished for her and signaled the waiter for the check.

Anett tried to say something, but burst into tears instead.

"I'm sorry," she hiccupped. "I'm just... so happy!"

"I can see that." Viktor nodded, satisfied, then added with a straight face, "But you're weird. I mean, you women. How you express these things. With tears. You'd think—"

Anett suddenly threw her arms around him and squeezed with a strength he wouldn't have guessed she had. He shut up. Partly because something had grabbed his own throat too—from being moved, and from her closeness.

After all, he was witnessing—no, actively participating in—a family reunion.

On the first day of Operation Shake Zsolt, he'd driven Anett to Mici néni's in a borrowed taxi, eyes fixed on their pursuers' car in the rearview mirror. He'd produced the fake paternity certificate with a word processor—not to mention the serious-looking official stamp he'd made using a three-thousand-forint kiddie printing set. At the final confrontation, when everyone gathered in person at the girl's rented apartment, Viktor had waited outside in a car, headphones on, hearing every word through the tiny microphone hidden in a lamp.

And if things had gone wrong—if Zsolt had overreacted—Viktor would have triggered the remote-controlled car alarm planted near the apartment entrance, capable of the same deafening shriek as the museum fire alarm they'd set off a few hours earlier, and burst in himself: police ID in one hand, cocked weapon in the other.

Thankfully, none of that had been necessary. Everything had gone exactly as Dénes planned.

And now it had gone that way again.

They were one hundred fifteen million forints richer.

Not bad for barely a week's work.

* * *

"I've grown fond of that girl," Mici néni said over her tea.

"Because she's like you were." Dénes shrugged, then added with an innocent look, "A hundred years ago."

"There is a resemblance," his aunt said, deliberately ignoring the cheek. "But what do you think will happen to her now?"

"You mean after she gets her son back?"

"Yes. It's possible that as a full-time mother she'll decide it's too risky to keep working with us."

"I don't think she'd happily go back to hairdressing."

"What if she does?"

Her nephew sighed.

"Then we'll get our hair cut at her place."

That might be for the best, Mici néni thought. Before the situation soured.

The situation Dénes clearly had no idea about. Men were always blind to these things. Until a woman climbed into their lap, panting *I love you, darling, you're my everything,* they rarely noticed she was strongly attracted to them. And yet there were signs. Dozens of them. Too bad they didn't know a single one—her nephew certainly didn't.

Of course, in this case that blindness might be a blessing rather than a curse. If he didn't know—and hopefully Viktor didn't either, who sometimes looked at Anett with the poorly concealed devotion of a puppy—they might still stop things before they escalated. If they could nip it in the bud, everything would work out.

Hopefully there was still time.

"It would be a shame to lose her," she said, optimistically.

"I think so too. We really are a good crew."

"I'm glad you think so."

"And Viktor seems to have warmed up to her too."

The old woman closed her eyes and sighed. You have no idea, Dénes dear. Just how much. Thank God.

"You think?"

"Absolutely. He wasn't angry with her anyway—just with her gender in general. Because of that whore who cleaned him out."

"We could track that woman down sometime."

"I mentioned it to him. He didn't want to. Not yet." He paused. "As for Anett, she'll decide what's next. And now you could finally tell me."

The old lady furrowed her brow.

"Tell you what?"

Dénes sighed. He knew she was playing with him. He had

to play along. Otherwise he'd never get what he wanted.

"How you figured it out. All of it."

Mici néni didn't answer right away. She studied her nephew, then decided to make him wait.

"You'll find out soon," she said, stalling. "But first tell me why you weren't surprised when Sólyom blackmailed us too."

"Because it was in the cards. Based on what Bálint found out about him, it fit. He'd put people on us, and once he knew who we were, he'd want to buy the goods firsthand. So I figured we should cover ourselves. Let him get something too if he tried to cut in from the right. Luckily he did—and it cost him the same seventy million as if he'd dealt with Oszkár."

"Except this way the money came to us," the former Bride said, nodding.

"Most of it would've come to us anyway."

"But if he'd bought from Oszkár, we wouldn't make this much."

"True." Dénes leaned forward. "But now it's really your turn. What gave me away?"

His aunt held his gaze for a long moment—then showed mercy.

"The table," she said. "The one you bought from that horrible creature."

* * *

"What's he doing over there?" the director asked, puzzled, as he shook hands limply with the security company rep, who had just returned with yet more mysterious equipment.

"Uh... no idea," the rep said, his forehead creasing to match his tone.

They both started toward Csaba, who was kneeling beside the vitrine, eyes narrowed, fingertips gliding along the edge.

"Leave him," the investigator said, stopping them. "Let him concentrate."

"On what?" the expert whispered, lowering his voice to match.

The cop shrugged.

"I couldn't tell you," he said honestly. "But I think he's figured something out."

Csaba didn't look up.

He ran his fingers along the edge again—slow this time. Pressed. Released. Listened. Then he shifted his weight and slid his thumb along the underside, where dust collected and no one ever cleaned.

"Director," he said hoarsely. "Could you come here for a moment?"

* * *

"Without him we couldn't have pulled off the Antal Ács job either," Dénes went on, continuing to list the merits of Karcsi, whom his aunt had labeled a horrible creature. "All that horse manure would've taken weeks to collect."

"Exactly," Mici néni said, nodding.

Dénes paused, thrown.

"What do you mean, *exactly?*"

"What I'm getting at, my boy, is that the table couldn't have been any easier to source either. I'm certain a rarity like that can't be found in a matter of days—if it can be found at all. Of this curved-leg, red-velvet-inlaid, intricately carved Rococo vitrine—with the glass top fixed at the center—there are perhaps a dozen in the entire country."

Right, Dénes thought sourly. And most of them were in museums or manor houses—places you could only remove furniture from by force. The single decommissioned specimen had been sitting in a rural community center no one knew about, which meant Karcsi had to activate relatives scattered across the country just to locate it. Even then, it had taken more than a month.

Worth it.

Because this was the key to the entire operation. The table was the exact twin of the one in the Giants Museum—the one beside which the minister had sworn six months earlier, in front of the cameras, that he'd acquire the Beethoven manuscript for the nation, so it could be admired under glass...

"And how do you know all this?" he muttered, genuinely puzzled.

His aunt shrugged. "The internet. You taught me how to use it."

"No good deed goes unpunished."

Mici néni smiled. A decent riposte—and in this line of work, improvisation often mattered.

But with the vitrine, there had been no improvisation at all. She'd understood that the moment Dénes arrived with the table. Not modified, really—more like surgery.

"By the way, hats off to whoever took it apart so cleanly," she said aloud.

"Supposedly the best carpenter in the city," her nephew said, recalling the man's expression when he'd been asked to scalp that beauty.

Shaving off the glazed top layer without damaging it—while ruining everything beneath, which afterward, like the elegantly curved legs, was only fit for firewood—was no small feat. But Dénes needed only the vitrine's intact upper section, reinforced with a metal plate so it could stand on its own. He'd also requested a thin, nearly invisible border, allowing it to be seated on another matching table as if it had always belonged there.

Until then, the seventy-by-forty-centimeter, five-and-a-half-centimeter-tall, glass-topped—therefore fragile yet surprisingly solid—openable box-like object (not so small, really) had to be hidden somewhere. Without attracting attention.

Not simple in a museum packed with cameras and guards—unless the object was mounted to the backrest of a suitably sized wheelchair and concealed beneath a blanket and an elderly lady. From there, Viktor and Dénes—after extensive practice—could extract it in one smooth, coordinated motion and transfer it within seven seconds onto the table concealing the Beethoven manuscript, perfectly covering the original glass top.

Even with their eyes closed.

Or in thick smoke.

All that remained was for Mici néni to strike the empty fake vitrine top with her cane. One good blow—and the scene resolved itself: glass shards, apparent looting, no sheet music. Which of course hadn't really been there anyway—or rather had been there, just five centimeters lower.

Only the four of them knew that.

Everyone else trusted their eyes. And their eyes saw exactly what the crew suggested: that the nation's most valuable Beethoven page had vanished.

Thus the perfect crime—one without even a suspect. There couldn't be one. No search would ever turn up anything, because nothing had actually been taken. The manuscript was right where it had always been; they never touched it, nor the original glass protecting it. Had they done so, the German-engineered alarm—flawless, of course—would have dropped the cage instantly.

Instead, the police and experts were left with a puzzle they couldn't solve in the first round.

The crew needed only that round.

Just those few hours—while adrenaline still charged the air—to sell the copy to an eyewitness who, having lived through the chaos, would never question its authenticity. Two eyewitness-buyers were even better.

That was why Dénes had asked Mici néni, just to be safe, to

make one additional forgery. Anett stashed them in the Sugar Cube's women's restroom, where the artist later retrieved them, hiding them in her walking stick—one in the shaft, one in the tip if needed—before setting out on what turned out to be the final two missions.

Both reproductions sold. No complaints so far.

Likely there never would be. Explaining things to the authorities would be... awkward.

Mici néni had carried nothing compromising into the museum, so even a thorough pat-down—including the cane, one of the parade's most important props—would have revealed nothing.

The real solution was the slightly modified top five and a half centimeters of the vitrine.

Courtesy of the city's "best" carpenter.

"He did it skillfully," Mici néni said.

She studied her nephew. "And so did you."

She meant it.

"Come on." Dénes waved it off. "We'd be nowhere without you. Nobody else could've produced forgeries this good. I just regret..." He paused, thoughtful. "In hindsight... that you didn't make three. We definitely could've found another buyer. These obsessed collectors are child's play."

His aunt stared at him, appalled—

—and then he grinned.

"Relax. I'm kidding." He patted her knee. "I know when to stop."

*   *   *

"I don't see anything strange about it," the director said, his nerves showing. He was already picturing the other man on a long vacation.

Csaba didn't answer. His face had gone distant as he continued running his fingers along the vitrine's side.

"I don't think it used to be this..." he muttered. "You know. Thick."

He shifted his grip, then pressed both palms against the table's surface.

It moved.

Frame and all, the broken glass and velvet lining slid aside—then farther—until, with a heavy crash, the false top dropped to the floor.

The original vitrine lay exposed.

And beneath its gleaming glass top sat the equally original, untouched Beethoven manuscript.

No one spoke.